Designer Baby

Underlying Crimes

Joann Mead

First Stillwater River Publications Edition 2019.

ISBN-10: 1-950-33943-2
ISBN-13: 978-1-950-33943-3

1 2 3 4 5 6 7 8 9 10

Written by Joann Mead.
Published by Stillwater River Publications, Pawtucket, RI, USA.

Designer Baby

To my designer babies
Jim and Gina

1

My Mai

"**Y**ou are mine. You are my Mai." He chuckled. "Mai, Mai." Repeating over and over, he laughed at his alliteration as he clapped his short, thick hands in time with his rhythmic chant.

"Only tonight. No rough stuff. Just what we agreed, Vlad. Promise?" For Mai Tran, this business has rules that must be followed. Her patrons were usually compliant. Most were lonely businessmen with too much money and time on their hands. Most had pedestrian tastes. But this client was not typical—more brutish and less refined than the Scandinavian men, and with none of the sophistication of western Europeans.

Mai keenly observed the differences in her clients. She was a quick study. This patron was decidedly coarse with his disheveled hair and beefy body. She comically thought the size of his head must be inversely proportional to his intellect. He didn't strike Mai as a man who got by on his wits.

Yet, his piercing blue eyes seemed to soften when he stared into her eyes. Perhaps Vlad was more docile, less threatening than he appeared. She wouldn't otherwise have gone with him to his hotel room. She decided this hulking beast was most probably harmless.

Quick to satisfy him, Mai was thankful it was over. When she sat upright at the edge of the bed, he grabbed her arm forcing her to lie down. His greasy hair, a dirty hay-yellow, fell on her

1

face and with one foul-smelling breath he demanded, "Mai, Mai, I give you money for one week."

"No! One night." Mai would never let any man own her for that length of time. And she could make more money with brief encounters. She had her method.

Again, she rose from the bed to gather her clothes. But without warning, Vladimir pinned her face down on the bed and straddled himself across her thighs. He pulled her hands behind her back and tied her wrists with a loose luggage strap. Struggling to no avail she tried to yell. But before she could project beyond a weak gurgle, he squeezed her throat and growled, "No loud mouth."

Mai froze. She feared things would not end well.

"Vlad, you did not pay me. Pay now and untie me." Mai tried to project calm.

Vlad pulled a bundle of euros from his jacket that lay on the bed. Unrolling the bills, he counted out ten large euro denominations and tossed them on the nightstand. "For one week, you are mine." He slapped her bottom, much too hard to be playful.

Mai grimaced with pain. "Stop! I did not agree to this." Appealing to his inner angel—should there be one—she praised him. "Vlad, you are a good man. You would never hurt a woman." For a few moments, Vlad seemed to listen but his penetrating blue eyes and playful smile deceived her. She had almost believed he was a decent person.

But instead Vlad grabbed her neck as if to strangle, threatening what might come later. He laughed as he smacked her harder, leaving red welts. "You take what I give you."

Mai recalled the beating her mother took from an abusive client years ago in Shenzhen—her blackened eye, the circular bruising on her arms, the raw red streaks down her back. Mai knew she should have listened to Mother's warning, "Sometimes you get more than what you are paid for."

Mai mumbled to herself, "I have become Mother." She painfully remembered the day she explored the contents of Mother's knapsack: the lingerie, the jewelry, the cosmetics, and other exotic tools of the trade. When Mother woke to find Mai fondling the lingerie, she flew into a rage and beat her. She slapped her face and whipped her legs with a bamboo rod.

But now, Vlad's abuse made her regret the turn her life had taken. Mai thought that things like this couldn't happen here. Not in this beautiful, safe country. After all, this is Sweden.

Mai pleaded in vain for Vlad to stop. She hoped he wouldn't go too far. But it seemed her worst fears might become a reality. The choking abuse intensified until she passed out from the near strangulation. Vlad took a break and swigged cognac directly from the bottle.

When she came to, Mai wondered if she could take one day of this, let alone one week. Vlad was probably the vilest man she ever encountered, and she'd come across quite a few other bad men. She'd kill him if she could. But she had no weapon.

Vlad told Mai, "I trap you, then release. I pay you money."

He picked up Mai's purse and rummaged through it. He plucked out a wrapped sweet and inspected a golden-yellow hard candy.

Mai couldn't believe her luck. She tempted him, "Would you like a 'Honey Sweetie'? It's very tasty. Suck it slow, it will ooze honey in your mouth."

He placed the sweet on the nightstand. "But first, we have more fun."

Mai hoped he would tire of his frightening play, but he punctuated his sadistic fun with a blow that split her lip. Blood trickled on to the sheets. Vlad ignored her whimpers and picked up the yellow-gold candy.

Again, Mai tempted him, "Honey Sweetie? You will love it." This time it was Vlad who complied. He unwrapped it and popped it in his mouth. His blue eyes rolled with pleasure. Indulgence was just one of his vices. Whether sweet, savory, or savage, he loved it all. But little did Vlad know, that Mai's honey candy was laced with a bioweapon, the Tiger Flu.

"Mai, Mai. Honey Sweetie. Do you have more?" Vlad dumped the contents of Mai's purse, disappointed at not finding more candies.

"No, it's the only one," Mai said and smiled. She knew he wouldn't last the week.

"For now, my honey pot, you make Vlad very happy. Little Mai, Mai."

Three days passed. Mai couldn't escape Vlad's cruel tastes. His vicious routine of partial strangulation, poking, thumping, and battering was unrelenting. He controlled her. He kept her tied, tethered to the bed. He escorted her when needed. Showered with her on occasion.

He asked not to be disturbed. Vlad's large meals were left in a hallway by hotel staff. Mai fed on what he gave her. "Keep up your strength." He insisted she eat.

He chided her if she dared complain of anything. Telling her how lucky she was. "You are trapped. But you are alive, little butterfly. You are not so fragile, are you Mai, Mai?"

That evening, Vlad complained he felt hot. Was he was coming down with something? A cold perhaps?

On the fourth day, Vlad was congested. Feverish. Mai promised she'd nurse him back to health. "It's only a cold or the flu. After all Vlad, you paid me for one week." Mai feigned affection and obedience. He untied her tether.

Room service left what Vlad asked for in the hallway—strong cold and flu medicines. Mai dosed him with a codeine cough mixture. The staff avoided their sick guest.

Mai reassured Vlad that he was getting better. No need for a doctor.

She mumbled words too cryptic for Vlad to understand, "Tiger, tiger burning bright", the words from William Blake's poem.

"Turn off the bright lights. My eyes, my eyes. I'm too hot. My chest burns." Vlad labored over every breath.

"In the forests of the night," Mai recited.

"What are you saying, Mai?"

"What immortal hand or eye. Could frame thy fearful symmetry?" Mai continued her recitation of the poem.

"My throat is sore. Give me more medicine." Vlad drank entire bottles of the codeine cough syrup. He swooned, dizzy and delirious.

Mai teased the nearly incoherent Vlad. "By my hand, by my eye, I framed thy fearful symmetry. I turned the little birds into tigers."

Confused by Mai's simple words, let alone decipher any obscure meaning, Vlad swiped his hand in the air just missing Mai's face. "Shut up about tigers and birds. My head hurts."

4

"Vlad, you have a slight fever." Mai could almost not contain her glee.

Diarrhea kept Vlad on the toilet. His strength sapped, he crawled slowly back and forth to bed.

Mai dabbed Vlad's runny nose with a tissue. She commended herself, knowing she'd been wise to inject the honey candy with the deadly flu strain. But not a contagious variety. She'd forgotten that a lone "Honey Sweetie" lay at the bottom of her handbag. How lucky that Vlad found it.

The malaise soon set in. So lethargic, Vlad couldn't even think of food, let alone sex.

His breathing labored, Vlad lapsed in and out of consciousness. Mai knew he wouldn't last long. Maybe another day or two, but he'd be dead by the end of the week. Mai mused with hateful glee, "Let him suffer as he slowly descends into a dreaded coma."

Mai took a long relaxing shower. Hairbrush in hand, she rearranged her blond wig that Vlad carelessly tossed on the bathroom floor. She gathered her belongings—the euro bills on the nightstand and what was left of Vlad's money roll—and stashed everything in her large purse along with her lace top and skirt. She dressed in jeans, a sweatshirt, and running shoes.

"You fool, Vladimir. I turned the little bird flu into a lethal weapon, the Tiger Flu. You don't stand a chance. My Honey Sweetie released the tigers," Mai said to the comatose Vlad. She relished the power she exerted over him and control over his very existence.

"You deserve what you get!" she punctuated, deriving as much sadistic pleasure as Vlad did with her.

"In what furnace is thy brain?" Mai recited, asking Vlad to answer to his fate.

Oblivious to everything around him, Vlad was delirious with fever. Brain death was imminent.

"*Do svidaniya*, Vladimir." Mai wouldn't wait around for his last dying breath.

Vlad would certainly not be flying home to Moscow. He would soon be arriving in hell.

2

Mai's Lies

The next day, Mai took a train from Stockholm to Gothenburg. A few days later, she read a news article about the mysterious death of a Russian tourist found comatose in a Stockholm hotel room.

"Uh, oh." Mai cringed at the thought of what peril she might now be in. She read that his post mortem diagnosis was pneumonia. Although foul play was not suspected, an investigation was ongoing.

Mai recalled with shades of regret her first victim, Lian, the Chinese-American woman who succumbed to a mysterious flu after returning to Seattle from Hong Kong.

"A woman like myself," she said with a sigh, feeling a kinship with her.

During Mai's previous life as Mei Wong, a lab scientist, she infected the unsuspecting Lian with Tiger Flu. World Genomics was the gargantuan lab in Shenzhen where she concocted her "Honey Sweeties". She remembered watching Lian's orgasmic expression as the honey center burst in her mouth, unaware of the sweet sorrow and agony that lie ahead.

She soon left China for a fellowship in Denmark. It was in Copenhagen that she seduced her second victim, Albert. She thought him a typical American research scientist. Like so many men, so easy to manipulate.

"Have a Honey Sweetie? Suck it slow. It will melt in your mouth." She lured him into her tiger trap.

Mai recollected how he drooled over her legs and that leopard-print skirt she wore so tight. She smiled at the nerd-like image she conjured up, his box-like jacket, pocket protector, and Khaki trousers. Her smile soured at the thought of what she did to him. Albert died days later after returning home to Boston.

Both Lian and Al suffered the same fevered delirium and dreaded fire to the brain. Brain death was inevitable. She'd given her two test subjects a lab-created strain of Tiger Flu—not a contagious variety that could spread to others, but very deadly never-the-less. After all, she thought, "I needed to prove it could be done." Mai told herself to assuage her guilt that it was "all in the interest of science". She never once drew a connection to the Nuremburg Trials on human medical experimentation. Her diabolic experiments were no different.

It was not surprisingly that Mai had absolutely no qualms about Vladimir's demise. She felt he more than deserved what he got. Mai reckoned she saved other women from his abuse and she felt vindicated for administering her own form of justice. His execution.

Mai breathed only a partial sigh of relief, for now she was not implicated. Or was she?

Mai knew things had to change. She told herself, "No more gold stiletto heels. And no more Russians!"

Now draped across the bed in a cheap boarding room in Gothenburg, Mai's new life in the West was not what she'd planned on. Back in China, the one million euros for her Tiger Flu creation seemed like a fortune that would support her for years in a life style of luxury. But her naiveté and her euros quickly disappeared, not just on pricey hotels and fashionable attire, but the biggest expense came with her transformation. The surgeries, the private hospital, the fake passports, and all the incidentals, like the cash bribes she doled out for the surgeons' discretion. Those big expenses sucked cash from the private stash she'd secreted away in her knapsack.

Mai's mind chatter was incessant. "At least I found the Tong in Paris," she thought. They forged a new passport, Mai Tran, a French-Vietnamese reincarnate. She was no longer the wanted bioterrorist, Mei Wong. But she worried, "What if I need to shift, to change, to morph again? There is no one to help me. I have no protection, only abusers."

"At least Kahliy looked after me." Mai smiled at her memories. "Ah, Kahliy." Her thoughts then shifted, "But it was *your* plot. *Your* students. *They* would carry the highly contagious Tiger flu. *They* would fly on planes to US cities. Infected human time bombs!" Mai's eyes widened, as if in horror. Millions of people would die. Or so she promised. She smirked and sighed, not from guilt, but from the relief that she didn't do *her* part in carrying out *his* plan.

She mocked Kahliy as she mumbled her thoughts, "Oh, Kahliy, you silly man. I never loved you. I used you. You satisfied my urges. You were a tool for me to make money." Mai paused to audibly reflect, "I could never destroy what I love. Life in the West."

Mai pondered the question of what the future might hold. And at that moment, Mai had a glimmer of her next big idea. She thought that if we truly love ourselves, as most of us do, then we would relish the idea of creating a perfected image of our self. We want perfection in ourselves, but no matter how much money we have, perfection is unattainable…unless….

"Ah, yes, I understand what men want most." Mai's eureka moment arrived, she laughed out loud at her audacious tagline: *I want a more perfect me, just as you want a more perfect you.*

A more perfect me. And what would that be? Mai's mind, enthralled by her fantasy, swirled in a sea of ideas. A flawless reflection, a perfected replicant…in our children.

She wondered how much people would pay for their dream child. Just how much is a perfect child worth? And it was there in that grungy bed, in a marginal boarding house, that the inception of Mai's next business venture was conceived. "No longer will I be the slave of men, when I can offer them their own perfected child. They won't buy me. They'll buy a perfect baby!"

Mai drifted off again with visions of "designer babies" created in the perfected likeness of their father. She would offer men a custom-made child; they'd choose from a list of enhanced traits. She'd offer a perfected prodigy, "a more perfect me", as the answer to the age-old question: What do you really want in life? It could be the answer to their quest for eternal life.

Mai needed a better plan, or a better scam to sustain the life-style to which she'd grown accustomed. With her money running critically low, she knew she had some thinking to do. She would visit coffee houses, not bars. She could wear new clothes—business professional. Find new clients. And something else, she could use her skills in editing genes.

Mai mused some more, "Editing genes in microbes is child's play. But it's too risky. And dangerous for me. *No more death and destruction. No more Tiger Flu!*"

Mai asked herself, "Why create death when you can create life?" Mai's mantras and personalized aphorisms drove her desires.

Mai thought of her pitch, "Design your own super-baby. A perfectly edited version of you!" Chuffed with her brilliant self, she fed her oversized ego.

With Mai's scientific methods perfected at World Genomics labs, she knew she was more than primed—she was credible and experienced. With gene-edited babies now a reality, disease-free embryos were created with "gene surgery". Babies immune to HIV now lived in China, made possible with a simple CRISPR tool, DNA scissors that clip out the bad genes.

Mai wrote down her sales and marketing ideas: *Your babies will be free of disease, no HIV, no cholera, no smallpox, or other diseases. Your children will grow up immune. Inherited diseases will be nipped in the bud. But that's not all. Besides removing bad DNA, we can insert new and improved DNA!*

At World Genomics, Mai learned about gene editing, its unlimited potential for designing DNA in humans. For babies, their traits could be changed, fixed, or exquisitely embellished before being born. Super-humans were the next big thing of the future. A total redesign.

"Why be a lowly 'natural' when you can be an 'enhanced' elite?" Mai asked, knowing the answer.

No longer limited to fantastical science fiction movies, beyond those imaginary super-heroes, these super-intelligent, strikingly handsome, beautifully athletic human-gods would be real. But perfection would be limited to the wealthiest among us.

Financial eugenics. Survival of the "fittest" would be those with the most money. Those with foresight into a utopian future. Those who could see the promise of a phenomenal family with perfected offspring.

Mai dreamed about a new successful business. She would try out her selling points on desperate men with deep pockets that would empty into hers.

Mai thought some more. "I don't want to kill any more people. And I love little babies, when they belong to someone else. Perhaps there is something auspicious in that? And my services will bring in *huge* amounts of money."

A feeling of euphoria enveloped Mai's very being. She knew she could capably pull it off. She never doubted her powers of manipulation and ability to con people. She could convince any man that she held the key that would unlock the door to his innermost desires. "I could give men what they really want, although sex might be part of the bargain," she thought. "After all, I might need to collect semen samples."

It was in Gothenburg that Mai began her tour of upscale coffee houses and tea rooms. She toyed with new business slogans and taglines. She rejected "Mai's Babies". No identifiers. More generic. "Designer Babies"? No, too generic. "A more perfect you?" or "A more perfect me?" Better. "Buy a Baby." Maybe. Or simply, "Buy Baby". After all, it was all about selling a dream baby.

3

Unusual Proposal

Mai loved the looks of Scandinavians. The taller, the blonder, the better. By Scandinavian standards she was average in height, but Mai towered over most Chinese women. She confidently glided into the coffee bar and removed her winter coat, revealing a business professional suit that accentuated her shapely figure. More eyes than one gazed in her direction including a middle-aged man who sat cross-legged on a leather sofa, sipping black coffee from a huge ceramic mug. As she walked in, she noticed the well-dressed man and his suave veneer. He was obviously a man of means.

Like most Swedes, Lars' coffee or *fika* break was accompanied by a favorite pastry, his choice, hazelnut coffee cake. And like most Swedes, strong coffee in both the morning and afternoon is a way of life. He often came across beautiful women in Gothenburg, but none with the exotic yet elegant look of Mai. In hotel bars, attractive women trolled for wealthy men, either for marriage or barter. He usually avoided them. He didn't need any complications. But this young woman didn't fit that picture. Perhaps she was not quite what she appeared to be. He thought he detected a note of deception in her guise. What was it she was trying to hide? She glanced his way more than once. He suspected some form of entrapment.

Mai blatantly observed his reserved manner. She knew she had his attention when he momentarily held her gaze, equally curious of her. She slipped into a comfortable lounge chair at an adjacent table.

Catching Lars' eye again, she sipped her cup of unadorned green tea. Leaning in his direction she asked, "Do you speak English?"

Surprised by her directness, he answered, "Of course. But I don't hear well, at this distance." Lars was just testing, but it worked. She picked up her tea cup and joined him on the settee.

"Do you live here? Have a family?" Mai asked.

Amused by her candid questions, he uncharacteristically engaged her in dialogue. "I come often to Göteborg, but my home is Stockholm." He was surprised by his own spontaneity with this stranger.

"Do you have children?" She played her sweetest game.

Lars couldn't resist her interest in him. "Unfortunately, no."

"But why not?" Mai was never shy about probing too deeply into the personal lives of men. She found most were willing to divulge their deepest secrets in hope of intimacy. Seduction was a game she perfected over time, only now she would try a different tactic. She wanted men to reveal what they really wanted, beyond any sexual desires. She was practicing her new marketing approach and business plan.

"Why no babies? You are so handsome. So tall and blond." Mai encouraged him, feigning curiosity, as though she found him fascinating. He mentally flinched at the flattery. He knew he was no oil painting, average in looks, but handsome? No. His once-blond hair was now thin and gray.

Lars thought her appearance was mixed, an Asian-European fusion. Her unnatural curvature, to his professional eye, was voluptuous and likely augmented. Her eyes seemed artificially round. He leaned towards her as if unable to hear, but only to get a closer look. He detected small but visible incision lines, the tell-tale scars of surgery to remove part of the eyelid for a rounder, more oval shape. It only heightened his curiosity, he wanted to know more about her. He knew plenty of women in his line of work. Cosmetic surgery.

Lars suspected that Mai was not the same person she once was. Augmented and altered but not obscenely so. He tried to imagine the original shape of her eyes. Her long legs appeared flawless but not likely adulterated. He couldn't be sure if she had other procedures. Well-shaped hips, he thought, but no evidence of a Brazilian butt lift. She had no excess fat to spare.

"I'm Lars." He avoided her family questions, wondering why she persisted at prying into his personal life.

"I'm Mai." She paused only slightly. "Why no children, Lars?"

"I inherited a bad gene that I would not inflict on any child of mine." He could see no harm in divulging his secret in exchange for the attention of such a charming yet mysterious woman. Lars, by choice, never had children. He carried a dangerous mutation, a heart defect. The odds were stacked against any offspring he might produce.

"Oh, I am sorry, but you know there are ways that genes, your DNA, can be corrected now, don't you?"

"But, of course, I know. It's often in the news. Editing genes in embryos has been performed in Sweden. But it's only experimental. It will take years before the technology becomes freely available."

"Many countries use gene editing tools, like CRISPR. Lars, I'm a scientist, I've changed the DNA of many animals and microbes." She squirmed, stroking her neck as if to sooth stiff muscles, then cleared her throat. "And what do you do, Lars?"

Ignoring her question again, he doled out a compliment to see her reaction. "You are smart as well as beautiful."

Mai didn't acknowledge what she had heard so many times before, she wasn't easily distracted. She persisted with a singular focus. "And your job is?"

"I run a business in Stockholm. Often, I come to Gothenburg to meet with clients. And in the harbor I have my boat."

"A big boat?"

"Not big like an ocean liner, so I suppose you would say it's small." Lars teased.

"A big boat for a family? You can still have children." Mai tried to imagine the size of his wealth.

Lars laughed at her persistence. "My oh my, Mai, you are relentless." Her recurring frown perplexed him. He was drawn to intelligent women who had a vulnerable side. Lars was mystified by her charm.

"Your bad gene is not a problem, Lars. I can analyze your DNA in my lab. Perhaps we could perfect it for you? And IVF clinics can implant perfected embryos in your wife." She suggested.

"But my wife is not young, she has no viable eggs left to fertilize. So, I'm afraid this is not possible…"

Mai interrupted him. "That's not a problem."

"And why is that?" He encouraged her as she honed her sales technique.

"Do you want something new? Do you want a more perfect you?" She pitched her hook, testing it on her prospective client.

"A more perfect me?" he asked and chuckled.

"Yes. A more perfect you." Mai knew she piqued his interest.

"Is this science fiction?" Lars playfully probed, wanting to hear more of her selling points.

"No, it's not fiction. Or fantasy. Certainly, I can help you with this," she persisted.

"Perhaps, but it's not legal. Only approved labs can experiment and edit DNA in embryos. But they're not allowed to develop into babies." He hesitated, then added. "At least, not in this country."

Mai stood up, smoothing her skirt to purposely distract him. Lars gray-blue eyes panned her silhouette, her image was impeccable. But it was her performance that most impressed him, she emanated confidence with her facade of a professional business woman. Not unlike those saleswomen, the pharmaceutical reps who frequent clinics and hospitals. Intrigued, he was drawn in.

She looked around and saw no one within earshot. "Ours are not made from scratch. Synthetic babies, I tell you, are science fiction. Well, maybe someday. But why start from scratch when you already have a lot to work with? We can keep the best of you, but enhance with extra special traits. Your choice." She sat down closer to him.

Lars continued to humor and cajole her. Not only was he captivated, he wanted to know what motivated her.

"If I had a choice, I would prefer children that resemble me. Tall and blond, but much more handsome. And free of disease, of course."

"Removing bad genes from embryos is easy, I have a very experienced team of scientists who can do this. They can snip out DNA for your heart disease. A simple procedure. But you must want more? Most people want more."

Lars pondered for a while, what more would he want? It was an entertaining, speculative game for him. "In Scandinavia, we admire the tall and athletic. And brain power. Superior intelligence. Very healthy, perhaps with extra immunity to fight diseases." His grin beamed across his face, well aware of the fanciful dream she was trying to sell him. He knew all about enhancement, after all his business revolved around cosmetic changes driven by the desire for youth and beauty. And he knew more about narcissistic obsessions than Mai could even imagine. "And what do you suggest?"

"High intelligence is most important. In China, the genomes of geniuses have been identified. And likely, the next generation of babies will be enhanced to make them super-smart."

"How do you know this, Mai? Are you Chinese?" Lar suspected she might be.

"No. I am not Chinese. I just know these things. I study. Do research. And my lab techniques are superior." She deflected his suggestion and pressed on. "How about strength and athletic ability? Stronger bones and muscles? A stronger heart? And a longer life."

He smiled and nodded, encouraging her. "*Ja*. Of course, yes."

"Good looks are a real social asset. Parents want children to resemble them, but only more perfect. A more perfect me. Or a more perfect you." Mai fine-tuned her pitch as she went along, then joined him again on the sofa."

"But not synthetic babies?" Lars egged her on.

"Someday scientists will create babies without parents. Build them with three billion DNA blocks, like Lego toys. But it is not easy. Far-away, in years to come." She babbled on.

"I don't want a clone. No mini-me for me." He cupped his big hand over her thin delicate fingers but Mai seemed unfazed.

She knew she had Lars nearly trapped in her web. To lure him in, she looked deeply into his faded blue eyes. "No one wants a clone. Now we have better methods. A child like you but edited to perfection. No flaws, no diseases. But enhanced. Superior intellect. Unparalleled beauty. And strong. Tremendous strength."

"How do you create this perfect human life? How can you do this? You're just toying with me."

"This is not the creation of human life. But it's the perfection of you. A more perfect you." Mai insisted.

"My perfect child. I can only dream." Lars sighed.

"I can make your dreams come true, a son with your image and likeness. We can now take sperm cells and edit their genes to replicate a more perfect you. Those cells can divide, as if they are an embryo. They grow and change, go through all the stages, and become a perfect replica of you." Mai was eager to impress him with her knowledge of the science.

"You're saying you have new technology?" He was incredulous and excited but he didn't let on.

"This method is unique, no fertilized eggs are needed. It requires the most advanced techniques and superior skills in our private labs. It's time consuming to coax these cells. And very expensive. Only for the wealthiest clients." Mai noticed that Lars did not bat an eyelash.

"So, my cells can be turned into a perfected embryo? Not a clone, but a perfect me? So, it is me, but enhanced. And those superior genes can be passed down to future generations. Hmm." Lars said.

More than intrigued, Lars could see the potential for many millions of euros and dollars sequestered away in offshore accounts. He quickly approximated what his clients would pay for this type of perfection. This goes far beyond the superficial changes in plastic surgery, he thought. It could generate untold personal wealth for me and this curious stranger.

"Surely, there must be risks, but think of the possibilities for the next generation." Lars found himself not just acclaiming but enthusiastically endorsing Mai's unusual business proposal. "What a great benefit to all of mankind. Our future is in your hands." But he was thinking about people, his clients, who would pay a small fortune for this type of service. "Tell me more."

"As you say, all of mankind. Your offspring will be a magnificently designed variation of you. We start with you and then your son becomes whatever you want him to be. The custom-made designer embryos can be implanted in surrogate mothers. It's easiest and most secretive with surrogates in eastern countries." Mai paused for him to take in the possibilities.

Lars felt drawn to Mai's intellect and to what she had to offer. But he could also see a lucrative business venture. And an escape from a life of unfulfilled dreams, catering to superficial wish fulfillments for neurotic people. He wanted so much more.

"Lars, privacy is essential for the next step in the process." She lowered her voice. "A cash deposit is required." Tearing off a corner from her notebook, she wrote a hefty amount in Swedish Krona.

Lars said with a wry smile, "It's a small price for perfection."

4

Three J's

My mind is wandering when I hear Jeremy's voice. He's good at interrupting my thoughts.

"Are you mad?" He repeats his question twice, trying to get my attention.

"What do you mean?" I knew where Jeremy was going but I played along. "Yeah, crazy mad."

"Well that too." Jeremy said with a grin. "Are you still mad at them?"

"Of course. But it's always about them, isn't it? They take all the credit. We're never in the limelight."

I'm jealous of the accolades that went to the others. The heroes venerated by the media. I concede they foiled a bioterror attack on America and captured the mastermind behind it. But we were the ones who uncovered the clues they would have never found. I can't get beyond feeling cheated, but it would be bad to reveal our unofficial role. That much I know for sure.

"Would you really want the notoriety? Isn't it better to live in anonymity? Hey, and they paid us well. So, it's off to India we go. Our own private celebration." Jeremy thinks I need a reward. I just want flattery. But we're sworn to secrecy, something I've never been very good at.

"Hey silly nuts, remember to keep it buried." Jeremy warned. "We're better off if no one knows about our role. Let's hope it stays subterranean." Another earthy metaphor from cryptic guy, Jeremy. He always falls back on his geography background when he searches for metaphors. At least it wasn't one of his obscure Wittgensteinian stories.

"Yeah, of course, you're right." I agree. Bullshit, I think. I want to be feted and loved by all, says a little voice in my head.

"Don't worry about it. On the scale of things, it doesn't matter." Jeremy peers at my computer. "You're working on your talk, aren't you? You've only got three days to go, grasshopper."

Jeremy advises me like some kung fu master with his childishly ignorant student. Then he taps on my head too many times. He can be so annoying. I silently scowl.

"Yeah, I'm getting there." I stare at my computer and think I'd better get focused. The clock is ticking. I can't talk about the ongoing investigation, the manhunt for Mei Wong. Manhunt? Or is it a womanhunt? Whatever, she's a formidable fugitive. Sometimes I feel like cheering for her, the woman clever enough to evade US and multiple intelligence agencies. She's managed to elude the FBI, Interpol, Europol and all the other assorted "Pols". It's not often that a woman ranks in the upper echelon of most wanted terrorists. Yeah, I know she's a murderer, but she sure has managed to outsmart the big boys and girls. At least for the time being.

I never did like public speaking but now I've been roped into it. My topic for the Forensic Science seminar: How to find the source of a bioterror attack. I'll tell them, you must look at the microbe's genes, it's genetic make-up. It's better than a fingerprint. It's like using human DNA to find a killer.

Case in point: There are two Tiger Flu victims, one infected in Hong Kong, the other infected in Copenhagen. Now, those two victims were nearly eight thousand miles apart. But both were infected by a flu virus nearly identical to the one that killed tigers in a Chinese zoo. The tigers had eaten dead chicken.

Did either of the two victims visit the Chinese zoo? No, they were nowhere close to that zoo. Is it just a bizarre coincidence? I doubt it. So, I query, did the mutant Tiger Flu come from the same lab? Possibly from the same test tube?

"Just where was it created?" I mumble aloud.

Jeremy looks over my shoulder. "Looks like gibberish. What's with the letters?"

I ignore his jibe. "This shows gene sequences. How the Tiger Flu was tweaked in a lab to make...."

Jeremy finishes my sentence, "...to make it more deadly?"

"Not only more deadly but really contagious. It's just too damn easy to create biologic weapons." I hear a hint of hysteria in my voice.

"Well, I'm sure you'll scare the crap out of them." Jeremy teases as usual.

"Hey, the recipes are out there. You've heard the warnings. Terrorists can easily create bioweapons." I stare at him with bug-eyed emphasis. "I could do it in our basement."

"But we don't have a basement. How about our garage?" Jeremy eggs me on.

"Yep, plenty of do-it-yourself rogues already doing that. And besides, Mei Wong is still out there. Who knows what she's up to now. Or who she's working for." I dive back into my presentation and don't come up for air until finishing the final slide.

I've read my notes over so many times I could probably re-cite them in my sleep. The auditorium is filling up and I see Jeremy in the front row making faces at me. He knows how to help with my stage fright. Make me laugh. I hope no one else sees his goofy faces—a ridiculous grin, a tongue panting like a puppy in anticipation. I poke out my tongue at him and hear a few spontaneous giggles. Oh no, there goes my credibility.

Older than most of the students, a handsome guy eases into a wooden lecture hall chair. He pulls up the half-table used by students who in times past actually wrote notes. Although most attendees play with their smart phones and tablets, he opens a laptop. This lecture seminar is open to the public, it's a series now twenty years since its inception. The always popular title is Forensic Science. Something about the word forensics always draws people's interest. Some students take the course for credit, others have a special interest. The slated subject was publicized locally. The title "Microbial Forensics" managed to lure a few in.

I look at the young guy, having singled him out from a crowd of about fifty and catch his eye. I wonder what he's thinking as he looks at me, a woman who barely sees over the podium. He's probably questioning what I have to offer. I'm no expert, just a writer of speculative fiction and a few journal articles.

But then the lights dim. My cheat notes are embedded in the slides. I've added cartoons and sarcastically make light of the fact that "We are all going to die." The audience laughs at all the right places and this makes me happy.

I breathe a sigh of relief as the lights go up nearly forty minutes later. Jeremy smiles. Gives a thumbs-up. A half-dozen people ask questions, then the audience mostly filters out. A few linger. The attractive guy is one of them. He waits until all the others have had their say. I couldn't help thinking, if only I were a decade or two younger. Enthusiastic, he talks about his interests in synthetic biology and gene editing. Right up my alley. I'm thinking I'm in love. Of course, it's just a fleeting fantasy. But I'm not dead yet.

Jeremy listens in and surprises me. The not very bashful blond gets an invitation to dinner at our place. As it turns out, Jack, surname Asbell, has a PhD in microbiology and an obsession with genomics. I'm surprised we haven't heard of him, especially here in the tiny state of Rhode Island, where everyone is either related or knows someone you know. It's really that incestuous, as anyone will tell you who has ever lived in the miniscule microcosm. The state is just one big extended dysfunctional family.

And so began our relationship with Jack.

5

Designer Baby

Mai opened a small case and pointed to a variety of test tubes.

"For processing skins cells." She removed a swab from a culture kit. "Please open your mouth."

Lars sat down and complied with his mouth wide open. Mai gently scraped the swab over his inner cheek, she collected his cells.

"The next steps in the process are very intensive. The DNA analysis. Growing your skin cell cultures."

Mai then retreated to the bathroom. Lars was not totally surprised when Mai walked out draped in a sheer robe.

"The next step is collecting your sperm. You have the payment?" Mai wanted the money upfront.

"Your fees for specimen collection are in this envelop." Lars handed a thick wad of cash to Mai. She slipped it below the rack of test tubes at the bottom of her case.

Lars untied the loose ribbon tied around her waist and bent over for a closer inspection. "You have scars that show your breasts have been augmented." He hefted each one with his fingertips as if calculating their weight. "Your hips and buttocks look and feel natural. Your thighs are firm and muscular." He poked gently at her as if she were a clinical specimen or client.

Mai thought him very odd. "We need to collect your sperm sample." She hoped he was just weird and not dangerous. Her last client in Stockholm always lurked in the back of her mind.

Lars ignored what she said. He looked at her eyes, not an intimate gaze, but he inspected the contours, the re-shaping. He gently probed and stretched her skin, her upper eyelid in particular. His spidery fingers explored her facial details. "Your correction scars were obvious to me when we first met."

"Why are you looking at me like this? How do you know these things, Lars?" She wondered if he had some strange fetish or fascination she hadn't yet come across in her multiple contacts with men.

"I have many clients." Lar stated, matter of fact.

"I don't understand. Do your clients have scars?" Mai was confused, still thinking him peculiar.

"This is what I do for a living. Augmentations. Corrections."

In a eureka moment, Mai tossed her head back and said, "Ahhh, now I understand. You do these surgeries. Cosmetic surgery is your business. You're interested in the work I had done in Paris." Mai laughed as she realized the opportunity. She was quick to assess the potential for what Lars might have to offer. "You have clients. Perhaps together we can start a business?"

"Perhaps. But first, you must finish collecting the specimen sample, Mai."

When Mai dropped the robe to the floor, Lars noticed faded yellow bruises on her arms, back, and legs. He suspected someone had recently beaten her, but he said nothing. Lars worried that she was a vulnerable, troubled young woman. He felt a strong desire to protect her from abuse.

"You could stay here if you like." Lars gestured with a hand wave at the one-bedroom flat. "No fees or bills for you. I use it only on occasion. More often I stay in hotels where I meet with my clients."

"Lars, really?" Mai could barely comprehend her luck and the turn of events.

"I own this building. These are not luxury apartments, nothing special. I bought them a few years ago. An investment, but sadly the price has barely increased."

Mai looked around at the quality Scandinavian furnishings. The rooms were spacious compared to the crowded Chinese apartment she grew up in.

Only one thought went through Mai's mind as she collected Lars sperm sample. *This must be my lucky day.*

Re-dressed in casual spring attire, Lars looked fashionably professional. He asked, "Do you have a laboratory where you bring these samples? Or is everything not quite what it seems to be?"

Mai flinched at his question but ignored the inference. "I have many resources but need to build my business. I'll contract lab scientists, there are plenty of people with the right technical skills. But I need investment money from you for my business." Mai corrected herself. "Our business."

"You don't really think I believe you. You'll take my money and run." Lars teased Mai. She was embarrassed he found her so transparent.

"I am not a fake." Mai said in her defense, but even she could see the irony in her newly designed body.

After Lars first met Mai in the coffee bar, he read up on the new field of gene editing in human embryos. He could see a strong consumer demand for it. Beyond the cosmetic enhancements he offered, many people now wanted genetic enhancements, especially for their children. It could be a lucrative business.

"Listen Mai, many of my clients look for more than what I can offer them."

Mai saw where Lars was going. "There are now countries that edit DNA in human embryos to remove birth defects and diseases. But we could promise a better dream. Superchildren!" Mai's exuberance was infectious.

Lars mused for a while, thinking about this uncharted territory. "I know I have clients with the desire and money. Perhaps some may be willing to take the risk?"

"I've nearly perfected the genetic menu of enhancements and selling points," Mai said with enthusiasm. She pulled out a menu list from her oversized purse and read some of the basics.

"Appearance traits like eye, skin, and hair color. Of course, children that are defect free with increased resistance to disease. There is so much more to offer."

Lars scratched his gray-blond scalp. "My clients believe everything I tell them. I can only do so much perfecting of faces and bodies, they always want more. Most want the promise of the fountain of youth. A longer life span and..."

Mai interrupted. "Their children could live forever. DNA editing can delay or turn off aging in humans. It's not just a dream but a reality. Designed to perfection in so many other ways."

Lars loved her pitch, the dream of immortality. "What other ways, Mai?"

"Increased intelligence. Even smarter than me." Mai bragged. "Smarter, stronger, and faster!" She created a new mantra borne by her vision.

"So cognitive skills can be boosted. People will definitely want that. Strong athletes. Very fast too?"

"And the best, but most expensive are the self-clones, available only to men. Sperm and cheek cells can be edited for superior dominant traits. This has already been done in experimental labs." Mai beamed with self-proclaimed brilliance. "They are the best to buy. My best embryonic creation, a "superhuman man".

"Certainly, they would be best sellers." Lars stroked Mai's hair in approval.

"But the most expensive." Mai grinned at the thought of more money.

Lars warned, "We don't want to promise a dystopia of superior people. It must be credible, but fanciful, induce them into a dream state."

"Biologic superiority, that's the ultimate selling point." Mai lit up and flashed a big smile.

"Mai, we must be convincing."

"I'll create marketing pieces for 'human upgrades'. Beautiful children with athletic power, intellectual ability, incredible memory. What most people don't know is that many traits are polygenetic, controlled by lots of different genes."

"My clients don't need to know that. Designer babies for the rich? This could be a rewarding business, for both of us." The gleam in Lars' eyes came from the bright future he saw ahead.

"Lars, I can put together a small team. We need a lab to act as a front. They don't need to know the details. I've used people like this before." Mai couldn't contain her excitement.

Lars already figured she was using him too. But his desire for more money and his infatuation with Mai ran deep. She made him feel like the man he wanted to be. He still glowed from her expert attention.

Mai bantered on with buzz words. "Babies by Design. Offering custom designed embryo edits."

"We have other things to think about. Surrogacy. IVF clinics. I have contacts in eastern countries. We may need them…or not. But we will offer the complete package." Lars' contribution to the business plan unfolded before his eyes.

But euro and dollar signs were all Mai could see. "How will I be paid, Lars?"

"I'll set up accounts in safe places. I know of paradise islands where we can go some day."

"Safe places?" Mai asked.

"Secret accounts." Lars nodded.

"Cash now. Islands later." Mai had little faith in delayed gratification.

6

First Supper

Dinner at our house is a spicy curry whipped up by Jeremy. From our garden I concocted a cucumber mint raita. A mix of beers, Indian and Asian varieties along with Jack's selection of New England craft brews to quell the heat of Jeremy's chicken vindaloo. I can always find an excuse to overindulge in booze, food, and men.

We bore poor Jack with too many tales from our years living in exotic places. He doesn't seem to mind. In turn, he talks about his work with microbes.

My eye's glaze, over as do Jack's, when Jeremy goes on about the magic of algorithms and the joys of the internet.

Luckily, our stories carry the evening—in particular, our years in Zimbabwe. Animal anecdotes usually interest friends, so we use them liberally on social occasions and tell Jack some of our best adventures.

Jeremy says, "At a watering hole, we came across a herd of elephants. They're drinking, splashing, bathing. Rolling in the dirt, dusting themselves…"

"..like talcum powder after a bath." I finish his sentence.

Jack asks, "How close did you get? African elephants can be quite dangerous."

I point at Jeremy. "You haven't forgotten the day you got us stuck in the mud. After a heavy downpour during the rainy season, the sky just opened up with torrential sheets of rain."

"Uh, oh. Here she goes," Jeremy warns "my sins will be revealed."

"I kept yelling at you, Jeremy. 'Don't slow down'. But, of course, you didn't listen. You braked in that pool of muddy water, dum-dum." Jeremy flips me the finger but I don't take any notice.

I go on. "It took us ages to pile sand around the tires. But then a big bull elephant came out of nowhere. He danced around on all fours, his huge ears fanning, flapping with rage, really threatening us…"

"A bloody huge male, must have weighed seven tons," Jeremy says and embellishes with, "you should've seen the size of his dong." I groan at the image Jeremy provoked. Then roll my eyes at Jack, as if shocked.

"Really, Jeremy." By now we are all sufficiently fueled and our conversation is revving up. I love how we share our memories.

Jack didn't stand a chance, but his expressive eyes showed his amusement.

"The elephant charged at the back end of the van, but I managed to get some traction. We escaped with only moments to spare," Jeremy says with wildly animated gestures.

I segue and say, "So many adventures, like that herd of cape buffalo in Wankie game reserve. There were easily a hundred of them, way too close for comfort. They're unpredictable and extremely dangerous. They kill hunters and even lions." I'm hyperventilating and excited, but it's got nothing to do with the cape buffalo.

"And don't forget that troop of baboons. We're walking in the bush and we end up right in the thick of some fifty of them foraging for food," Jeremy says.

"Would they attack you?" Jack asks.

"A couple males showed their big front teeth at me, just a warning, but ready to attack if I provoked them. I knew enough not to smile or show my teeth. They can be very aggressive." Jeremy grins displaying his big front teeth at Jack.

"Their powerful jaws can break your bones," I say and raise my eyebrows at Jack.

Jack gets in a few words. "Those baboons must've been terrifying."

"Actually, my worst encounter was with guerrillas," Jeremy says.

"Gorillas? I didn't know there were gorillas in Zimbabwe." Jack tilts his head.

"No, not the animal kind. Ger….rillas. Guerrillas. As in terrorists. A roving band of irregular fighters with AK-47's and an RPG, a rocket-propelled grenade. The guy with the missile launcher on his shoulder aimed it at the front of our bus. He was swaying, drunk-as-a-skunk. It looked like an ambush to me, about a half dozen guys saluting with AK's, waving their weapons up and down the side of the school bus. I told the kids 'shut up and don't move'. They froze, scared shitless."

Jack asks, "But why were you with a busload of kids?"

"I was doing a favor, helping coach high school kids for a tournament in Botswana. The players were remnants of the Rhodesian cricket team. It wasn't long after the war for independence. Luckily, the gentlemen let us go."

I remembered being afraid when Jeremy first told me his bus story. Frightened about what happened, what more *could* have happened.

"Lucky you," Jack says.

"But 20,000 people weren't so lucky," Jeremy says. He shakes his head and tells the sad story. "When we lived in Zimbabwe during the early to mid-1980s, Robert Mugabe sent in troops to put down the Matabele opposition. The Fifth Brigade, trained by the North Koreans, were utterly ruthless. They conducted a series of massacres against our neighbors, the Ndebele civilians."

"Ethnic cleansing," I say. I didn't know what else to call it.

"We saw the soldiers. Rounding up people on the road to Victoria Falls." Jeremey confirms with a nod.

"But we didn't understand at the time," I say. "We didn't know what was going to happen to those people."

"It wasn't long after that we left…" Jeremy trails off. We all shake our heads and say no more.

Once sufficiently inebriated, our mood shifted from the horror of atrocities to lighter tales.

"Imagine a warthog drunk on fermented Marula apples trying to back into his den," I say and we chuckle.

Then Jeremy talks about his near miss with a crocodile while fishing on the Zambesi River.

Jack laughs and slaps his leg, then punches Jeremy lightly on the shoulder. They seem to have some camaraderie going. Nothing like wars stories to get that macho thing and testosterone flowing.

And there's nothing like a double dose of testosterone to get me going. I could smell the male pheromones that permeated the air, even more potent and pungent than the spicy curry sauce with red chili peppers. And, I'm fantasizing, here are two men who could serve up a tempting taste-filled desert.

Then Jeremy opens the refrigerator and brings out a bowl of Rasmalai, my favorite Indian desert. Soft fluffy Indian cheese rasgulas, flavored with saffron, swimming in a sweetened, thick clotted cream. Jeremy serves up desert bowls with two cream-colored balls in the juicy liquid. On top, he sprinkled pistachio nuts.

"These are absolutely indecent," Jack says.

"Delectable, delicious," I purr.

"Salacious, lascivious, libidinous…" We laugh at Jeremy's licentious alliterative rant.

A competition ensued, who could be more naughty, lewd, ribald or just downright dirty. And I'm loving every minute of it.

And then Jack comes up with the most wanton of them all. "Lubricious."

It's a word with so many possible meanings. And I'm feeling a mix of all permutations. I can't help being enamored with Jack. And simultaneously with Jeremy. Two men, just the thought makes me lubricious. Jeremy often teases me that I am a wanton woman.

I think about a movie I'd recently seen. A *ménage à trois*. Three lovers. But unlike in the movie, a classic male fantasy of one man with two women, in my fantasy the roles are reversed. I'm too self-indulgent to want to share with another women. I want to be the center of attention. The one desired, the point of focus, the love or lust interest. Feeling light-headed, I'm sweating from a mix of alcohol and hot peppers. Running my fingers through my dark curly locks, I tug on my hair as a warning sign. Not wanting to embarrass myself, I retreat to the bathroom and splash cold water on my face.

On exiting the bathroom, I find Jeremy waiting in the hallway. I comment that I'm, "just cooling down." I know I look guilty of something, even if it's just my thoughts.

"No more wine, peachnut." He knows my limit with booze.

Jeremy is full of endearments that are often derogatory. A derogatory endearment may sound like an oxymoron because, well, it is. Jeremy applies them liberally, usually in jest or as affectionate gestures. Sometimes, they're warnings or admonitions.

Jeremy seldom uses endearments like "love" or "sweetie". Instead he gravitates toward those weird affectionate "P" terms like "poppet", "puss" and, the one I hate most, "pussums". "Passion-puss" is kind of cute but only when used by an Englishman. "Snookums" is archaic, diminutive, and creepy. Lamb chop, cutie-pie, and sweetiekins are just cornball.

Then, there are the vegetables like "pumpkin", "my little cabbage", or "little petite pois". I don't mind the occasional fruits or flowers, like "sweet pea" or "petal". But when he calls me "peachnut", I know that he means that I'm not a peach, as in succulent, sweet, or fleshy and pink, but the nut inside.

I complain to Jack about Jeremy's never-ending array of endearments. They go on and on. Ad infinitum. Some refer to my physical attributes. Others refer to my sporadic bouts of ridiculousness and insanity. "Miss Curly Wurly" or "cheeky chops" are cute alliterations. "Silly nuts" or silly willy", are just plain silly. Jeremy calls me "guzzle guts", if I pour a second glass of wine. And "grumpie girl" if I wake up and grunt first thing in the morning.

Jeremy doesn't use English animal endearments like "dove" or "lamb" or "duck". He goes straight for the huge beasts with "my little water buffalo", if I go for a swim. Or the anatomically cheeky and rude "hippobutamus", if I happen to bend over.

I most despise his insult "stunted little dwarf" as politically incorrect and insensitive. This derogative reference to my short stature has just got to stop. He thinks he is funny. But me, not so much.

I don't mind if he says I'm the "bees knees".

Windbag that I am, I've blown the guys away with my blustering monologue. Jack's fallen asleep on the living room couch. All the better, since he shouldn't attempt to drive. Jeremy removes his shoes. I bring a pillow and blanket. Retreating to our bedroom, we're too wired to fall asleep.

Jeremy insults me, "You really are a silly moo." And he starts to giggle.

"And you're a sarky monkey." *Touché.*

7

Mai Meets Hong

"**S**orry if I was staring at you, but I can't quite place where you're from. I seldom meet people who look like me." Hong sat himself down on the bar stool next to Mai.

Mai could see a resemblance, but his features appeared natural, not altered.

"What language do you speak?" Hong asked.

"I prefer using the language of science." Mai gestured at the décor that pervaded the unusual hotel bar and restaurant. Models of molecules, a poster history of graphene, flasks with flowers, and beakers with wine all referred to scientific facts, models, and mathematics.

"Nothing shocks me. I'm a scientist." Hong read from an airplane banner that trailed behind a yellow model biplane hanging from the ceiling.

"Nothing shocks you?" Mai echoed. "I'm a scientist too."

Hong ordered two colas.

"And how are you with mathematical equations?" Hong pointed under the bar top at equations scribbled on a chalkboard below.

Hong gazed at Mai's exposed legs dangling from her barstool. It was unseasonably warm so wearing shorts was not unusual. Much of Scandinavia sweltered in a heat wave with record highs. Yet another reminder of global warming.

Mai bent her head down to see the math equations inscribed on the faux chalkboard. Hong focused on her loose cotton summer top that draped open, exposing an exquisite set of globes. He quickly shifted his gaze to a metallic sphere, a Van de Graaff generator. An array of scientific instruments in a wall display littered the lounge.

Hong lifted his drink and turned to Mai. "My name is Hong. And yours is?"

"Mai." She paused to drink from her beaker of cola. "Your accent is American?"

"Yes, it is. But it's funny, I'm seldom asked if I'm American. People always insist that I'm Chinese. Or one of the other "Neses". So many ignorant people out there, they really don't know the difference."

"Were you born in America, Hong?"

"I'm Euro-Asian, Chinese dad, English mom. They married in Hong Kong before emigrating to the US. I was raised in Rhode Island."

"Where is this island?" Mai had no idea where he was talking about.

Hong chuckled. "It's a tiny state, not an island. It's between Boston and New York. But many people have never heard of it. You can easily miss it, it takes less than an hour to drive across. Other people confuse it with Long Island, which is really just part of New York and is a real island." Hong could tell he was confusing her. "And you Mai, where do you live?"

"I live here now. For a while. But I'm never mistaken as European. I describe myself as a 'Pan-Asian-Euro fusion'." Mai smiled like a reptile, Hong thought her a chameleon. She appeared to change and blend in with the background.

He laughed. "You're like a buffet restaurant that panders to all tastes."

Mai snapped back, "It means I can be whoever I want to be." She frowned, unsure if Hong was making fun of her.

Hong continued to laugh at Mai's dismay. "Well, that's one way of doing things."

"I do as I wish." She abruptly stood up as if to leave.

"Please, Mai, don't leave. We Americans like to kid around."

"I'll be back." She wandered off in search of the *Damer*.

As she combed her newly styled short hair, she wondered if Hong might be useful to her in some way. Perhaps he was a visiting academic in science or technology? Judging by the décor of the hotel, his leanings seemed obvious, besides his interest in her legs and cleavage.

Mai returned and perched on the barstool. "Are you staying at this hotel?"

"I'm in Gothenburg on a two-year job exchange. Sharing technical expertise in modifying DNA. I work in a lab near here. Editing animal embryos. And you? What are your interests?"

Mai couldn't believe her luck. "I'm interested in editing human DNA. Quite a few countries in Europe, even here in Sweden, edit human embryos. Mostly, they knock out bad genes that cause genetic diseases."

"Wow, I would never have thought you and I were such a perfect genetic match," Hong blushed and quickly added, "well, you know what I mean. How likely is it that we would both be interested in the same thing?"

Mai agreed. "Yes, how intriguing. Just think of DNA editing possibilities with human babies."

Hong scratched his head as if deep in thought. "I don't think it will be anytime too soon that gene-edited babies are legal. At least, not in this part of the world."

"In China, there are edited babies." Mai put out a feeler.

"Yes, China were the first with gene-edited children. I don't see any problem with that."

Encouraged by Hong's sense of ethics, Mai prodded him. "In this country and others, gene-edited embryos are not allowed to grow into babies. Many countries edit DNA in embryos, but only grow them for a couple of weeks."

"Too bad. They're missing a big opportunity. Countries with designer babies will control the human race."

"Hong, how experienced are you with gene editing techniques?"

"It's child's play. I do micro-injections. I'm a great technician. I teach techniques here at the university. Besides working in my lab, I'm organizing the upcoming international gene editing conference. Right next door."

"Oh Hong, I'd love to attend the conference, but the fees are beyond my means."

"That's not a problem. For you, perhaps gratis?" Hong moved in closer, his forehead just centimeters from her. "But you still haven't told me about your genetic mix."

"Hong, I'm such a hybrid. I already told you."

"So, you're a mutt?" Hong teased.

"I don't know that word. It must be short for mutation."

Hong laughed again. "My lab is near here. If you have time, I'll give you a quick tour before I get back to work."

They walked to Hong's lab in the science and technology center adjacent to the Riverside hotel.

Gowned up, Mai could have been any one of a number of students. Hong not only wanted to impress her but was curious to know more about her. She signed in on his visitor log under the name, Mai Tran. Tran, a common Vietnamese name, might as well have been Smith or Jones. Hong didn't think Mai Tran quite fit the mold. But then again, neither did he.

Hong Min Chan, an Anglo-Chinese racial mix, was ethnically hard to identify, but he got his best features from both of his parents. It was also his blended looks that helped make him a master at deception. He could easily fool others.

"Let me take your photo, Mai." She flinched at Hong's suggestion but realized it would be hard to identify her in a lab coat, N-95 mask, hair cover, and plastic eye goggles.

Mai, happy with the photo, asked him to text it to her. "It might be a good for PR."

Hong, thrilled to get her cell number, could barely wait to connect with her. He thought her PR comment strange but didn't want to appear nosy. There'd be time to quiz her gently. First, gain her trust by not being snoopy or aggressive.

"Can we get together later this weekend? I'll pick you up for dinner?"

"My room is only temporary." Mai sidetracked. "Can we meet at your place?"

"Mine's nothing exciting, a studio flat near here. Why don't we meet up at the Riverside hotel restaurant? I'm sure you'll like the menu." Hong would probe her later. There was something odd about Mai, she seemed too perfect to be true.

8

Hot Sausage

I It's a hot, sticky summer evening, when Jeremy gets a call. "An algorithm problem. Don't wait up for me," he says, heading towards the door.

"But I've cooked cavatelli with hot sausage," I yell from the kitchen. I'm miffed that I just spent ages cooking my home-made sauce. It's been simmering for two hours. And I've just laid the table. Not to mention all the cutting up of vegetation for the tossed salad. I'm irked but there's not much I can do. But, I think, oh yes there is.

I text Jack that Jeremy's been hauled off on business and there's an empty place at the table.

⫘⫘

On the veranda, there's a welcome breeze. A reprieve from the semitropical heat of the day.

I'm satiated from having stuffed myself with sausage and now I'm guzzling pinot noir. Jack prefers knocking back his cold local brews. Our conversation drifts from cooking marinara sauce to cooking up microbes. Topics we both have a common interest in. And now I'm thinking about Tiger Flu.

I say to Jack, "You know about the capture of the infamous Kahliy, don't you?"

"Of course, in Italy. He topped the list of most wanted terrorists," Jack says.

"Yep, in a deck of cards, he's the king of spades right next to the queen, his accomplice and lover, Mei Wong."

"Ah yes, the elusive Mei Wong. A real Mata Hari so they say." Jack draws the analogy.

But I disagree and shake my head no. "Mata Hari was an exotic dancer turned spy. A seductive double agent." And I'm thinking that Jack's exotic blue eyes are just as seductive.

"Then, would you say that Mei Wong is more like Villanelle?" He suggests and raises his eyebrows.

"Mei Wong is real. Not a fictional character like Villanelle." I counter. "And Mata Hari never actually assassinated anyone. So, what do you know about Mei Wong?"

"That she's still at-large, wanted for murdering two people. She infected them with Tiger Flu and conspired to murder millions more."

"And Kahliy?" I ask.

"Mei and Kahliy plotted a 9-11 style bioterror attack aimed at America." Jack, like everyone else who followed the news, knows about the dynamic duo. It topped the headline news and even managed to usurp the daily barrage of political dysfunction, mass shootings, and sex scandals.

Jack talked about Kahliy. How he manipulated his 19 students. How he indoctrinated them with his own brand of nihilism. How he put them on flights from Europe bound for US cities. How he sexually manipulated them. And in the end, he promised them an orgy of death and destruction as they infected Americans with the Tiger Flu.

"I'm impressed," I say. Jack seems to have a good handle on the narrative details.

Jack then adds a few tidbits. "Mei Wong actually designed the bioweapon in a lab. Lucky for us, things didn't work out as intended."

"Yep," I agree, "thank goodness the Tiger Flu outbreak never happened."

"Not that a successful bio-attack couldn't happen in the future. It's just so easy. I could do it." Jack gives me a look as if everything is easy for him. He could do it if he really wanted to.

And I'm thinking that a guy like Jack will always get what he wants.

I nod along, then blabber with abandon. Jack could see I'm getting drunk as a skunk and might just throw discretion to the wind. And I do when I reveal how we worked with the "The Partners". How Jeremy and I pieced together the cryptic clues that revealed the 911-style plot.

Jack is enthralled by my tales, so I ignore the adage, "Loose lips sink ships."

With no holds barred, I narrate my loosely scripted stories. After all, I trust this young guy. And I rationalize to myself that so much of what happened is in the public domain anyway. Except for mine and Jeremy's actual roles.

I tell Jack, "I speculated. I created wild scenarios that, at the time, seemed more like science fiction."

"So, you build scenarios. Hmmm.." Jack hums in amazement. I think he must wonder if I'm just feeding him bullshit.

"And with Jeremy's help, we uncovered social media clues...buried in plain sight. Jeremy used some pretty unorthodox methods. He found the thread that lead to Kahliy's capture," I say proudly.

"Jeremy? So that's what he does. Hmmm.." Jack hums with his hand pressed against his mouth.

"We teased out this tangled web and never got any recognition. No credit for our roles." I shrug.

I still feel slighted that no one acknowledged what we did. No gratitude. No Accolades. Those people, "The Partners", continue to underscore their own roles as I wallow in self-pity, forever destined to oblivion. My ego just won't let up. Damn, I'm so insecure. I still crave recognition and flattery, unlike Jeremy who's content with himself. I wish I had his self-assured confidence.

"I think you shouldn't be telling me all this," Jack says and laughs at having caught me out.

I'm hot-flushed from the wine, blithering fool that I am. My alcohol-soaked brain won't stop obsessing, regurgitating, dredging up more horror stories of death and destruction. More doom and gloom.

"It's all those bioweapons. They must be stopped." I wave my hands, commanding that all that evil must come to an end.

Of course, microbiologist Jack knows far more about the scientific details than I do. But he indulges me and doesn't finish my sentences like Jeremy does.

"They're not like chemical agents. Not like nuclear bombs. These bioweapons self-propagate. They reproduce. They breed, they bubble, they froth, and they grow in people. Human biore-actors!" I rant *ad infinitum* and I'm increasingly anxious.

Jack adds, "and they don't discriminate... they spread... they're airborne... just a sneeze or a cough..."

"Or a kiss away." And, I think, did I really just say that? My loose lips could be put to better use.

When I finish blathering, Jack adds more fuel to my fears. "So many scary scenarios for our ultimate demise. Did you know that pox viruses can be constructed from scratch? You order the parts on-line and they're mailed to you. Horsepox, monkeypox, or smallpox anyone? How about a weaponized Ebola?"

"Nobody is safe." My excitement is hard to contain. Jack's really got me riled.

"Unless you're on an island where you can hunker down. Like on Nevis with all those billionaires." Jack smirks. "That's where I'll be." Jack stretches out his long legs and they nearly touch mine. Like a piece of eye-candy, he's tempts my sweet-tooth.

We talk about Bill Gates, how he warned that a terrorist could create a synthetic smallpox or a deadly strain of the flu. "Hundreds of millions of people could die." I say and toss my hands in the air.

Jack goes on. "There are superbugs being synthesized that we don't even know exist. And another potential threat, what if some unstable genius decides to attack us at our genetic core?"

"A genetic attack?" I'm not sure where Jack is going. "Do you mean like something inside us? Something stealthy?"

"You tell me, Jo. You're the speculator. If you were a rogue terrorist, what devious ways would you attack us?"

"Go after something to make us vulnerable? Something that finds its way into our DNA? Destroys our immunity maybe? Something insidious." I gasp in horror at the thought that we could be wiped out by some sinister scientist.

"Perhaps. But there's something new. Something very dangerous. On the cutting edge of genetic science."

"You mean a new biologic weapon?" I cringe at the possibilities.

"Sort of. But it's a new category of biologic weapon. Not a conventional one. It's R-N-A editing." Jack grins. Maybe I'm just imaging but Jack's eyes seem to light up like blue LEDs. I'm hoping that bright glimmer in his eyes is for me. But then he says, "right up my alley. I do RNA editing."

I still don't get it, so I ask Jack, "I know about DNA editing, but how could RNA editing be a bioweapon?"

"Not many people are aware of so-called 'genetic weapons'. We're at an early stage of discovery. Like the invention of nuclear bombs or hydrogen bombs. But genetic weapons are sort of like neutron bombs."

"Neutron bombs? They kill people and leave buildings standing?" I start to get the picture.

"Similar. But genetic weapons kill some people and leave others standing. They're very selective. They target ethnic groups." Jack pointed and wiggled his finger in my face.

"Ethnic? Can they target a race of people?" I thought Jack had to be kidding. "Racist neutron bombs?"

"Look. Different RNA messengers control your brain, heart, kidneys, liver, lungs. If you target those RNA messengers and disrupt them, well you know what happens, don't you?"

I shake my head to clear the booze clouding my brain. "Those organs get shut down."

"Yes, like your heart. These weapons can make your heart stop beating," Jack says and leans in towards me. My heart races.

"Or your lungs. You'll gasp for air." Jack was so close he took my breath away. "But there is something else. Something more. I have a dark secret," he says.

"So, what's your big secret? What's it you're not telling me, Jack?" I pat the arm he's draped across the table. "Trust me."

Jack blushes with what might be embarrassment. I think he'll divulge some sexual exploit but instead he dives into a lengthy monologue.

"When I was a kid, I'd hang out with my buddy in my grandparent's basement. We'd set up a lab where we toyed with chemistry sets and microscopes."

"You lived with your grandparents?"

"Yep, my Grans. My mother died in childbirth. She never married. A few years ago, I inherited the family home after grandpa died."

"Oh my, I didn't know." I feel sorry for this poor orphan and more drawn to him. Is it something maternal? No, that would be incestuous. But then I get aroused.

"We tinkered in more than one sense of the word. I still have barrels of Tinkertoys. We constructed models, molecular creations. Fast forward, I now own the house and we build a do-it-yourself micro lab in the basement. Got a DNA synthesizer and design harmless but bizarre bacterial creations. Scented bacteria like *E.coli* that smelled like bananas or wintergreen mint, instead of shit."

We both laugh and Jack continues, "also glow-in-the-dark bacteria. With fluorescence genes from green jellyfish."

"You're a biohacker, naughty boy." I tease Jack and wonder if he glows in the dark.

"Until we became biohackers *in extremis*, creating the next generation of bioweapons."

Jack just dropped the motherload. I tried not to look ruffled and nodded. "And did you?"

"We thought we had the right recipe. Got the ingredients to concoct a cocktail for a lethal bioweapon. After all, it's not rocket science, is it?" Jack winks at me.

"Very naughty indeed." I understate. Sexier that sex, his sinister streak is downright scary.

"My buddy Hong managed the animal colony at the university: the mice, rabbits, gerbils, guinea pigs, and ferrets. On his trips to visit family in China, he collected influenza samples from dead chicken. We tinkered and toyed with a promiscuous mix of viruses. Tried to create a deadly bird flu that could easily infect people."

"Very promiscuous boys, you two." I wave my pointed finger as if I'm admonishing. "So, you're the idiotic rogues playing with death."

"Welcome to the dark side. We thought we had a weaponized strain. But lucky for us, we had a mishap that proved us wrong."

I gape like a dead goldfish but Jack doesn't stop.

"Now this is really weird. Late one night a remote-controlled plane flies above the animal building. In its cargo hold was C4 explosive. Surprisingly, it did little damage, but enough to fry the ferrets we hid in the attic."

"Fried ferrets? Whose plane was it?" I ask.

"Would you believe it was another rogue group? SLAC. Stop Lab Animal Cruelty. In the end, we autoclaved our viruses. We were so idiotic. What a fucking stupid experiment."

"Very fucking stupid," I say with the emphasis on fucking. "Don't you feel guilty about what you did?"

Jack shrugs his shoulders and reaches his hand across the table. He walks his fingers up my arm, tickling my skin like a spider.

And then Jack says, "Guilt is something I don't do."

9

Hum Dinger

The next morning, I tell Jeremy about Jack's new breed of WMD. Targeted genetic weapons. A few years ago, I wrote articles on weapons of mass destruction: the chemical, biologic, radioactive, nuclear, and explosive agents. My writing on explosives later hit too close to home at the Boston Marathon.

Jeremy called it my "blood and gore" phase. It wasn't for the faint of heart. I wasn't an expert on bomb blast injuries, but I worked for one. Always a bridesmaid but never a bride.

Jeremy tracked the myriad of chemical, radioactive, and biologic weapons used on British soil. Everything from spiked-umbrella attacks with Ricin pellets, to radioactive Polonium in cups of tea. And nerve agents like Novichok, spread around the streets of Salisbury. Jeremy also kept track of how Russian military intelligence targeted turncoat spies, double agents, opponents, journalists, and anyone else who threatened or exposed them.

"I've never heard of genetic weapons." Jeremy was definitely interested.

"Yep, Jack will talk in Sweden about RNA edited viruses. They can target and kill ethnic groups. Apparently, different races and ethnicities have very unique RNA sequences. So, you can send out a genetic weapon designed to target and annihilate a group you hate. Nasty thought, isn't it?"

"Sinister stuff." Jeremy mused. "Just think what a neo-nazi or right-wing racist group could do with a genetic weapon. Extremists and supremacists could target people they don't want. A quicker form of ethnic cleansing. Not a happy thought."

"Or rogue terrorists could create a genetic plague, tailor a virus to activate in certain groups of people. Jack really surprised me with that one." I trail off, remembering the feel of Jack's spidery fingers. Less pleasant in hindsight.

"Yep, what d'ya know. The Neo-Nazis might someday fulfill the Aryan dream after all. If they target two ethnic groups, they could conceivably eliminate Israeli Jews and Arabic Muslims. Both in one go."

"Yikes! Now, that's a real hum dinger." I shake my head at such a diabolical thought.

Then Jeremy switched gears. "So, what else did you and Jack get up too?"

I shrug my shoulders. "Not much."

Jeremy taps his knuckles against his lips. I know that when he does that, he isn't satisfied with an answer.

Later that afternoon, I stare out the open bedroom window and watch two hummingbirds probe the honey suckle vines. Both are males with bright iridescent red chests. I can hear the beating of their tiny wings as an audible buzz. They both covet the same orange tubular flower. When they get too close, they ferociously accelerate into high gear. They alternate with buzzing, diving, and attacking. Each aggressively pokes his thin beak forward. Their game is intimidation. Both retreat to a tree branch, perched in two adjacent oak trees. A third hummingbird whirs, a female who lacks the male's bright colorful display. She probes the tasty red bee balm.

Jeremy startles me from behind. "Amazing how angry hummingbirds get when another one stalks their breeding territory. These little birds can store a lot of aggression."

"Hummingbirds don't mate for life. The male mates with many females. Romance has very little to do with it."

"Do they now?" Jeremy hints with an ironic smile. "I mated for life. How about you? Do you mate for life?"

"He's too young for me." I dismiss his question.

"So, if he wasn't so young, would you?"

"Hey, he's a young stud muffin. He can get all the girls he wants. I'm not sure I'd want to be one of his many. Like those female hummingbirds."

Jeremy pokes his finger against my nose. It's not an affectionate gesture. "You don't need a boy toy."

I pretend to ignore him but I'm flattered by his jealousy. We watch the hummingbirds and hear their hum, the ultrafast beating of their wings. So quick, it's a visual blur.

"Their wings beat up to 70 times a second." I whisper, conjuring the biologist in me. "They can see ultraviolet, so for them life is more colorful."

"Is that what you're looking for?" Jeremy smiles but I see anger.

I strike back. "Hummingbirds like the hotter colors. Like red, yellow, and orange. They avoid blue."

"So what color am I?" he asks.

"You change like a chameleon." I'm careful.

"You didn't answer my question. What color?" he insists.

I indulge him. "Red hot."

End of question.

We watch as one of the males descends to a patch of red bee balm flowers, probing deep into the funnel-shaped blooms.

"Hummingbirds lick the flower's nectar with their speedy moving tongues." Jeremy intimates.

I laugh at his innuendo.

He pulls my arm, spins me around. Pushes against my clavicles until my knees buckle, I fall backward onto the bed. He scolds me. "I think you need to be disciplined."

Days go by and Jeremy seems in fine form. I thought he might have been up to something. He's been so secretive lately.

"I think it's time we celebrate our part in foiling terrorist plots. You know I've always wanted to go to India. And you know the story about my father and grandfather."

Jeremy hoped to follow in their footsteps. During World War I, his grandfather missed the trenches of the Western Front and landed in India for the war's duration. After World War II, his dad was stationed there during the Partition when it was divided into two separate states, India and Pakistan.

Jeremy says, "My dad had the choice of seeing a five-hour Hindi film or visit the Taj Mahal. You won't believe this, but dad chose the film. So, a few years ago, he took Mum to the see the Taj Mahal. It cost him a fortune."

Now, Jeremy wants to be the third generation to visit India. He lays out a packet on the kitchen table with an itinerary.

"I've booked it. Before we go to the North, we fly in to Mumbai and head for the Central Indian highlands. In search of tigers." Jeremy can hardly contain his excitement.

Customized, our month-long Indian adventure meant it was just the two of us. We wouldn't be herded with a busload of other tourists.

"And we won't make the mistake my dad made by not visiting the Taj Mahal," Jeremy says.

Jeremy's always been an avid reader of world history and literature. He'd bring everything he knew about the Raj and British colonialism tucked in his head. Jeremy, a true renaissance man, sucks up knowledge the way wealthy plutocrats suck up money.

I'm not too surprised that Jeremy would book up this holiday without my prior approval. Being the control freak that I am, I would want to scrutinize all the options, debate every decision, obsess over every detail. But what can I say? There's nothing to stop us. We're independent agents and have no employment contracts. No indentured servitude that other poor devils have.

Jeremy knows how much I love safaris. I photographed the big cats, lions, and cheetahs in Tanzania and Zimbabwe. Why not add some tigers and leopards to my collection? And then there's the grazing deer and antelope, the birdlife, and the ubiquitous monkeys that never cease to amuse.

So, I agree, we deserve some time off, let's get away from it all. There are no pressing world crises that demanded our attention. We're on nobody's radar. On the scale of things, we're expendable.

I'm anticipating our escapades ahead, the tigers and leopards and wildlife, oh my. We'll surely encounter them in the largest tiger reserves in the heart of India. And it will be a dream vacation for both of us. Once the avid naturalist, I got waylaid into the dark side of biology. Enough doom and destruction. Stop with the murder and mayhem. No more blood and gore. And forget about weapons of mass destruction. At least, for the time being.

10

The Variables

Mai dressed in casual chic to blend in as an Asian academic. She wanted to mimic the understated style of the engineers, mathematicians, and lab geeks. No matter where they are from, their style is the same.

When Hong arrived at the bar lounge, he hoped she'd be wearing something alluring. She'd be quite the gold prize to flaunt. But Mai got there first and nestled into a pale-yellow leather sofa. She wore a subdued blue cotton frock with a lacy white vest. Her conservative attire did little to hide the shapely figure she cut.

Hong was thrilled that she actually showed up. It was early for dinner and there was time for a drink. Hong ordered two Swedish beers from the bar.

"You must try this local brew." Hong insisted as he handed her a beaker of beer. It matched the hotel's science and technology themes. Mai grimaced at the bitter taste, she wasn't a big fan of hops.

Hong cozied up next to her, making sure other men knew she was unavailable. He felt quite pleased that he snagged this exotic fish. Hong draped his arm along the back of the yellow sofa as a gesture of ownership. He wasn't going to let this catch get away.

Hong looked around at the marine specimen that were sprinkled throughout the lounge.

"That's a sea anemone shell with an octopus base," he said and pointed to an end table. A large lit candle was centered in the shell. He gestured towards another, a multi-towered white coral on a round end table. He hadn't really noticed these aquatic artifacts before, but he thought them apropos for his fishing expedition.

Eventually, Hong and Mai made their way to an intimate table in the far corner of the restaurant. Mai ordered a glass of pinot noir, much more to her liking than the beer.

"According to the menu, this is a meeting place for visionaries and dreamers." Mai read the enticements designed to flatter its egotistic patrons. The academics thought their brilliance was reflected in the décor and motif.

"Yes, and innovators and contrary thinkers. It blurs the lines between genius and insanity." Hong taunted. "Which one are you, Mai?"

"That's for you to find out. Genius and madness. It's all the same." Mai didn't look up as she perused the menu.

Almost on cue, a clock distracted them with the sound of a common cuckoo call, perhaps warning its guests of excess hubris. You too are crazy as a cuckoo.

"Wow, look at this menu," Hong said with a grin. "The Variables, Fundamental Principles, Constants, and Sweet Conclusions."

"Oh, Sweet Conclusions. I love dessert." Mai often lived on sweet pastries.

"Shall we start with 'The Variables'?" Hong showed her the list of small dishes, what are most often called appetizers or hors d oeuvres.

"I'll have Sashimi. And for my Fundamental Principle, the grilled flank steak." Mai played along with the math inspired language. She wanted something hearty, meaty. Something she could savor with a glass of red wine. She left the beer drinking for Hong's more plebian tastes.

"I'll have one of their Constants. I'm torn between a hamburger and fish and chips." In Gothenburg, Hong knows the fish is always the better option, usually a fresh cod or other seasonal fish. And Hong's second beer would go with either. Hong chose the latter. "We can decide on Sweet Conclusions later." Hong winces as he wonders if he's gone too far.

Mai eyed the crème brulee and the chocolate mousse. She starved herself all day so she could indulge in whatever might appeal to her. But she was more preoccupied with what useful purpose Hong might fulfill.

Hong seldom ate at the Riverside restaurant. His lab technician job only allowed for an occasional splurge and Sweden was not cheap. His usual fare was grilled Swedish hotdogs and home-cooked ramen, his favorite faire regardless of more exotic and expensive options. Tonight, he'd tap his US account to impress Mai.

The tone of the meal was light-hearted. Hong amused Mai with his wicked sense of humor, although she often laughed at inappropriate moments. He wondered if his American sense of humor confused her. He found himself unsure of the impression he created with this wonderful but mysterious woman.

When it came to hobbies, running and biking were two they both had in common. Hong thought she was more attractive than him, yet he believed he could lure this mermaid with his bait. She seemed to find him entertaining, he turned on the charm. He felt like he might have a chance at some kind of romantic involvement.

As he listened to Mai talk, her mellifluous voice, a mix of savory and sweet, struck him as soft, delicate, soothing. Hong watched her succulent lips, so wet and perfectly full. He was lost in a somnambulant dream, as if he were sleepwalking, he hoped he'd never wake up.

Women usually found Hong's boyish good looks and lithe body appealing. Mai imagined his athletic ability might play out well beyond the running track. She assessed that Hong had much to offer with the magic combination of genes and more genes. He was not just an interesting genetic mix but he had the ability to edit genes. Now what is the probability of that? The whole package excited her and she imagined what else lie under his attractive guise. And what else he might have to offer.

Hong knew his mixed ethnicity opened up a much larger playing field when it came to attracting a variety of young students. At the Rhode Island college where he worked in the animal research facility, he knew his way around campus. He frequented locations where hook-ups and rendezvous with women were likely. On a typical weekend, he showed up at party houses off-campus where he found plenty of alcohol-fueled underclass-man willing to "shag", a term his Anglo-mother sometimes used. Hong didn't find it hard to find a lonely drunk co-ed that would be willing at the mere suggestion.

But Mai Tran was in a whole other league, he wondered who she really was under that veneer of a woman of science. Oddly beautiful and certainly strange, but Hong needed to find out more, before jumping in bed with her. He didn't want to ruin the exploration of the evening. He was having too much fun just anticipating what might come out of a relationship with this fascinating woman.

11

Sweet Conclusions

After dinner, on a walk along the harbor, Mai said what was really on her mind. "Hong, my business partner and I have paying clients for a very profitable service. I believe that you could partner with us. Together we have all the right skills."

Hong was confused at Mai's blunt offer. He flung his hands out in a what-are-you-talking-about gesture. His splayed arms spoke louder than words and Mai picked up his meaning.

"Would you agree, Hong, that designer babies are something that captures everyone's imagination?"

"Designer babies? So, where did that come from, Mai?" But Hong nodded for her to go on.

"It's the future of reproduction, sculpted neonates, babies by design, engineered to perfection."

"Sculpted neonates? I like the sound of that. Even with the right skills, there won't be too many opportunities for editing the genes of human embryos. At least not for quite some time."

"Hong, you know it's done elsewhere in the world. And rich people already have their pets enhanced. You've seen those Beagles with the strong muscles, haven't you?"

"Sure, designer pets are already the rage among animal lovers. Like those miniature versions of big dogs as lap pets." Hong struck a pose, a pathetic panting puppy.

Mai giggled, then changed over to a wry grin. "But think of the possibilities with humans," she said.

"The Chinese have genetically engineered children in their midst. They're way ahead of the rest of the pack. But western scientists always debate the ethics of designer babies. It will never be legal in the West." Hong shook his head 'no' and shrugged.

"Exactly, Hong, but think about the wealthy one percent of the world. Those with huge amounts of money to buy anything their hearts desire. They'll willingly depart with a few million. They just can't resist, it's a cheap price for a superhuman of the future." Mai could see Hong's expressions change once he realized she was selling a fantasy. Hong's eyes shifted to the river's horizon where the iridescent water and yellow-gold lights reflected in his eyes like the glitz and gold of Mai's wealthy clients.

"You see the promise in it? People will believe whatever you tell them." Mai bent in close to Hong's face, as if about to kiss him. "Tell me what people want."

"What's new. What's innovative. Especially if it gives them an advantage over others," Hong said. "It isn't always money that drives people. Sometimes it's something else. Not money, but something people are passionate about. Something other than inanimate possessions. But something their children will inherit. The best genes, superior DNA, that'll be passed down to future generations to come. Like gene-edited super-athletes that win Olympic medals. Or super strong, like those muscular Beagles." Hong laughed at the thought.

"And if men make the choice, they'll want a perfected, enhanced reflection of themselves. Not just a child, but a perfect son." Mai probed Hong on gender. She knew that improving the genetic stock of mankind would most likely be a male prerogative, for a multitude of reasons.

Hong got it. "A son, a more perfect me. A new edition. And a gift that keeps on giving through generations to come." Hong chuckled but Mai failed to capture the humor. "Look, they are 'Edits', not babies. A new breed called 'Edits'." He got more and more excited following his own trail of ideas. "How's this? A 'Perfect Edit of You'!" Hong was on a roll. He thought it all a fanciful joke.

"Hong, that's brilliant. Who could resist a redesigned edition? A designer child. A perfect 'Edit'."

"But it's illegal here, so how do you get away with it?" Hong wondered aloud.

"Hong, selling a product that's illegal can make it even more desirable." Mai's total lack of scruples, made Hong wonder where she really came from. She didn't fit into the norms of eastern or western society. She seemed totally devoid of any moral compass. But it was something about her, beyond her eloquence, it was the way she could persuade you that she had the elixir for those men with unfulfilled lives.

Hong led Mai by the hand to a park bench on the water. As they sat, Hong indulged her fanciful imagination. On his phone, he looked up something Stephen Hawking once wrote.

Hong read Hawking's words to Mai. "Some people won't be able to resist the temptation to improve human characteristics, such as size of memory, resistance to disease and length of life."

"Irresistible, isn't it?" Mai cooed, not like a dove but like a mythological siren luring a sailor to his doom, shipwrecked on a rocky shore. Or perhaps like Circe, an enchantress, a sorceress, a nymph. Mai was skilled in the magic of mutation. But she had more power than mere incantations. She could change humans into wolves or lions. Or men into pigs.

"Here's another Hawking quote for you. 'Once such superhumans appear, there's going to be significant political problems with the unimproved humans…who won't be able to compete'." Hong looked at Mai's face to see her reaction.

Mai saw nothing wrong with that thought, nor the idea of someone's pipedream of equality. "In the future, unimproved humans will cease to exist." Mai arched her brows and remarked with a shrug. "Who cares?"

Hong jaw dropped at Mai's prescient thought, that the future of the "unimproved" was extinction. He hadn't thought about it that way. Hong said to Mai, "Some races of people will survive."

"Perhaps, some." Mai already knew who. And so did Hong. They knew that China would be the first to mass engineer people, gene-edit a superior race with every conceivable survival advantage. But superiority was not for everyone. The masses would have design limits. Edited with specific traits suited for their purpose in life. To be better soldiers, or to be compliant workers.

Hong remembered another thing that Hawking wrote. "Hawking also thinks we're on the cusp of a new phase, what might be called self-designed evolution. And we'll be able to change and improve our own DNA."

"Ah, so we are on the cutting edge, our business venture could be very, very lucrative." Mai fondled his thick hair. "And think about the benefits of our business partnership." This time Mai kissed him, a brief but direct message that didn't need an explanation. He turned around, holding her hand as they walked back towards the hotel. At the reception desk in the lobby, he booked a room for the night.

Amazed by the room's interior design, Mai pointed to the unique wall-paper with strands of DNA, carbon molecules, and a sketch of Albert Einstein. They both admired the mix of scientific themes and how the motif was applied to every detail.

Hong hadn't stayed at the hotel, although it was next door to his lab. Many academics frequented the hotel, often for conferences or just to meet up with colleagues. The entire hotel, even the bedrooms, sported science and technology themes that amused scientists and visitors alike.

A spartan studio flat within walking distance was provided with Hong's lab position. He couldn't possibly bring Mai back to his electric griller and packets of ramen noodle. Not to mention the bed that doubled as a sofa. Maybe later, but tonight he splashed out.

"Please take my photo, Hong. This is a perfect background. I can use it for business promotion." She handed her phone to Hong. Mai felt confident that her newly designed face and body didn't resemble her previous self. In many ways she preferred her reincarnation as Mai Tran, unencumbered by her Chinese origin in the Urban Village, the ghetto in the outskirts of Shenzhen.

Always a good eye for composition, Hong angled a lamp for the best lighting. He tried to accentuate her lovely eyes. He posed her to feature her best attributes, those mathematical curves and spheres. Like foreplay, it heightened his anticipation of what could come later.

"Perhaps you can be my right-hand-man?" Mai walked her fingers down his arm to grab her phone, then placed it in her black leather sling bag.

"And you can be my right-hand-woman." Hong watched Mai retreat to the bathroom with her sling bag across her shoulder. His eyes fixed on a bright yellow ribbon that secured the zipper shut.

When Mai emerged, she was wearing an opaque baby doll nightie. The pink polka-dots made her look like confectionary candy, sweet enough to eat.

Hong pulled her towards him. "Are you ready for dessert?"

Mai knew she provoked the desired effect. "Sweet conclusions? I'll have an extra helping please."

Surprised at Mai's directness, he held her tight against his chest. Closely intertwined, they seemed a perfect fit. But he found her curved body unnaturally hard and firm.

"Hybrid vigor." Hong mused aloud. He wondered if he was falling in love.

12

Indian Highlands

There's a feeling of foreboding mixed with excitement that makes me nervous, as I sit low in the back seat of Jack's car. I stare at the tops of swaying trees. The heavy wind strips the leaves that offer little resistance.

At Jack's insistence, he drives us to Boston's Logan airport.

"Hey, it's not out of my way. I'm meeting with my MIT buddies." He tells us his friends dabble in synthetic biology. They make new creatures, piece by piece, from scratch. "*De novo*, starting from the beginning, they assemble snippets of DNA and RNA. I want to catch up with the latest."

Boston's MIT and Harvard are right on the cutting edge, per-haps a razor's edge when it comes to genetic modification.

At Terminal E, Jack man-hugs Jeremy and kisses me on what would have been my cheek had I not turned so abruptly. Just grazing my lips, he nearly bites my nose. I'm thinking how awkward it was.

"We'll meet up next month," I say. We planned a stop-over in Sweden after our Indian adventures, and Jack will be in Gothenburg at an international gene editing conference.

"Hope you catch a tiger by the tail," Jack cracks.

"I have no intention of getting that close." I think I've al-ready blown it with Jack there.

"And don't come back with Tiger Flu," Jack banters on. He always makes lame jokes when flustered.

"I won't be kissing any tigers." I can't get kissing out of my mind. Jeremy gives me a side-long glance.

"I'll feed her to the tigers if she misbehaves." Jeremy threatens. I know what he means.

In a Mumbai hotel, we spend the night entombed in a what feels like a monolithic mausoleum. We sleep like the dead for a few hours and then the alarm rings at 3 AM.

I wake up with a groan and complain, "It's not even daylight."

Jeremy says, "Good morning, sunshine."

Then I whine and moan at Jeremy, "I hardly slept a wink. What sadistic travel agent planned this?"

Jeremy gleefully reminds me, "We have a 5 AM flight to Nagpur."

I'm not enthusiastic and sarcastically comment, "Oh yeah, the gateway to tigers."

We fly into Nagpur and are picked up by our driver for a seven-hour journey through the central Indian highlands. As expected, the road is sprinkled with cars and highly decorated buses. And then there's the unexpected farm tractors and ox-driven carts. Our driver is dodging the rickshaws, who are dodging small motorcycles and motorbikes, who are dodging the bicycles who, all in turn, dodge the pedestrians, wild pigs, and holy cows.

I grab Jeremy's hand with every near miss with people piled on motorbikes or crammed into three-wheel auto rickshaws. But now I'm absolutely stricken with fear for the family of four packed on a small motorbike, until I see a baby in the handle bar basket.

"Five! Jeremy, there's a family of five. A baby is in the basket." I try not to gawk like the obnoxious tourist that I am.

Wealth is relative and here the difference is obscene. But the intricate-patterned saris with their intense and colorful dyes, the brilliant orange chains of marigolds, the organized stacks of green and yellow melons, and piles of neatly arranged vegetables, some I can't name, make me gape in wonder. It's a heady mix of beasts and beauty compared to what I left behind.

"Are there any rules of the road?" I ask Jeremy.

"Apparently not," he says in his understated droll way. "There doesn't seem to be any rules but somehow our driver has mastered the necessary survival skills."

Our driver weaves through, what to me and Jeremy is insane chaos. At the same time a similar mix of oncoming traffic, over-loaded vehicles full of produce and people, barrel at us at twice the usual speed.

I ask Jeremy, "How does he manage to avoid it all? This barrage of obstacles, coming and going in every direction?" Jeremy doesn't have time to attempt an answer when our driver swerves to miss a giant rock and a huge pothole in the middle of the road. I exhale with a sigh of relief when we don't fall into the massive crater.

"Nothing surprises me, I'm numb to it all," Jeremy says, he looks as wacked-out as I am.

We finally end up at our destination, Kanha, and pull in to our wildlife lodge. There's not enough time to wash up before dinner but we splash water on our faces and change into clean shirts.

It's early in the tiger viewing season and we're the only visitors booked in the lodge. A special table awaits us for snacks and before dinner drinks.

"I feel like a high-ranking British colonial," Jeremy mutters under his breath as they indulge us with aperitifs. But unlike colonials, we didn't bring our rifles and pith helmets, nor would we collect tiger trophies during hunting expeditions.

Our safari guide introduces himself but I don't catch his name. A naturalist, he shows us maps of areas we'll explore tomorrow. I peruse the lists of mammals and birds, snakes and reptiles, trees and plants. There was nothing about the insects, of which there were plenty. Our guide tells us where he is from, a place I've never heard of.

When it comes time for him to leave, I ask, "Are you going home to your wife and children?" I'm a bit too presumptuous. I have no idea why I asked. I follow up with a hasty "Sorry."

He replies, "I would never do that, I love gentlemen." He smiles, nearly laughs. "I will meet you early tomorrow morning."

In the pitch blackness of the night, a young boy guides us to our bungalow by flashlight. We settle in and wash away the sweat from a very long day.

"These cottages are great. Very eco. But I'm not too sure about the shower," I complain.

"Where the pebbles too rough for your delicate little feet?" Jeremy teases.

"Haha. No, it's just so dark in there, I could barely see myself." I know the bungalow runs on a generator.

"Lucky you, pussums." Another offhand insult. I hate when he calls me pussums.

"Ha!" I flip him off and fall into a comfy bed. "We leave at 6 AM." Must get up early for our first game drive, although the only shooting I'll do is with my new telephoto lens. Just like those colonials, neocolonial Jeremy indulged me with a high-ranking camera.

During our early morning safari in the forest reserve, we bump along in an off-road land rover but see no tigers.

After our mid-day meal our lodge manager, Deepak, asks us, "Would you like to see our organic garden?"

"Sure," Jeremy says and I nod 'yes'.

It's just a couple minute walk to the garden where vegetables, herbs, and fruit are grown for our meals. Every bit of food we eat is either cultivated on site or living in the wild. With so much game, from the gigantic buffalo to the tiniest barking deer, and all those birds—the wild pheasants, red junglefowl, plump gadwalls and geese—we never knew the exact species of mystery meat they served us. With the savannah grassland so full of all-natural, organic meat and poultry, there's no going to the supermarket for grocery shopping.

After our garden tour, Deepak says, "We have time before the afternoon safari. Would you like to take a walk to the 'buffer zone'?"

"Yes," I say, then ask, "What do you mean by buffer zone?"

"It's where the tribal people live," Deepak answers.

I'm curious and wonder what life is like living on the edge of the game reserve. Then, I look down at my feet and hope it's a short walk. Before lunch, I'd taken off my hiking shoes and put on sandals.

We walk for quite some time on a well-worn dirt path along the edge of the tiger reserve. Further on, we see a small hut that I assume is a tribal dwelling. There are no people near the hut, just a few fowl and a feral dog. As we approach the abode, a wild boar darts ahead of us and crossed the dirt path. He's so close he kicks up a cloud of dust that gets in my eyes. I get a whiff of his odor. He smells like a mix of motor oil and maple syrup.

"Don't get too close, they can be quite dangerous." Deepak tells us. We back off and heed his warning.

"Did you smell that boar, Jeremy? What a weird pong," I say and crinkle my nose.

"Like a greasy car mechanic eating a plate of pancakes," Jeremy says. We all think it's an accurate description.

We keep walking and come across deer and assorted game cavorting on the grassy meadow. Nearby, Langur monkey's eye us curiously. Luckily, we don't come across a hungry tiger, I doubt if I could outrun one. But in the wild we see all bovine creatures great and small, from the biggest bison in the world, the guar, to the tiniest barking deer.

"Now that's a bloody huge cow," Jeremy says to me under his breath. He points to a guar grazing in the distance.

We thank Deepak and return to our bungalow. I change from sandals into socks and walking shoes before the scheduled drive that afternoon.

That evening, before dinner, Jeremy manages to get on-line. Internet access is spotty at best, but he found an interesting nugget.

"Listen to this," he says and reads, "In happier times, before they were exiled from their ancestral home, the indigenous people used to live among the tigers in the bamboo and Sal forests. They were given a meager compensation and relocated to the perimeter, the buffer zone."

"So, those tribal people and tigers once lived together. But today their lives are very different." I tilt my head and frown. It just didn't seem right.

"Some of the people got jobs in the tiger reserve. But in the past, their lives weren't threatened by tigers. And vice versa." Jeremy tells me.

"As for the tigers, humans are the biggest threat. Their very existence is at stake." I ponder their future.

In 1900 there were 100,000 tigers in the wild. Today, only 3200 remain.

It's late in the evening when I shower. The generator light is so dim in the bungalow, it's hard to see what I'm doing. I love the rain shower, but hate the pebbles beneath my feet. But then I feel a bump on the skin of my right calve.

I crawl into bed and say to Jeremy, "There's a bump on my leg. Maybe a tick?" It's late, I'm exhausted, and Jeremy is asleep. I fall into a dream, where tigers burn bright and wild cows dance like frolicking fools.

The next day, the rare spotting of a leopard keeps me from focusing on the tick engorged on my right leg. So, in the grasslands and dark forests were "Leopards and Tigers and Ticks, oh my!"

A few days later, we drive many miles through villages and hamlets with people as diverse as the wildlife in their midst. In Bandhavgarh game reserve, we chase the alarm calls of barking deer and agitated macaques and monkeys. Then race toward the shrieking call and wait and wait. Eventually we move on.

Our guide stops and points at the dusty earth next to the tires. "Those are paw prints" he says, "the tiger must be somewhere near."

We wait again in silence and listen. Our guide points to the thick bamboo. And then I hear it. Is it a pant or a yawn? No, I don't think so.

"He's asleep," whispers our guide. We listen harder to a subtle sound, a guttural gurgle, a rumbling rattle. It's a familiar, intermittent snore not unlike that of a guy I know.

"I'm picking up good vibrations," Jeremy whispers in my ear and I try to control my joy of anticipation.

"He's asleep," says our guide. "We don't want to wake him."

"Nothing worse than a grumpy guy," Jeremy says, assuming he's male.

"So, he's a guy because he's big and powerful? Who says she isn't a tigress?" I wag my finger at Jeremy.

We drive on and head back towards the lodge. Our guide points to deep scratches on a tree trunk and says, "those aren't fresh claw marks."

So, despite the tiger claw marks on trees, huge paw prints in the sand, and even hearing one snore, we never did see the elusive tigers. They hid deep in the forest. Even the tiger trackers and mahouts, the riders on elephants, couldn't roust the snoozing beasts.

Tigers spend most of their day sleeping, 16 to 20 hours. Versus 12 hours for their pussycat cousins.

Unless, that is, the tiger is hungry. Then unlucky beasts, the weak and the young, become tasty morsels. It's a virtual smorgasbord for tigers and leopards on the grassy meadows.

13

Neonatus Perfectus

Lars texted Mai that he'd come today to check on his apartments. He didn't want her to forget the tremendous favor he did for her, letting her live rent free. Mai thought it a small price to pay for his, so far, limited demands. Always a gentleman, Lars was the perfect sugar-daddy. For Lars, a warm embrace sometimes meant more than a frolicking romp. But she knew how he loved exploring her curves and, even more so, her face. He would run his fingers delicately on her cheekbones, her nose, chin, eyes.

To Lars, Mai was still an enigma, he knew there was some deep-seated secret to crack open. Like a macadamia nut, she was almost impenetrable. He wanted Mai to think of him as her protector. He knew from her earlier tell-tale bruises that some vicious brute wreaked havoc with her body. He suspected there might be much more to that story. Perhaps she was hiding from someone.

〰◁▯▷〰

"I could change you." Lars mumbled, but Mai ignored him as she browsed the photos in her gallery.

"Lars, do you like my photos?" Mai handed her phone to Lars.

"Who took these?" Lars was more concerned she might have other admirers. Just who was her photographer?

"Our lab tech, I've hired him. Highly skilled at microinjection. He uses tiny glass pipettes to inject embryos. Our perfect frontman."

"Why a frontman?"

"The science behind our promise. He edits animal embryos, not human. Amazing I found him. His lab uses gene editing tools like Crispr and Prime," Mai said, she was irrepressible. "These techniques are very exciting."

"So, the leap to humans is credible, at least in the eye of my clients." Lars was impressed at how resourceful Mai could be. "I'll tell them it's called 'gene surgery'. They love cosmetic surgery. They will love gene surgery." Lars knew he had a creative flair, but he so seldom had reason to use it. Most of his work were predictable nose-jobs and sticky-out ears.

"Do you think the lab photos will convince that we're a professional business? For a small brochure, it might help lure your clients." Mai improvised her marketing plan. "Gene surgery. Cut out the bad, insert the good."

"You're a clever woman. You look quite believable in the lab photo, all garbed in protective gear. The only way I can recognize you is your eyes." Lars scrutinized the photos. "And this photo, your lab tech micro-injecting an embryo. It's very impressive. A convincing front. What did you say his name is?"

"Hong."

"Will he meet with clients if needed?" Lars wondered about Hong's role. But most of all, could he be trusted. "Can he keep our secrets?"

"Of course, he will. He'll do anything for me, given enough money. His services don't come cheap, but I can handle his payments with cash you give me. American dollars would be best for him, he's in Sweden on a two-year contract. He's a lab tech, a post-graduate pauper."

"He sounds like a good prospect. US dollars are not a problem. Some of my clients are Americans. They come as medical tourists. And for privacy."

As Mai nodded, a bright beam of window light caught the fire flickering in her eyes. All was going according to her plan. She could almost smell the money, just the thought of it enhanced her senses. She would demand plenty, supposedly to pay Hong, and keep most for herself.

"Is Hong his surname or first name?" Lar wondered.

Mai shrugged. "I'll find out his full name." She changed the topic. "I have more photos to show you. After all, a picture is worth ten thousand words. A Chinese proverb."

"That's ten times as many words as the American saying. For them, a picture is only worth one thousand words." Lars mooned over Mia's image, his infatuation bordered on obsession.

"Image is everything." Mai used another English slogan but was unaware of its origin.

Flipping through her cell phone, Lars came across a different set of photos. "What about this image? It shows your best traits."

Mai loved flattery. "The background is a good match too, wouldn't you say?"

"Yes, it's vaguely familiar to me, perhaps I've seen that motif before. The illumination looks professional, it sheds a good light on your beauty. But could it suggest you are part of the bargain?" Lars chided Mai. "I don't think so." He waggled his finger as a warning.

"Oh no, I am only yours, as we agreed. Don't worry. We can find other beautiful women to help collect semen samples. I am yours. Only yours. I promise."

Mai wouldn't let her sugar-daddy think otherwise. He was useful in so many ways, a definite "keeper" in her estimation. On a scale from one to ten, he was a 9. She assigned him a numerical value based on his practical worth, not on his physical attributes.

Lars asked, "Mai, where did you find this background for your photo?" He pointed at the DNA strands and carbon molecules. "I think I've seen this somewhere before." He couldn't quite place the wall design. It would come to him eventually. His memory was not compromised, but sometimes it took time to recollect the many images collected in a lifetime. But faces, he never forgot.

"Oh, it's in the science center." Mai's expertise at lying kicked in when she needed it. She didn't want Lars to think it was a wall paper design in a hotel room. She took her phone from him, turned it off and tossed it in her purse. She then sat on his lap and looked deeply into his tired blue-gray eyes.

"You love my beautiful face don't you, Lars?" She smiled her sweetest smile.

Lars stared at Mai's face, in particular her altered traits. He imagined what she looked like before the surgical changes. It wasn't too difficult for him. In his mind, he reconstructed her with Han Chinese features. But beyond her appearance, she was more like a Chinese puzzle box, full of secret compartments and hidden openings.

For now, he would explore those secret openings. Later could come those hidden compartments.

⚭

Lars' ability to remember faces never eluded him. He could pick out a face in a crowd. His memory of patients faces was nearly photographic. Lars' outpatient clinic cranked out face lifts, nose jobs, ear pinning, and facial reconstructions. He referred the breast enhancements, tummy tucks, liposuctions, and Brazilian butt lifts to other colleagues.

On odd occasion, there were complications but most were easily taken care of. Lars kept his practice clean and surgical unit scrupulously sterile. Over the years, there was the rare infection that required antibiotics. More recently, Lars saw an uptick of antibiotic resistant bacteria in patients with compromised immunity. It was an unusual event when a patient was admitted through a hospital Emergency Room.

Lars' meticulous attention to detail meant his practice ran as a well-oiled machine, but it didn't generate a huge amount of profit. He couldn't see much future for himself other than a sedate and ordinary life with a wife who had nothing but contempt for what she called his wealth-driven, self-centered clients. Lars, on the other hand admired and envied their life-style. And now he saw a better way to grab more of their money.

⚭

Mai didn't hang out much in Hong's small flat, she preferred the simple elegance and amenities of Lars' apartment. She usually knew in advance if Lars would visit her in Gothenburg, he seldom surprised her. He texted or called on the dedicated burner phones he'd bought. It was a common practice for those carrying on illicit affairs. Lars kept his wife in Stockholm and Mai in Gothenburg on separate radio waves.

The next time Lars was in Gothenburg, he called on his burner phone. He would come to talk about business.

When Lars arrived, Mai greeted him, waving her brochure. "I've created this menu of genetic options. We can use this to promote our new business." Mai was proud of her flashy sales piece.

"I'll handle our finances. Many rich people stash their wealth in tax-sheltered havens. They have off-shore accounts in places like the Caribbean islands, Malta, maybe the Cayman Islands. Money flows in the land of money, from one island paradise to another." Lars chuckles. "And you and I will be together on a paradise island."

"Multi-million-dollar babies." Mai nodded with delight. "A perfect scam."

Lars explained to Mai a simplified version of transferring money to off-shore accounts. "Everyone does it. It's called 'naughty' money. It's not quite illegal."

She mulled over the scheme. "It sounds like a confusing puzzle." Mai thought the plan complicated.

"But you are a Chinese puzzle too." He softly smiled. Mai, an intricate and complex game for the hands and mind, he wanted to explore every angle. Forever lost in her charm, her creative ideas, her abundant curves, her mutable features, he wondered from where did they come? What lied beneath Mai's exterior perplexed him. Her secrets were hidden within a box within a box within a box.

"I call our product '*Neonatus Perfectus*'. It reflects the elitism and exclusivity of our clients," Lars said.

"I like that, but for me it's simple. Buy your designer baby. I will hack your DNA." Mai shrugged her shoulders and grinned. "I'm a Baby Hacker. Show me the money."

Lars met-up with clients in top-tier hotels. Sometimes, he visited them on their yacht. Either way, they preferred discretion. With his new offering he found clients with a newfound interest, especially since gene-edited babies were now a reality. Customized designer babies were no longer a pipedream.

Lars soon realized just how deep self-indulgence and narcissism lay in his select group of people. Their obsession went deeper than their desire for physical beauty. It was buried deep down in the DNA blueprint that made them what they are. Along with their desire to right any wrongs with their genes.

Lars explained to his clients how the precise design and edits of DNA opened new windows to unexplored horizons. "The next generation of your babies will be perfect. Their physical health. Their appearance. Their mental traits."

Lars preferred using the more eloquent and refined word for newborns, neonates. "I offer you *Neonatus Perfectus*," he told them. The Latin-derived construct had that pretentious ring to suck his clients in.

With *Neonatus Perfectus* his clients would someday have exquisitely perfected children. No rich, acquisitive narcissist could resist the temptation. Lars collected big fees for the promise of DNA-edited embryos. His clients invested many millions. A Scandinavian bank passed the funds through the Baltics. From there the money was hidden away in tax-sheltered havens.

The final product, super-charged, superb babies, would be payable upon delivery. A fanciful hoax that clients would never divulge, lest they expose their own money laundering schemes.

In the world of money, you might not always win, but you can't lose.

14

Psychedelic Journey

It's been a week since the tick buried itself, injected its juices and sucked my blood. Before I could register how dangerous the minuscule beast might be, it dropped off. After all, with so many macro-beasts, the leopards, tigers, and wild buffalo that could really inflict some damage, why sweat the small stuff?

We lived in some pretty wild and wooly countries and survived the big cats, elephants, crocs, hippos, vipers, mambas, and cape buffalo of Africa. I never really worried about being attacked, despite a few close calls. I have little fear of animals. People, on the other hand, always worry me.

In northern India, we seldom stay longer than three nights in any one place. I laugh hysterically while I try to hang on to the rickshaw's railing. At the same time, I snap photos helter-skelter. The rickshaw puller, oblivious to my manic motions, follows Jeremy and our guide in the lead chariot.

At the Old Delhi market, Jeremy asks the shop keeper, "What's the difference between first-flush and second-flush Darjeeling tea?"

"The strength of the tea varies when picked at different times of the year. It's all about taste." He points to each one.

Jeremy loads up on a selection of exotic strong teas. He then picks a variety of spices. Jeremy loves to cook curries, but the thought of food right now makes me queasy. My tummy is turning, but I ignore my belly ache as just a small glitch. I didn't sample the street food, so I tell myself it's an anomaly at most.

The next day, I dismiss a bout of diarrhea as "Delhi belly."

Just days later, my watery, blurry eyes, I blame on the smoky funeral pyres at Varanasi. The smoke has an exotic smell of charred flesh and incense. My inflamed eyes worsen after that mystical evening, a spiritual burning, with the bodies of the dead heaped on blazing fires. It's a sure ticket to heaven. But I'd begun my descent into hell.

"It must be the smoke that makes my eyes run. Isn't it?" I ask Jeremy. But my eye puddles become rivers and run deep with gooey silt.

The next morning, pilgrims bathe in the Ganges along the steep steps known as *ghats*. I watch in horror as they cup their hands and drink the water.

I tell Jeremy, "I just don't get this spiritual cleansing."

"Some profess that the water is full of oxygen and has self-cleansing properties." From the expression on Jeremy's face, he's a skeptic.

"Well, maybe at one time, but what about the risk of hepatitis, typhoid, cholera, amoebic dysentery, just to name a few?" I wasn't convinced either.

"They must have a stronger constitution than I." Jeremy parodies as he splutters and coughs. My nagging cough, on the other hand, is quite real.

I didn't sip or bathe in the healing water. I couldn't be much worse off if I had taken a dip. Perhaps I should have joined the pilgrims soaking and sipping in the Ganges. It might have healed me.

I try to climb those wide *ghats* but my knees act like rusty hinges. Jeremy pulls me up those steep steps and teases about my lead weight. But as I struggle my knees ache, they throb, they engorge over time.

In Agra at the Taj Mahal, I can barely walk, my joints are inflated like soccer balls. So tired, my legs feel elephantine. Near collapse, there's no amount of sleep that can conquer my overwhelming fatigue.

By the time we get to Jaipur, a light pink polka-dot rash rages over my body. Only my face is spared.

In walks Doctor #1 to our hotel room accompanied by a bell-boy who stands like a sentry at the door.

Jeremy says, "Thank you for coming here to see my wife." The young doctor gives Jeremy his card but says nothing to me.

Doctor #1 talks to Jeremy as if I'm not there. "What are your wife's symptoms?" he asks. I'm thinking this doc really has an odd bedside manner.

Jeremy looks at me and says, "Jo, tell the doctor what's going on."

I begin with "I have a rash." The list of symptoms is so long, but I've got to start somewhere. I'm thinking he should look at my legs, my back, my arms, but I await his instructions.

The doctor lifts my long sleeve, ever so slightly, and reveals my wrist covered with spots. He exposes barely two inches of skin. I wonder how he can imagine what my rash looks like under my clothes? But he seems convinced that the rash extends to remote parts of the great unknown. I try to lift my sleeve higher but he pulls it back down. To avoid a tug-of-war, I give in.

I tell him, "My joints are swollen and sore." But Doctor #1 is not interested in looking at those parts.

When I complain, "In Delhi, I had diarrhea," it became the doctor's default, his malady of choice. Doctor #1's diagnosis, a rash and a bellyache.

The doctor leaves me with a probiotic, Vitamin B and an antihistamine. He seems to have come prepared to treat me, no matter what symptoms I had. That common medicinal mix must be his standard treatment for tourist's digestive disorders.

When the doctor leaves, his sentry follows. Jeremy scratches his head. "That was hardly a thorough body exam. He must have had religious or cultural issues."

That evening, things only get worse with frightening nightmares followed by bizarre, but somewhat pleasant hallucinations. I laugh when a chair transforms into an animated wild boar. Its Mohawk hair flashes like bolts of lightning, its eyes radiate with electric red beams. Like a dose of LSD, I chuckle aloud as I watch the spectacle of psychedelic illuminations.

I drift in and out as I lay with my head at the foot of the bed. My toes fondle Jeremy's face but he doesn't complain. The next morning, I describe what felt like a blitzed-out acid trip.

Jeremy, with his droll English accent, says, "Toxin-induced, I presume. Maybe I'm not convinced of the doctor's diagnosis."

He calls the front hotel desk, asks for a second doctor.

Doctor #2 arrives and claims to be President Bill Clinton's doctor-on-call during his visit to India. So, if he's good enough for Bill, I should be honored to get India's best. At least he's more thorough with his body exam.

He sends a lab tech, or was it a vampire, to collect my blood. Still lapsing into a cyclic toxic acid trip, reality had become a series of bad dreams and nightmares.

Doctor #2 returns a few hours later with his medical bag full of tricks. His diagnosis for the rash is an upper respiratory infection. I still have that persistent dry cough.

"Remove your clothes," he demands. I comply as if he were a military commander. I think he is, or something very similar.

Jeremy whispers, "He's the police."

My first reaction is confusion. At first, I hesitate, but Jeremy nods affirmative. I modestly leave on my bra and panties.

He pulls out his injection kit that looks like a hypodermic needle prop from a horror movie. He lowers my pantie exposing my big white cheek. Now, I'm thinking I'm doomed. I'm really doomed.

With all good intentions and butt injections with god-knows-what, a mishmash of meds, antibiotics, antacids, and a cough syrup tasting of cardamom—the treatment did little to quell the assault of whatever is ailing me.

With my insides on fire, knees and ankles ballooning, a muddled malaise, disturbing delirium and a lack of equilibrium. And a never-ending cough. It's an unrelenting cascade, a deluge, and I'm sucked into a downward spiral, a swirling eddy of death and destruction.

The vicious cycle of symptoms worsens when the rash thickens into deep pools of dark red and purple-black. And my, oh my, my photophobic eyes. I'm blinded by the light.

"Close the shades, Jeremy." I'm no longer able to stand the light of day.

15

Hyper Traits

"Hey, Hong Min Chan." Mai didn't bother to glance at Hong, who sat at his desk pecking away on his computer. Mai was lost in an electronic fantasy, engrossed in designs of imaginary young women. She lay on Hong's bed with one hand on her e-notebook and the other propping up her head.

"How funny, your last name is the same as Min Chan, the Japanese anime character." Mai connected his surname with the school girl, Min Chan, a foul-mouthed beauty popular among teenage girls. Mai looked up at Hong, he grinned and shook his head 'no'. He thought her infatuation with anime childish and immature, but he gave her a smile and nodded as she babbled on.

"She's my girl hero. A strong and beautiful woman." Mai mooned over the animated drawings. She saw herself in Min Chan.

"Some are brave and daring fighters, yet pretty and intelligent. Like me." Mai facetiously batted her eyelashes. She knew Hong thought her silly and vain, but it didn't deter her fascination with child-like avatars and their many different personalities. Mai thought she encompassed the lot of them.

"Others are aggressive and quick to attack." Mai sneered, her lips no longer smiling. Hong thought her deadpan stare signaled a vague threat.

"Aggressive and quick to attack?" Hong feigned a frightened face, bug-eyed with fear. "Should I be afraid?"

Not a word out of Mai, not even an easy smile. Oblivious to his attempt at humor, she ignored his question and resumed her imaginary life where anything could happen. With her new app, she drew virtual world anime characters with her own designs, manipulating them with just the right features. It was her idea of fun.

Mai's fanciful escape was a dimension Hong had never seen before. She seemed like a child, he would need to watch over her and keep her under his sway. He still thought her the most intriguing woman he'd ever met. The rest of her life was muddled and vague. She revealed so few details, no memories, no reflections on her past.

Hong leaned back in his desk chair and gazed at her as she lay on his bed. There was little other furniture in his small flat.

"You know what my name 'Hong' means, don't you?" Hong asked, referring to his Chinese name.

"Ah yes, of course, it means big or great. Or a flood," Mai said.

He wondered why Mai, who is French Vietnamese, would give the Chinese translations "great" or "flood". He ran a quick search and found the Vietnamese meaning of Hong. Most often it's a girl's name and means "pink and rosy". He let his question rest while it went through his mind. Thoughts are something you hold close, not to be shared with anyone. And intimacy with this woman didn't change Hong's rule.

It was those subtle inconsistencies that Hong was trained to look for. Those telling details that make you wonder if you can trust what you see and who you meet. Is she for real? Hong asked himself. He quickly dismissed any suspicions since what he really wanted from Mai was the fantasy of love. He did worry that he was hopelessly hooked, absolutely fucking head-over-heels in love.

Hong opened a decent bottle of sparkling wine, one of Mai's favorites, and filled his two stemmed glasses.

Mai raised her glass for a toast. "To our business partnership. May we be rich and a great success."

Fixing a soft affectionate gaze, Hong added, "and to our future commitment to each other. A gift for you, Mai." He handed her a box from a lingerie shop in Gothenburg.

She was less than enthused with Hong's declared love, but the finery impressed her. She peeled open the box and ran her fingers over the intricate lace. Hong lifted the large veil of black Chantilly lace and unfolded it for her.

"Shall I take off my clothes?" Mai asked and Hong nodded enthusiastically. Mai stripped down and draped the lace wrap over her shoulders. Modeling with ease, she held the veil like dragonfly wings as she flaunted her best assets.

"Hong, you have no full-length mirror," Mai pouted, annoyed that she was unable to admire her reconstructed beauty. She never went without one, no matter where she happened to reside.

Hong grabbed hold of the sides of the lace veil and pulled them tight around her, binding her arms in the black netted lace, as if he were wrapping a mummy. Ignoring her protest, he restrained and constricted her, enveloped like a cocoon. She was trapped in a web of Hong's making. He pulled his captive towards him. Hong, the spider, captured a fly in his web.

Sometime later Hong untangled the tight swaddling wrap. Mai tossed the lace veil on his desk and changed back into her jeans and sweater. She found two clean mugs and poured a pot of green tea. As she opened a packet of Swedish *pepparkakor*, she sniffed the crispy-thin spice cookies before neatly arranging them on a platter. While Mai busied herself with their tea break, Hong slipped the black lace web into his desk drawer.

"How is the list of traits coming?" Getting back to business, Hong quizzed Mai as she sipped her tea.

"Nearly finished." For Mai it was like compiling a list of anime traits, but only the very best of them. She handed her e-notebook to him. "Help me, Hong, I have the standard gene improvements but what about other upgrades?"

Hong scrolled through the traits. "You can derive attractive upgrades by adding the prefix 'hyper'." He thought it obvious.

"Hyper-fast, hyper-attentive. Hyper, hyper, hyper… How about hyper-sensitive? Just think of the advantage for people who are quicker to react to everything around them." Mai was thrilled at the potential.

Mai played with more traits, adding them as advanced options, extreme traits to entice those clients who could afford the enormous fees. Enhanced gene editing could hook the gullible ones, those with more money than sense.

Hong spoke in fast forward. "They could have highly evolved brains, superior intellect, perfect memory."

"How about scientific and mathematical geniuses?" Mai asked. "Everyone thinks they want an Einstein."

"Don't forget athletic. Strong and muscular." Hong flexed his biceps.

"Smarter, stronger, faster! My new mantra." Hong never saw her so pumped up about anything.

"And if you combine that with sexual prowess, they could be sexy geeks." Hong nearly choked himself silly. His goofy laugh annoyed Mai to no end. So, who's the child now?

Mai returned to her designs, not the anime of girlish fantasy, but the list of possibilities for designer babies, gene-edited to perfection. She turned away from Hong and ignored him while she tweaked her list.

After a while, she turned back to Hong and said, "Someday I'll create the perfect designer baby. DNA is just so easy to hack." Her face beamed with smugness and confidence. She truly believed she was capable of anything.

"You want to be a baby hacker?" Hong snorted at the perfectly apt meme.

Mai thought how the branding of "Baby Hacker" clearly revealed the dark side of hacking human life. Its violence. Its control. Its domination. Not elitist like Lars' *"Neonatus Perfectus."*

"Baby Hacker? Ahh perfect." Mai could see nothing wrong with hacking the DNA of humans. After all, she designed microbes with edits to make them more deadly and contagious. And hacking the genes of people yet to be born intrigued her. Who could argue with wanting to perfect the human race?"

"Baby Hacker!" They laughed in tandem, but they were amused for different reasons.

"I'll edit baby DNA for rich people who pay me." Mai said, knowing that someday it would be more than just a passing fantasy. Someday, she could play at designing what it means to be human. She privately dreamed of fame and fortune rather than tawdry scams for money.

Mai thought to herself, someday that money will finance my secret dream. My own designer baby.

16

Sven's Yen

Lars enlisted a hefty number of investors in their business, *Neonatus Perfectus*, but he was especially keen about this newest one. Years ago, Lars performed a facial reconstruction on his client, Sven, a rocker from a famous metal band. The surgery was intricate but Lars did meticulous work. Sven broke his nose and cheek during a drunken smash-up in his early metal days. Lars saved his face from a deformed shattered cheekbone and a comically twisted beak.

When both Lars and Sven were in Gothenburg, they sometimes met up for drinks in Sven's favorite bar. One evening, Lars vaguely proposed his human gene editing business. He couldn't believe his luck when Sven came up with a crazy idea, his outrageous vision of a future band that would follow in the footsteps of his aptly-named band, Ethereal Angels.

"Wouldn't it be great to design a replica of our band?" Sven asked. "Tantalizing thought for the future, isn't it?"

Sven invited Lars to his yacht moored in the Gothenburg marina. Compared to Sven's yacht, Lars' fifty-foot cruiser with its three staterooms was an old fishing trawler. Sven's yacht, over two hundred feet long with six cabins, could easily sleep a dozen people. But when in Gothenburg, Sven kept his private life and a series of lovers out of the public eye. For intimate encounters, the privacy of his yacht was just right to avoid the sensationalist press who hounded him in public. For a break from the bedlam of his nomadic life on the road, his floating palace was a perfect retreat.

Lars was totally blown over by the scale and the opulence of the luxurious "little boat", as Sven called it. Lars' Swedish reserve masked his awe. But he was absolutely gobsmacked at the "little boat" and its estimated worth of about seventy million euros.

As they continued on the tour, Sven waved his arm. "The master bedroom suite." He then pointed to the private sundeck. "I lounge out there when the weather is warm. And when I visit the Islands." Lars was more impressed with the sculpted leaf framed mirror above the bed than the panoramic view of the ocean. He imagined that Sven put the mirror to more use than the sundeck.

"I'll show you the upper deck. It's not too inviting at this time of year."

They ascended a staircase rather than the elevator. It was bitterly cold on the deck, but Lars peeked at the plunging pool and sunbathing area. He imagined lounging on a warm, sunny day, cruising the islands, the Mediterranean, Caribbean, or South Pacific. The choice would depend on time of the year to avoid typhoon and hurricane seasons.

They retreated to the main cabin lounge and bar where Sven poured Lars expensive single-malt whiskey. He fired up the sound system and played a sample of the band's current music. Sven, lead guitarist, studied classical guitar in his youth. Like other influential metal guitarists, he merged the two in his music. He'd begun improvising with more melodic guitar riffing and less shrieking and amplified distortion. It was a departure from other heavy metal bands.

"I think you'll find this more to your liking," Sven said. "We've tempered our music with age, mellowed it like this whisky." Now in his forties, his metal band had become more harmonic over time and less of the death-metal band of its youth.

Lars listened to the blend of alternative rock and heavy metal, somewhere between Nirvana and Metallica.

"Yes, I can understand most of the words. The singing is cleaner." Lars wasn't being sarcastic, he was well aware that besides being more commercial, Sven's band was about ten times more popular with this mellower sound.

Sven poured out his vision to Lars along with another single-malt whiskey.

"I have a dream and so do my band members. We want to perpetuate the legacy of Ethereal Angels. What we want is…." and Sven continued with his well-thought-out futuristic scenario, surprising Lars with its brilliance.

Lars listened, thinking how cerebral Sven was at articulating their fantasy. His mad genius and vivid imagination went well beyond his outstanding musical talent. Sven didn't just dream big, he had the means to do it. Beyond the band being wildly successful, Sven was also the only child of a banking magnate. He inherited a sizable family fortune and hadn't even begun to spend it.

"Is it possible to replicate my band and all their talents with your new business offering?" Sven just opened up an incredible opportunity for Lars. With six members in the band, Lars could see a huge single payoff.

Lars paused to remember his pitch. "I can do better. How about a perfected version of your band?" The whiskey warmed his inner being. As Lars peered out over the sea, he saw huge amounts of money on the not too distant horizon.

"A better version? Perfected? What do you mean?" Sven licked the rim of his crystal glass. It rang a high pitch.

"Embryos can be gene-edited, we can offer you standard designer babies. But they aren't exact replicas of you."

"But I want an identical replica. Is that possible?" Sven envisioned an exact copy of the band. He was ignorant of the actual possibilities of today's tech.

"We have better methods. My scientists can now create superior, enhanced baby boys from sperm. We can edit your sperm DNA with 'prime editing'—a more powerful technique with pin-point precision. Very safe too." Lars revealed a side Sven had never seen—a highly animated version, different from his usual reserve.

"Woah, an improved boy child created from my sperm?" The idea left Sven awestruck. His wide-eyed stare was almost orgasmic.

Lars could see the excitement, it brightened up Sven's cosmetically enhanced face. He admired his expert nose and cheek reconstruction and how he erased the worst of Sven's lines and wrinkles, those that aged him most. Too many years of sex-and-drugs-and-rock-and-roll had taken its toll, but Lars managed to reverse the ravages of time.

"I want a boy. A perfected me. From my sperm." Sven was now determined to have what he wanted for him and his band.

Lars advised him, "A bigger investment is needed for your perfect gene-edited boy. If you wanted a girl, the simple procedure is easier, less expensive, but a woman's egg must be fertilized."

"But you said that sperm-edited babies are best for a boy like me. Right?" Sven insisted, he wanted the best.

"Yes, they are. They're actually self-clones," Lars pointed at Sven "a perfect you!" Lars paused as Sven took it in. "They're edited to perfection. *Neonatus Perfectus* is the most expensive product we have. And your progeny will perpetuate a perfect you." Lars knew he could tap into Sven's narcissistic desires.

"Money is no object." Sven shrugged his shoulders. Cost never came into consideration. Sven grew up indulged by his mother who was now sequestered, dementia had taken its toll.

"Make sure there are no genes for dementia. Or other inherited problems."

"But of course. My team of experts will run every one of your 25,000 genes through an analyzer. They'll identify any flaws. With prime editing we can correct the tiniest DNA flaw safely. And we can replace other genes with the best traits possible."

"Cut, copy, paste. Simple as that?" Sven didn't understand the details of gene editing, but it seemed to make sense. "Make sure nothing escapes attention."

"Your sperm DNA will be purged of bad genes and edited for excellent health, longer life, immunity to diseases."

"My eyes are bad, 20-20 for my kid?" Sven pursed his lips. He rubbed his eyes and squinted.

Lars nodded. "Of course, we can do that. Consider your inborn defects corrected."

"Wow, that's incredible." Sven shook his head in amazement.

"But what about advanced options for your designer babies? Other specific traits in your reincarnation?" Lars prompted.

"Well, musical talent. How about perfect pitch when it comes to musical notes?" Sven asked.

"Perfect pitch? Some call it absolute pitch. Sometimes it runs in families. It's rare but we have the genes in our collection. Your children would be special. Exceptionally talented. In an instant they'll identify tones, match them with musical notes."

"How common is this trait?" Sven asked.

"About 1 in 1500. So, yes, your boys will be unique. Just think about the musical advantage they'll have." Lars paused for Sven to realize the full impact, the incalculable value. No amount of money could ever be attached to it.

As Lars thought about the pipe-dream he offered, Sven gazed at the sea imagining the possibilities. "The Ethereal Angels of the future will inspire awe. Angels, eerily like otherworldly ghosts, not just superhumans but supernatural beings."

Sven pictured the new metal band, improved and perfected, becoming a world phenomenon. "It would be like watching ourselves in retrospect, only infinitesimally better." Sven trailed off, lost in a daydream of futuristic images of his band's progeny. "Prodigal sons. But let's hope their talents not be squandered."

Lars needed to keep Sven focused on the dream. He dismissed Sven's inference to riotous living, how talented musicians too often self-destruct.

"We'll collect cheek cells and semen from you and your band members. My assistant is very adept at that."

17

Intelligent Sex?

Mai woke in Hong's bed, but she didn't know how long she slept. Her mind drifted to the past when she worked at the Chinese biotech company, World Genomics Labs. For one special project they recruited gifted people with 'high cognitive ability'. By running the entire genomes of the most intellectually gifted people, World Genomics looked for unique sequences of DNA that were common in ultra-high-ability geniuses. They hoped that if their research could identify the DNA that made people so special, so intelligent, so brilliant, then creating exceptional, super-smart Chinese people was achievable in the near future.

The scientists presumed that once they identified these genes for genius and the unique DNA for intelligence, these traits could be added to the ethnic gene pool. The Chinese nation could then become incredibly powerful. It was a national goal worth pursuing.

Mai's DNA didn't make the cut for the project. Her genome was added to the larger control group with normal mental abilities. Controls were necessary for comparison.

But Mai thought there was more to intelligence than genes alone. Mai knew she had the edge when it came to manipulating people, especially men. That ability would be a very desirable trait, especially for leaders of authoritarian regimes. After all, there are powerful leaders in today's world with average intelligence who are masters at manipulating their people.

Mai remembered a Chinese geneticist she knew. He told her about his secret research lab where they gene-edited embryos. They knocked out one gene from an embryo, the CCR5 gene, and made babies resistant to HIV. An extra bonus was that these "knock out" embryos might grow into people who are quicker learners, have better memory, and improved intelligence. He boasted to Mai, "They will be the very brightest students."

As she lay there, Hong was busy searching on his computer for articles on cognition and brain-smart genes. He summarized one for Mai. "A study in New York says there are about 70 specific gene locations for brain smarts."

"Hong, there are genes that can be removed easily, like the gene that makes babies HIV resistant. And it also makes people smarter. They learn faster and remember things better. Smarter, faster, better."

"Ah, yes, the CCR5 gene. Would they do better in school? I could've used that." Hong grinned.

"Me too." Mai agreed.

"But there might be problems that come with it. Possible downsides. And some of these experiments were done on mice. Are you a mouse, Mai?" Hong laughed and said gleefully, "I'm not."

"Hong, do you think our world leaders could be designed for the future? What advantages would they need over others?" She knew where she was going with her questions. "What are the desired traits for a possible new world order? For dictators to control people?"

"Mai, you never cease to amaze me. You're asking if it's possible to take down one group of dictators and replace them with…what, another group? Would this new group of despots be more ruthless and savage?" Hong tried to provoke Mai. What exactly was she thinking?

"Perhaps, that might be a big advantage." Mai said matter-of-fact, she saw nothing untoward.

Hong got his answer. He thought, this woman has no scruples. She wants the advantage at any cost. He chuckled at Mai's deviant ways. "You really want to live in a world run by tyrants designed by you and me?"

Mai said nothing.

"What about sex?" Hong asked, looking for something other than a scientific treatise.

But Mai took him literally. "Should a 'He' or a 'She' rule?"

"He. Leaders should always be men." Hong held up his chin with a measure of arrogance.

Mai nearly laughed but bit her tongue. She didn't want Hong to feel judged for his macho mindset where male superiority was a given. As Mai once told Lars, the best and most expensive designer babies are self-clones where sperm are DNA-edited to create superior baby boys. Men can be made in their own image. The newest technology itself dictates the male prerogative, the male advantage.

"So, chauvinists rule the world? Should only the dominant sex be given the genetic privilege of leadership?" Mai coyly questioned Hong's biased opinion.

"That's a done deal, everywhere in the world, men are the protected species." Hong believed what he said, although he expected Mai to come to the defense of women.

"So, who needs women, except to carry men's preconceived embryos?" she asked, challenging Hong's convictions. But Mai was no feminist, she used men's feelings of superiority to exploit them. With so many narcissistic misogynists in the world of power and money, she would capitalize on their fantasies that would bring in capital. It was all about the money, after all.

Hong playfully nudged Mai. "You misunderstand. By sex, I meant something else."

But Mai ignored his innuendo. "Ah, yes, virility matters. And you're right, there are genes for sexuality and stamina."

"Hmmm, interesting, in the next generation new genes for sexual stamina could be passed on." Hong speculated, thinking he already had plenty.

Mai thought of other, more pragmatic consequences. "In wealthy Northern countries like this one, there will someday be an elite class of perfected people. What do you think will be their idea of perfection?"

"Exceptional people…with indigo blue eyes? This begins to sound like a pure Aryan race in Nazi Germany. Don't people choose their own ethnocentric idea of a superior race?"

"So, who will make the choice for future babies?" Mai asked.

Hong reflected. "The baby would have no choice in the matter."

"But what baby has choice now?" Mai asked the bigger question.

"True." Hong shrugged his shoulders. "After all, who has ever had any say in their own DNA design?"

"Not me. Not you. And in the future, what will happen to the rest of us unedited people?" There was no end to Mai's questions.

"Maybe we'll end up like those fools who self-inject DNA in their basement labs. Self-edited by our own design." Hong was half serious.

The art of self-design was out-of-control. Both Hong and Mai knew that reckless idiots experimented on themselves. Self-inflicted gene therapy had become the new craze in do-it-your-self labs.

"I saw that silly guy injecting himself." She'd seen DNA hackers with hypodermic needles full of concocted DNA edits. "Bigger muscles." Mai flexed her biceps, sometimes she liked to compete with Hong's humor.

"Others try to change the color of their eyes, skin, hair." Hong added.

Mai chuckled. "Rainbow colored people."

"There's that nutjob injecting new genes to enhance the size of his dick." Hong laughed. "I don't need that." He stood up and put his hands on his hips.

Mai wrinkled her brow. "Really?" Then she smiled. She left his male ego intact. She knew enough about men to never insult the size of their manhood. "There's no end to what men will do for super-male traits. It's insane the way bio-hackers are self-editing."

"It's the wild, wild west of genetic freaksters," Hong said with a quirky grin.

"Self-editing could someday create very bizarre people. Like you." Mai teased and pointed at Hong.

Hong screwed up his face and wiggled his tongue like an alien serpentine monster, making Mai laugh hysterically. "I've hacked myself." Hong nearly choked on his forked tongue.

Mai calmed herself to a chuckle, she couldn't resist a dig. "You will hack you. I will hack baby."

"Ok, baby hacker." Hong said as he slithered onto the bed. It was time to give Mai a good hacking.

18

Emerald Serpent

"Mai, I'll pick you up tonight at our apartment. Bring your sample collection kit with extra supplies. We'll meet with people on their yacht in Gothenburg harbor." Lars called on his burner phone. He'd never asked Mai to meet with clients before.

"Lars, who are these people?" Mai asked.

"I can't tell you their names. They're from the entertainment industry. We need to collect multiple male specimen."

Mai seemed surprised at Lars request. "Multiple?"

"They're extremely wealthy and have invested in our business. Six gentlemen from a music group. I assure you they're not beasts."

"Do they know which traits they are interested in?" Mai was curious.

"They've reviewed the menus and paid big deposits. They haven't decided traits yet, but I'm expecting some unusual enhancements."

"I'll promise them anything and everything their hearts desire. I'll sell them their dream babies."

"You are my dream baby. You need to look your best. There's big money in this for us, I am anxious to get this sale. They are trendy sorts, so wear something with flare. That emerald green gown I bought you would be ideal." Lars had a vision of how she should look, enticing but not a tart, elegant but not off the red carpet.

"Not my business professional suit?" Mai teased. "I'll put special coloring in my hair. It's best to be a little disguised."

"Perhaps, but nothing extreme. Something that goes well with the emerald green dress. Mai, I wouldn't ask you to do this, but it's worth the effort. It will secure our future together. A life neither one of us could ever imagine with what they pay us."

Mai's eyes lit up at the thought. Her life-long dream that alluded her was finally within reach. Not only would Lars protect her, he'd provide a life of extravagance and luxury.

"I'll look my very best."

Lars arrived in a limo carrying a large box. He was early but wanted time to go over their preparations for the evening.

"What's in the box?" Mai asked.

"You'll see later. But first let me look at you."

That afternoon, Mai added bright red-orange highlights to her hair, creating the appearance of flames emanating from her head. With multiple male specimen to collect that evening, six musical "gentlemen", as Lars described them, she needed to ramp up the level of allure.

"Your hair is brighter than I expected, but it will certainly get the attention of these musicians. Bring me your eye make-up kit." Lars had his own ideas on what impression he wanted Mai to make. "You know I do cosmetic work, not only surgery but make-up too."

"You don't like my eyes?" Mai pouted. She wore her usual thin eye liner and mascara. She'd been wearing a more natural look to blend in with the academic crowd.

"Your foundation looks good, but I can do better with your eyes." Tonight, Lars wanted a more dramatic look to her face. Something striking. He would emphasize her glamourous side as an appealing Asian delight.

Lars started with emerald green eye shadow, the brightest he could find in Mai's collection. He then applied a thick black eye liner to enhance what was left of her Chinese ancestry. He finished with a black, lash-building mascara applied at a sharp angle.

"You're good with make-up, Lars." Mai was surprised at his cosmetic skills.

Lars looked at his watch. "Now, go put on your emerald dress. Then you'll see what's in the box."

Mai went to the bedroom to dress. She felt more than ready for the evening in anticipation of what riches the night would bring. She surmised the musical group was someone she might recognize or at least have heard of. Judging by the eye make-up Lars applied, the band would appreciate a more exotic offering.

When she walked into the front lounge, the plunging neck-line and side slits of her emerald satin gown drew Lars eyes towards her serpentine shape. Punctuated with her golden stilettos, he thought her disturbingly snake-like, yet classy and elegant. The emerald green satin created a striking contrast with the con-flagration of blazing red-orange hair—as though she might ig-nite at any moment.

"You look like an emerald tree boa." Lars seemed enthralled with her image.

Mai wasn't surprised at the comparison. She'd been com-pared to a snake before in her past life. Propped on a barstool in an iridescent green snakeskin skirt, a client whispered in her ear, "She smiles like a reptile and lives on her back." His name was Vlad. And she knew how that turned out.

Mai didn't smile. It was a time she didn't want to remember. A time when her money ran out and her client turned toxic and down-right evil.

"Is it a poisonous snake, Lars?" She asked, knowing just how venomous she could be.

"No, not at all, but many people are afraid of it. The females are larger than the males—over two meters long. The emerald snake is a boa, she lives in the South American rain forests. She kills her prey by holding them with her mandibles and wrapping her body around them. Once immobilized, she squeezes her prey until it can no longer breathe. Her victim dies from asphyxiation. She has the power to constrict, she strangles her prey to death."

"Why do you compare me to this evil snake?" Mai asked.

"It's the most beautiful snake in the world. Like you, Mai. The most beautiful woman in the world."

Mai breathed a sigh of relief. Things were so much better now that Lars held the key to her future.

Lars opened the box and pulled out a dark full-length hooded fur coat that once kept another animal warm. A label from a cold-storage unit showed it wasn't newly purchased. Lars helped Mai slip into the fur and turned her around. He admired her like a hunting trophy.

Lars pulled out a case with dark-rimmed women's eyeglasses. "Wear these in transit." He slid them above her ears and poked with his finger to balance them across her nose. He then pulled the hood of the fur coat up to cover her spiked glowing hair.

"Best not to arouse suspicion. Under the hood and glasses, you could pass for my wife." Mai gazed in the wall mirror, pulling a comical face. Tossing the hood back, she inspected herself. She thought her face resembled a child-like anime character, a spectacled young girl with brilliant sunset-colored hair.

Lars knew his wife would never miss the glasses. She had multiple pair, each worn as a fashion statement. As for the fur, it hadn't been out of cold storage for a long time. His wife had qualms about wearing it, afraid she'd be reprimanded and publicly embarrassed. Lars bought her the dark brown mink coat many years ago, but she now had misgivings about the inhumane use of animal pelts.

Lars checked the contents of the sample collection kit. He picked up the case and said, "It's time to go."

When the limo arrived at the harbor, Sven's yacht loomed large.

Mai asked, "Is your boat as big as this?"

"Oh, mine is so much bigger," Lars said with a chuckle. Mai didn't understand his subtle joke.

As they stepped out of the limo, Lars watched Mai's jaw drop, a look of shock and awe spread over her face. Exorbitant, obscene displays of wealth impressed Mai. She saw no value in living modestly.

Mai thought about what she left behind, growing up in Shenzhen's Urban Village. She would never look back at her family's poverty, it was best left in the past. She would never return to China, that she knew for sure.

19

Devils or Angels

Lars presented Mai as if she were precious booty on their pirate vessel. Sven forewarned the other band members not to attempt to plunder this emerald treasure. Mai would completely control the clinical collection of their DNA.

"No demands!" Sven admonished. "Go only as far as allowed." Although arousal was critical in delivering their seminal fluids, Mai would decide on the methods, not the group of mischievous rogues cynically misnamed the Ethereal Angels.

When Mai pulled back her hood, her red-orange flames seemed to illuminate the cabin. As if unwrapping a gift package, Lars helped disrobe her from the heavy mink coat. Mai stepped through the side-slit of her iridescent green gown to reveal a glimpse of what lie beneath. Under the cabin's stage-lights, her striking ivory-white leg looked like the melting wax of a Christmas candle. She stunned the roomful of men into silence. Seldom did they have a quiet moment, mostly they practiced riotously in the cabin full of high-end Moog synthesizers, guitars, and drums.

"I will hack your DNA. Edit it to perfection. I am your baby hacker," Mai said to everyone's amusement.

"Baby Hacker!" they chimed in unison, then laughed and whooped.

Lead singer Nils couldn't resist. "We know metal bands who'd love that name." They laughed lewdly again, but Mai didn't understand the humor. It was lost in translation.

"Designer baby, will you be mine?" Nils sang to a familiar tune and the others chimed in.

"She's not your designer baby. She's a scientist." Lars emphasized. He tried not to get angry, but he wanted the band members to respect her.

"She's not your *Sexig sak, miss Ting Ting*, remember your manners." Sven cautioned the boys she was not a sexy toy. "We'll party with the yacht girls later tonight."

Lars smiled at Sven, pleased that he chided the guys to behave themselves. "So, let's talk about traits." Lars cued Sven on the gene preferences they discussed.

Sven asked the guys, "Who can hum a 'C' note?" All tried but were all over the place with discordant sounds. They snickered at their own ineptness.

"Try again, how about a 'G'?" Sven asked, but their attempts made him cringe. "For your kids, it will be natural." All eyes were fixed on Mai as she struck a pose with her shoulders pulled back. Her emerald gown neckline plunged to incredible depths. Her stunning enhancements were spectacular.

"OK, *enough*." Lars got their attention. "Your children will have perfect pitch. They'll recognize sounds as most of us see light and color. They'll identify a musical note as if it were the color blue. In an instant."

"Our children will be far more talented than us." Sven scanned the group to see their reaction.

"So, my son will instantly recognize tones? Musical notes?" Nils piped up.

"Of course. Perfect or absolute pitch is inherited. A special trait related to the 8q24.21 gene," Mai said to impress them with her expertise. Mai knew plenty about human genetics. She'd show them that she was a scientist who happened to come in an interesting package.

Lars explained, "We've collected rare samples of the 8q24.21 gene from some highly talented European families. Their DNA can be added to your designer babies."

"How about rhythm?" the drummer asked as he thumped a few beats on his thighs.

"And quality of voice?" Nils asked, almost singing a melody.

"Excellent drum beats. Superior vocal cord genes. We have selected the best DNA." Lars assured them, then turned to Sven. "Your investment will pay off in dividends. That highly valuable DNA will be passed on in generations to come."

"It will keep on giving." Sven was intrigued at the thought of endowing extreme talent and unique genes to the future of music. "Our legacy. Our gift. Our sons will be the bleeding-edge band of the future."

Sven had transferred twenty million euros per band member, seed money totaling one hundred and twenty million. He couldn't think of a better investment. On delivery of the finished products, the designer babies, many millions more would transfer to Lars' offshore account. Expensive? Yes, but Sven envisioned his entire band replicated as self-clones. Something no other band would ever conceive of. Each member of Ethereal Angels would have their sperm DNA edited to create superior musicians.

"What about correcting physical traits?" Nils asked.

Sven goaded him. "Your baldness, Nils? Your boy will be called Harry. He'll have a mop." Sven patted Nils' hairless crown.

Mai emphasized, "Not just your self-clone, but a *perfected* one. Each one of you. A more perfect you."

Lars explained that there were plenty of surrogate "baby mommas" available in Sweden and he had connections with private IVF clinics, no need to go out of the country. He'd select well-paid baby mommas to carry their perfected all male "boy band". Members of the band would grow up close in age. If the IVF baby mommas ended up with multiple babies, there could be extra band members. Their "Designer Band" of cloned musicians and the vision for the future music world, whether metal or whatever, would raise the bar for performers to no end.

Lars asked again, "Do you want a more perfect you?" He mimicked the hook that Mai used to capture his attention when they first met during his *Fika* break. "You guys are a creative bunch, but with the *Neonatus Perfectus* menu there are no limits."

The band members brainstormed other changes, additions, and bizarre alterations. They fired off one idea after another. But of all the absurd and ridiculous genetic traits, penal size enhancement seemed to amuse them most. Lars could see them lustily eyeing Mai, she was ravishing. But as already agreed, she must not be ravished.

Mai was focused on the task at hand, a tool she was very adept at. Retreating to a bathroom, she removed her gown and donned a white lab coat. Starting with Sven, Mai used her clinical expertise to ensure the safety, quality, and sterility of the samples. She escorted each client in turn to the designated cabin, a clinical room where she collected multiple specimen of pure, unadulterated semen. Each specimen was properly labeled, their identity verified. For quality assurance, her cool kit stored the samples in segregated sections.

Before leaving, Mai used sterile swabs to collect the skin cells from their inner cheeks. Each band member's genome—the complete set of DNA with all their genes—was vital for the next step in the process.

Lars picked up the chilled case containing the clinical samples. "We must expedite delivery to the technicians at the *Neonatus Perfectus* lab." Both he and Mai were in a hurry to leave. "The samples must be processed immediately. Our technicians are waiting."

They returned to Lars' flat where he heaped a pile of cash on Mai. In her handbag, Mai had stashed another wad of generous tips from the boy band, in appreciation for lending them a hand.

Lars would stay the night. He told Mai he would always protect her and he meant it. Mai showered and washed the temporary red dye from her hair. She said nothing about the evening nor the chores she executed so flawlessly. To Mai, it was all a vital part of the job. She had no qualms.

Lars watched as she slept like a baby. Sweet dreams, he thought. She smiled like an Ethereal Angel.

20

It's a Knockout

Jack just finished breakfast, a minimal meal with vitamin supplements and a smoothie, a green concoction full of cat grass and kale. Except for anomalous departures from his routine, such as dinners with Jo and Jeremy, Jack watched what he ate and limited his drinking to a few social beers. Jack didn't like the effects of too much alcohol. Booze made him too vulnerable and easy prey for unwanted women. With Jack's looks, he seldom had to seek the young ladies. They found him.

Perhaps that's why he felt comfortable with a married couple nearly old enough to be his parents. He naively thought he was protected from any unwanted attention.

On rare occasion, he'd throw caution to the wind, but he could afford to be selective. He chose only the most beautiful, desirable, and readily available women. With his love 'em and leave 'em attitude, most often his relationships were short-lived.

Jack was drying himself after a shower when he heard the familiar Skype ringtone. He sprinted to his bedroom to answer the call. When the video screen popped up, Hong laughed hysterically as Jack threatened with his towel to expose himself. Neither could say anything until their hilarity died down.

"Save it for Gothenburg, there are plenty of liberated beauties here," Hong told Jack.

"So I've heard," Jack agreed enthusiastically. "Hey, let's go out for a night on the town."

"Take in the nightlife? Most definitely," Hong says, but he knows that, as an organizer for the Genomics and Gene Editing Conference, he's bound to be busy deflecting blows from administrative misfires and other disasters. There'd be little free time for carousing with Jack.

Jack and Hong hadn't seen each other for a while, but they kept in touch. Neither had lost their fascination with manipulating DNA. Years ago, in their do-it-yourself lab, Jack and Hong learned firsthand how to play with DNA and create mutant microbes. Such were their youthful, reckless days of indiscretion. Now they were the ones wary of cowboys, clowns, and unscrupulous scientists designing the next generation of biological weapons.

"Jack, you're on the agenda under RNA Editing." Hong held up the draft in his hand. "I'm lumped under DNA Editing Techniques. Gonna show off my micro-injection skills. How's this for a title? 'Methods and Madness in Editing Animals.' Pretty tame stuff these days."

"You haven't edited human embryos like your crazy Chinese relatives, have you Hong? Wait, wait, don't tell me. Probably. You're such a madman." Jack's wide grin nearly broke the computer screen.

"Hey, there's plenty of rogues out there doing it. Like back in the day when we were young and restless, or was is young and reckless?" Hong joked.

"What, me? A rogue? Never!" Jack innocently widened his eyes, as if butter wouldn't melt in his mouth.

Hong flashed his toothy smile, then Jack issued the one-finger salute, which Hong returned with both hands. Always trying to outdo each other, the two were irrepressible.

"We've got a motley bunch of DNA hackers on the agenda. Like those simian idiots who edit DNA in apes and monkeys. Great, hey?" Flaring his nostrils, popping his eyes out, Hong wedged his tongue under his upper lip and made a monkey face, driving Jack into another frenzy of laughter. The boys were always quick to resort to their wild and manic puerile past.

"You must be China's first human-monkey hybrid. Aren't they creating human-pig and human-rat hybrids too?"

"Yeah, of course," Hong said and broke into the song, "China does it, Russia does it, even little old Japan does it. Let's do it...."

"Let's fall in love." Jack nearly choked on the song's refrain. After more hysterical laugher, the two finally calmed down. "Are we being Cole Porter today?" Jack threw out his hands and shrugged his shoulders.

"Ok, Ok. So, what's your title? I've got to post this conference agenda next week."

"Mine? RNA editing". But should I add 'the Advent of Genetic Weapons' to the title?" Jack was curious how Hong would react. "It's the newest weapon of mass destruction," he said, matter-of-fact.

Nearly speechless, Hong gasped. "Woah! A new WMD?"

"Yep, target and destroy. Basically, you can target a specific ethnic group and wipe them out." Jack purposely carved a sinister grin.

"You sound like one of those conspiracy guys." Laughing as usual, Hong figured Jack was joking.

"Listen Hong, this is a ground-breaker. With RNA editing in viruses, anything is possible. And it will happen, believe me on this one." Jack was deadly serious.

"Like when the US dropped the bomb and nuclear weapons became...a reality?" Hong's smile still lingered.

"Genetic weapons are a huge threat. And someday, they will be used. Because they can." Jack was adamant.

"Holy shmoly. That's a far cry from our days playing with those damn ferrets. Nasty little vermin." Hong turned everything into humor. But underneath, a chill started to set in on the possible consequences of genetic weapons.

"Hong, we've known for a long time that if you can interfere with RNA, you can shut down vital genes in anything living."

"Yep, including people. I've just never thought much about the implications. So, you're saying that RNA can become a targeted weapon?" Hong had totally lost the laughter.

"It's like this. Some ethnic groups have very unique RNA sequences in their cells. Your ethnic Chinese relatives, for example." Jack grinned as he pointed at Hong. "If we disrupt RNA in people who are Han Chinese by infecting them with an edited virus, we can knock-out their key body functions." Jack paused. "Think about it."

For Hong, it was beyond a bombshell. "So, these are targeted bioweapons that kill people." He didn't need much time to understand the impact. "But it's an ethnic knockout...hmmm." Hong scratched his head and dropped his jaw, his mouth gapped open like a dying goldfish.

"A knockout and a knockdown, too," Jack said.

Hong no longer thought Jack was funny. Not only offended, he was angry. "So, hearts might stop beating or people might not be able to breathe? What the fuck. But why Chinese people? Who wants to kill my people with targeted bioweapons?"

"Who knows? Maybe another ethnic group? Such as, errr...Russians? They wouldn't be affected by the same nasty knockout virus." Jack paused. "So, maybe China doesn't want to piss off Russia?"

"Or the Americans. Like you, Jack," Hong said, punctuating with an accusatory sneer.

Jack shrugged his shoulders, playful rather than threatening. "Hong, just think of the possibilities."

"Interesting, so you can whack-a-mole people with genetic weapons. And the weapon will only attack and kill the moles." Hong chuckled just a little. "Hmmm...this could get interesting." Hong decided to play along.

"Yep, absolutely clobbers them. Shuts down their brains and hearts and lungs. Attacks one race of people and not others." Jack nodded. "Get it?"

Hong frowned. "Oh, shit."

"Yeah, that too."

"So, in theory, you could kill off the Han population of China with a targeted genetic plague? Sure, why not." Hong answered his own question. "A sinister swirling shitstorm. It sucks." Hong liked the alliteration but he was no longer trying to be funny.

Jack nodded and widened his eyes. "And think about other possible uses. There's so many more."

"How about the future of war? Could we be on the cusp of genetic warfare?" Hong wasn't joking. "Or is this more conspiracy theory?"

"Good question," Jack said and pulled out his lecture notes. "In 1999, a German group, the Sunshine Project looked into the future of targeted genetic warfare. They said, even if you could affect as little as 10% or 20% of your enemy, you could wreak havoc on their soldiers on a battlefield. And on the enemy's society as a whole. No one believed them, not until the warnings of 'genetic bombs' like Anthrax or bubonic plague that could be tailored to activate in one pure ethnic group."

"Just the purebreds. So, what about Americans, what happens to them?" Hong asked.

"Hong, we're such a mongrel mix, it would be like buckshot. You'd kill limited numbers, but it's a pot shot."

"So, all that diversity will work to America's advantage." Hong paced in a frenetic fashion. All Jack could see was topsy-turvy images of Hong gesticulating wildly.

"Now we've gotta add another category to C-B-R-N-E weapons, the Chemical, Biological, Radiological, Nuclear, and Explosives. Gotta add a G for Genetic Weapons." Jack teased, but he meant it.

"What? C-B-R-N-E-G. Who can remember acronyms with 6 letters? I've got a hard-enough time remembering LGBTQ. Anything over three or four letters just doesn't stick." Hong laughed nervously.

Both Jack and Hong worried about new gene technologies, but for different reasons. Jack worried about the risk of unintended consequence. There were the upsides, like treatments using gene editing in people with inherited conditions. Jack's grandfather was afflicted with inherited blindness and he wondered if he might also carry that genetic trait. The downside of gene editing meant that enemy rogues also had the same new tools to tinker around with.

Hong's greatest fear was made strikingly clear by Jack. He never realized that his DNA, that part that makes him Han Chinese, is vulnerable to enemy attack. He feared that, if provoked, an ethnically mixed population like the US could use targeted genetic weapons against a 90% ethnically pure superpower. But others besides the US might also have reason to go after China. Hong could only fathom the possibilities.

"Don't worry, Hong, I doubt if these weapons will be used anytime soon. And chances are, they'd be pretty hard to perfect. If things can go wrong, they will."

"Like releasing gene-edited mosquitos to eradicate malaria? They sterilize the females, don't they? And I don't see much difference when it comes to eradicating people." Hong frowned as he pondered over the threat to China.

"We've already opened Pandora's Box. Just think of all the gene-altered plants and animals out there." Jack shrugged. "The glow-in-the-dark cat is out of the bag."

"We're not talking about cats that glow." Hong closed in on the screen. "But genetic weapons will change the very nature of the human race. Why release something into the world we don't fully understand?" Hong sensed the hypocrisy in what he was saying.

Jack gave a dismissive shrug. "Why not?"

21

Comrade Hong

In all the years they'd known each other, Jack was unaware of Hong's tightly held beliefs. Hong, a fierce patriot, was a staunch believer in China. His loyalty to the Motherland never wavered but he kept this secret close. He masked his real allegiances, hiding them under a facade of incessant humor. Hong knew that if you joke about everything, no one knows your true feelings. People will dismiss you as a clown. No one knew, not even his buddy Jack, about his devotion to the ancestral land of his father.

Hong spoke excellent Mandarin but seldom used it outside his parent's home. If people spoke to him in Mandarin, he feigned a cursory child-like vocabulary. He would tell people, "My Mandarin is baby talk, like ga ga goo goo."

Hong's initial training consisted mainly of indoctrination by his father. His dad, a tough taskmaster, also trained young Hong one-on-one in several of the martial arts. Hong was enlisted at an early age by China's PLA, the People's Liberation Army.

※ ※ ※

When Hong first visited mainland China, he met his recruiter. It was in Shenzhen that Hong went through his first interrogation. Was he able to keep secrets? In particular, the nation's secrets? Was he trustworthy and honest? Could he cope with the stress of a secret life? Could he be compromised? Hong, primed by his father, was ready with his responses.

The recruiter asked, "What motivated you to join the People's Liberation Army?"

Hong answered, "I love China, its history, its culture, but primarily its ideals. My dad showed me where our loyalties lie." Hong truly was taken with China; he spoke from both his heart and mind.

Then the recruiter asked, "Why do you want to spy for China?"

"My duty to China is first and foremost. As a special agent, my goal is to become a spymaster."

"Do you want to be a hero?" the recruiter asked, trying to find out what really motivated Hong. Was it his ego that drove him?

"I hope my legacy will be that of a true hero. A nameless hero, I'm not looking for fame." Hong meant what he said.

The recruiter scrutinized Hong about his dedication and sense of duty. He then gave him money to cover his travel expenses, all in US dollars, that Hong easily smuggled home.

It was later that Hong travelled to a secret training camp in Suzhou. At the camp he would undergo a strenuous regimen to learn the tools of the trade.

Hong remembered his excitement on his first overnight train journey. It was over a thousand miles from Shenzhen to Suzhou. He slept much of his nearly 13 hours on a high-speed train.

The city of Suzhou, a popular tourist destination, was renowned for its beauty. Hong gave himself extra time to explore its canals, classical gardens, and zigzag bridges that connected tranquil ponds and manicured islands. He thought the 500-year-old Humble Administrator's Garden exquisite, it impressed him to no end. Hong wished he could take photos to share with family and friends. But no one could ever know about his clandestine life. And photographs, unless authorized, were forbidden.

During Hong's introductory session, a trainer presented an overview of the Ministry of State Security. "Our mission at MSS is to ensure the security of China by countering enemy agents and spies. Counterespionage."

Hong clung to the words of the instructor. He loved the vibe he got from the word 'counterespionage', it rang of intrigue and deception, and sexy, captivating people. Whether in James Bond movies or John le Carre novels, Hong was drawn to the world of daring deceit and duplicity. He thought of himself as a consummate conman. By using his charm, he knew he could seduce and manipulate people. He would gain their trust and use them to his advantage.

Hong sat in an iron and wood school desk which, in the United States, would be considered antique. He listened closely, enthralled as the instructor described the five types of spy agents. Hong's goal was to master all the spy trickery he could.

"Inside agents keep their spying eyes inside our great country on threats to our security and safety. We must protect our Motherland against dissidents and religious sects that do not conform to our Chinese ideals. Terrorists and nihilists must be stopped dead in their tracks."

Hong didn't know enough to understand the complexities. He made a mental note to find out more about these nefarious groups.

"Double agents, deception agents, expendable agents, and penetration agents have dangerous duties. But when successful, they are all invaluable." The instructor left much to the imagination. Hong knew that agents could be short or long term.

"An expendable agent will be killed if discovered passing false information," the instructor warned. It was something Hong vowed he'd never do. Why put himself in that kind of situation? He knew he'd never deceive China's People's Liberation Army and didn't understand how any true patriot could.

"Comrade 8" was Hong's assigned name. At the training center, comrades weren't encouraged to befriend one another, but Hong warmed up to one in particular. Although always wary of others, he could easily spot someone with a sense of humor, no matter how subtle.

When standing in line, Comrade 9 was always behind him. It might have been his fleeting glance, a glimmer in his eyes, or the curl of his lip, but Hong wasn't sure. At first Hong thought Comrade 9 might be flirting. Does he think I am gay?

One evening, after the shower room cleared out, a quick encounter brought them both the intimate connection they were looking for. The daily stresses needed to be alleviated somehow, Hong rationalized, with a pull, or a push, or just a quick wank, nothing too fancy. Just an expedient, effective release of bottled-up pressure from the day. Comrade 9 was the closest he'd come to any genuine relationship, one built on mutual gratification and trust.

"Sometimes," as they were told in deception training, "you will be called upon to compromise people. Use any means possible, including sex. Set-up and entrap those you will spy on."

Hong's own interpretation was, go for the balls, go after their vulnerabilities. Whether their inclinations are the same as yours or not, it doesn't matter.

On a cigarette break, Comrade 9 told him, "It's all part of the training. The art of deception means you can do anything to deceive."

"Anything?" Hong asked.

"Do anything to con those you wish to compromise," Comrade 9 said.

"So, I should compromise people to get information. Make them vulnerable. How so?" Hong asked.

"If you can blackmail them in any possible way, use it to your advantage."

Hong took the advice. He would hone his techniques. He aimed for perfection.

Hong felt safe in his encounters with Comrade 9. Neither would compromise the other. The stakes were high for both. And in a few weeks, Hong would return to the US. Neither he nor Comrade 9 would ever see each other again.

Or so Hong thought.

During the weeks that followed, the MSS trainers tested Hong, sometimes severely, but he withstood their grueling interrogations and arduous physical challenges. His specialist grooming continued with firearms, martial arts, driving, communications, and surveillance skills.

Early on, Hong reported about his rogue experiments in Jack's DIY lab, amateurish as they were. But they were on the cutting-edge of DNA manipulation at the time. They had first-hand experience in dual-use biotech. Technology that could be used for benefit or for harm. He and Jack tried to enhance flu viruses—their infectivity, their virulence, their lethality. It was not just child's play. They experimented to create pandemic influenza strains.

"China wants you to steal intellectual property and spy on the brainpower behind it." An instructor told him, "In the United States, your emphasis will be on surveillance. China's intelligence wants you to collect secrets about new and emerging biotechnologies."

Hong could see his opportunity. His advantage, he excelled at deception training. As an agent of MSS, his goal would be penetration of the US genetic engineering elite. In espionage jargon, he would become a "mole". And he was in it for the long-haul. He could cultivate relationships with American scientists for access to secrets that might give China a scientific and economic advantage.

The Chinese strategy, collect secrets by gathering fragments. What might seem like disconnected bits is a cumulative effort. Like adding pieces to a ginormous jig saw puzzle, eventually the big picture is revealed. And the Chinese make extensive use of Artificial Intelligence. Like the Americans, they use AI to identify patterns and potential threats.

As a deception agent, Hong had to be beyond suspicion. If exposed, Hong knew he ran the risk of long-term incarceration or death. Decades in a federal prison or expendable agent? Either one was a death sentence. Hong's role could become increasingly risky, but like a Chinese James Bond, just the thought of intrigue, the risk, and beautiful women, made him excited by his new life.

The US had been hitting hard against China for economic espionage and stealing trade secrets. In the tech sector, the US feared a Chinese telecom giant was spying with its electronic devices. Was the private corporation collaborating with Chinese spy agencies? The CEO's ex-military career heightened US suspicions.

Increasingly more paranoid, China thought the US was planning for a long-term war against them. They worried that the US was preparing for huge biowarfare efforts against both China and Russia.

Relationships among the triumvirate were at an all-time low. Trust was virtually non-existent.

Hong thought that someday, on the biologic front, he could prove to be quite useful.

22

Splendid Isolation

By the time we got back to Mumbai, the rash thickened. It grew into larger splotches, a deeper shade of red, then purple. My eyes glowed a violet hue, gelatinous and gooey. I could have been caste in Kiss of the Vampire.

I seldom left the hotel room. Malaise was my constant companion. When I could make the tiresome journey to the bathroom, toilet paper felt like a coarse-grained emery board. Forget about getting out of bed, I dropped down leaden and crawled on my hands and knees. Jeremy would try to pull me up by my arms, but I sunk back down, lifeless as Raggedy Ann.

On the flight from Mumbai to Stockholm, I'm buckled over with painful cramping, my seatbelt is like a sharp knife ready to sever me in half. My gut is explosive, like an over-pumped bicycle tire, my intestines are ready to blow. Unable to pee, I'm sure my kidneys have shut down. My self-diagnoses become more and more disturbing. I tell myself I'll most likely go blind.

Once we land, I cross my fingers and hope I won't get stopped or interrogated about my otherworldly iridescent eyes. I somehow pass the test baring zombies and vampires from entry into Sweden.

At the airport hotel, I'm unable to eat, my inner tubes are in knots, my knees are inflated like plastic beach balls. I drift in-and-out of consciousness. I'm indescribably delirious. If I have a fever, I do not know.

Jeremy undresses me. The purple-red islands have grown into massive black coral reefs. He touches my skin and groans in sympathy. Disease expresses itself in so many strange ways.

"We'll get you to a hospital."

Lars looks across at a man and woman, tourists most likely, as they stagger into the ER triage area of the hospital. It wasn't unusual for international travelers to seek help for various maladies. If Lars didn't know better, he'd think the woman was drunk or inebriated in some other way. Her partner helps her, holding her up with his arm wrapped around her waist.

Lars sits with an older woman, a patient who had a face-lift in his clinic. When she broke out with red inflamed skin, he suspected infection and told her to meet him at the hospital. Already seen by the intake nurse, they wait for blood tests to be taken. Lars seldom had post-surgery infections in his cosmetic surgery practice, but this was that odd occasion.

Lars never forgets a face. His uncanny ability is an asset in his profession. He easily remembers his clients' 'before' and 'after' facial images, indelibly imprinted in his mind. While he watches the man bring the woman into the triage area, he focuses on his face and expressions. The man, Jeremy, grimaces as if in pain. Lars knows the look of distress and worry. The woman, most likely his wife, is obviously very ill, perhaps dying. Lars could see the frightened look in Jo's zombie-like eyes.

A male intake nurse, masked and rubber gloved, pushes a wheelchair over to the couple. As the woman nearly collapses into the seat, her sweater dress hikes up and exposes her legs. A grotesque, mottled purple-black rash alarms everyone in near proximity. Lars had never seen a rash as thick and dense as the massive blotches on her legs. Things didn't look encouraging.

The nurse gives the woman a mask and tells her to put it on.

Lars overheard Jeremy say, "We've just arrived from India."

A triage nurse, without hesitation, wheels Jo away.

I don't remember much, other than being wheeled wildly through hallways. Jeremy gave our itinerary in India to the chief resident as I was inspected by a pack of young doctors in training. Each took gigabytes of cell phone photos of my purple-black ink spots and concord-grape eyes.

Many blood-draws later by a coven of voracious vampires, my exsanguinated body is transferred to a plank of cold metal. I wonder if I'm already dead. Perhaps I'm on my way to the morgue? Are the white-gowned beings the ghosts of others on their way to heaven or hell? Perhaps.

As my brain fog begins to lift, I can hear voices. Two hazmat garbed nurses, a TV, and call button mean I've been delivered to an isolation room.

At least now I can die in peace. I ask for DNR, do-not-resuscitate, I want no tubes. My lungs heave as I try to breathe but I don't complain. Everyone wears masks in what is now my darkened lair, I can't stand the light of day. And my, oh my, my photophobic eyes, I'm blinded by the light.

I rave at the ghosts, "Close the shades!" Like a vampire, I fear I may burst into flames. I'm convinced I have all the symptoms that prove demonic possession. The heavy weight on my chest, the rippling colors all around, the mood swings, the dry mouth. Did I thirst for blood? But the drip I'm now tethered to infuses antibiotics, not blood.

The next day, the soles of my feet throb. So sensitive, extreme pain, even the walk to the toilet is excruciating. I ask an orderly for help, most people speak some English. The cast of characters who visit me are caring and kind, but for one nurse I consider my nemesis. I feel violent urges at her very presence. She asks me for a shit specimen. Yes, she said "shit", but having not eaten in days, there's none to give. I would kill her and eat her flesh if I could. Then leave behind her remains excreted in a gigantic turd.

My mood shifts from anger to anguish without warning. Beware those who enter my cave, my darkened den, I will love you or hate you for no apparent reason. In the dark, my mind plays tricks. So do the poisons and toxins that strike me down after a diabolic microbial attack. They wreak havoc with my brain. I'm a ferocious flame, then I freeze like an icicle. I forget who I am. My eye color changes with my mood. Perhaps I really am transitioning to something wicked. If I'm not a vampire, then what kind of demon possesses me?

Later—perhaps hours or days, I can't tell the difference—another ghoul garbed in a white gown enters the room. He's not the usual nurse, or orderly, or doctor. Behind the mask his voice is muffled but oddly familiar. Perhaps another undead. But this demon's presence soothes me, he put me at ease.

"It's me." The ghost speaks softly.

"Jeremy, is that you?"

23

Comrade 9

"Holy shit!"

Hong did a double take when he came across an on-line news story. A Chinese intelligence agent seized in Belgium stood accused of trying to steal trade secrets from the US military. The US wanted him extradited for espionage—something that had never been done before. But it was the photo of the Chinese agent that made Hong bolt upright. When he zoomed in close up, a familiar but fearful face stared directly at him.

How Comrade 9 allowed himself to be lured was shockingly obvious to Hong. He knew it had to be sex. They'd been warned during training that sex was the ultimate compromise. It exposes people, their vulnerabilities, and their inclinations.

It was that glint in Comrade 9's roving eye that seduced Hong. So easily enticed, so easily enamored, just look at the way he fell for Mai. Hong knew that sex often lead to the undoing of people in high places—the politicians, priests, and professionals. No group is immune.

Hong reprimanded himself to be more careful, not to let his guard down. During his indoctrination, the caveat drilled in to MSS recruits was: "Do not make yourself vulnerable to entrapment." Obviously, Comrade 9 did not heed the warning.

"Holy fucking shit!" Hong added another expletive to the string. He felt the noose tighten and wondered if someday, he too might be thrown to the wolves.

Hong wondered, what about Mai? But he tried to put any suspicions out of his mind. Afterall, not only were they business partners, they were in love. Mai was no spy. A con, yes, but otherwise he thought her transparent. Her vanity drove her, yes. Money could convince her, true. But he saw a love no woman had ever given him so openly, so passionately. She consumed him. Like the sweetest of golden honey, he melted in her mouth.

Hong knew that Mai was no light weight when it came to brains either. He remembered when Mai told him, "Whoever controls the world's DNA will rule the earth."

Every living species on earth can have its DNA edited. Species will be designed to serve the wealthiest, most powerful superhumans.

And Mai reminded Hong, "The country that invests the most will gain control over life as we know it." Hong agreed.

In the game of DNA editing, both the US and China vied for global dominance to control the future of biology. The US considered China a long-term threat on many fronts. And China knew that the US was escalating towards a long-term war. World War III, should it come, would not be won with conventional weapons. The race was on.

Hong thought about how the next world war would involve a new weapon. One that would destroy groups of selected humans. He worried that Jack's RNA editing could one day be used as a "genetic weapon" against China. It was one of those life changing catalysts that inspired him to act. And fast.

Hong obsessed over his fear that the US would target his people, the Han Chinese. If successful, few would survive. They'd be exterminated. Wiped off the face of the planet. Hong couldn't get the thought of ethnic cleansing and annihilation out of his mind.

"Know the enemy and know yourself. In a hundred battles you will never be in peril." Hong remembered the advice of the ancient military general, Sun Tzu. But he wondered if he truly understood the meaning. And how well did he really know himself?

His simple directive from the MSS was: "To defeat your enemy, gather every piece of information and analyze it."

Hong's skills in covert surveillance and his role as information gatherer would be put to the test.

To prepare for the upcoming conference, Hong forged ahead in ferret mode. He scoured Gothenburg for spy devices. Since most transactions in Sweden are electronic, he found ways to convince a few stores that cash was still good—especially if they didn't want a record of their sales.

Hong hid a cache of tiny cameras on walls and installed audio devices. He covered the hotel and conference areas and paid special attention to the smaller rooms used for prep areas. They were prime places for scientists to rehearse presentations or meet informally with colleagues. As the conference coordinator, everyone assumed he would be seen everywhere.

Hong saw opportunity when it presented itself. The upcoming meeting would give him ample occasions to cultivate his peers and milk them for proprietary secrets. Academic espionage.

Hong had the task of gathering information from international experts, to leap-frog their scientific findings. The emerging fields of synthetic biology and gene editing held incredible promise, so he doubled down on surveillance. With his access as coordinator, he'd collect presentation materials, hand-outs, and pilfer any unattended notebooks. Hong's offensive was on. He went at it with a vengeance.

And Hong suspected he wasn't the only MSS agent attending the conference. Others would bug cell phones of notable scientific delegates, especially high-profile researchers. All agents were limited to a need-to-know basis. All possessed just tiny pieces of the gargantuan puzzle. Other agents monitored texts, calls, internet activity, and whereabouts of participants on GPS.

Hong had no idea about Jack's latest research until they talked. He didn't expect that Jack would need much surveillance; they'd never kept secrets from each other.

On the evening before the conference opened, Jack texted Hong: "On my way to Gothenburg. Let's get together later tonight."

But Hong complained: "Too much to do with all the administrative crap."

"OK, Day 1 afternoon." Jack texted and Hong agreed.

"Crappy conference stuff is driving me nuts." Hong added an emoji of an exploding toilet.

24

Purple Haze

My mind is muddled, my speech distorted. I tell Jeremy, "When I talk, words. No sense, they make."

"Do you mean nonsense? Since when did you become the Jedi, Yoda?" Jeremy chuckles, but under his mask I can't see if he's smiling. Always quick with a funny retort, it's something I've always liked about him.

Then I think about that tick that attacked me. A song keeps repeating in my brain and I sing a verse. "If it wasn't for that tick, I wouldn't be in this predicament." I trail off.

"Oh, you can sing. That's a song from They Might Be Giants. They've always been a favorite of yours." Jeremy keeps singing, "If it wasn't for that tick, I would not be in this predicament, not be in this predicament that I'm in." Jeremy is tapping his latex gloved finger in the air to the beat of the music.

My mind can't stay focused. I'm thinking about something else now. "Deep Purple, they are."

Jeremy tilts his head as he tries to follow the logic of my confused mind. "So, now you're talking about the band Deep Purple? Smoke on the Water?""

I toss off the mint green blanket and point to my feet. "Deep purple, the soles, my spots. Hurts, walking." I tear up and say, "Purple haze, not gray smoke."

Jeremy bends over to take a closer look at the bottom of my feet. "OOO..Ouch! Got it now, it's Jimmy Hendrix's Purple Haze."

"Purple haze all in my brain, lately things just don't seem the same." I'm surprised I can remember. But the word order is embedded in my memory.

"Things aren't the same, my love." This time Jeremy's endearment was sincere. I could tell from his quavering voice he was worried, despite his attempts at humor with musical history.

"Acting funny, but I don't know why." I pull another line out of the depths and wonder where it came from.

"Tomorrow you can kiss the sky, Jo." Jeremy paused. "I met Jimi Hendrix in London years ago." Alluding to his all-time favorite musician. Jeremy was a DJ in London in an earlier iteration of his life.

"You'll get better tomorrow." Jeremy prompted.

"Yes, the sun…something…tomorrow." I think of the music from "Annie", but my thoughts are fleeting. "It's the words. They disappear." I forget what I'm trying to say.

"Like a magic disappearing act?" Jeremy asks.

I can't hold an idea long enough before it is gone. Forgetting what I'm trying to say, the thoughts dissipate into thin air.

I point to the shades. "Keep dark. Purple Haze, the light, my eyes hurt."

"Purple Haze all in my eyes, don't know if it's day or night," Jeremy sings, trying to make light of my verbal malfunctions and my bat cave existence.

"I couldn't breathe. So heavy, my chest." Sad-faced, I shake my head no. "DNR, please Jeremy, no tubes."

"You told me to have you cremated, sprinkle your ashes at sea," Jeremy says in his droll English way.

"No funeral pyre on the Ganges for me." I manage to string together an intelligible sentence and recall our India trip. Things are looking up, we laugh together.

"You don't want to be floated down the river?" Jeremy wags his finger and stops short of poking my nose.

At that point, two women doctors arrive, surprisingly with no masks. "We'll move you to another room. Your blood test for Spotted Fever group is positive. It's not infectious." Their voices are familiar but now I can see their faces. Both pretty, one with light hair, the other wore a scarf but I recognize her enormous brown eyes. I thank them.

"Rocky Mountain Spotted Fever?" I ask. "But we weren't there."

"Similar bacteria but another species," says the doctor with the big eyes.

"No wonder you were misdiagnosed, it's rarely found in cities in India," the other doctor explained.

"The doctors who examined you were in a city. Jaipur," Jeremy says.

"So, I won't die?" I ask, feeling a mix of relief and love for the friendly ghosts.

"No, and you're not contagious, never were. It was the tick," they say together in random tandem.

The doctors have another look at my arms and legs. Not very sexy, in my estimation. I can see their smiles but lose track of who says what.

"Your spots are about 50% of what they were. You'll be transferred to another room. Perhaps released in a few days."

I fix on Jeremy's face as he's pulls down his mask and exposes a huge smile.

The doctors leave the isolation suite, but Jeremy lingers and holds my hand.

"How are you, Jeremy?" I finally realize how exhausted he is from the dark circles around his eyes. Usually a sound sleeper but now he's looking owl-like.

"Purple Haze all around, don't know if I'm coming up or down," he sings, followed by a harmonious sigh of relief.

🌀⬥⬤⬥🌀

A few days later we're back at a Stockholm airport hotel. Jeremy sets up a table with my antibiotics and treatments, including special drops for my zombie eyes. I've started to eat real food over the past couple days. My weight had dropped 4 kilograms.

"I've lost about 10 pounds," I say with a roll of my bug-like eyes.

"Well, you said you needed to lose weight, possum." Jeremy seems to have acquired a new endearment.

"Possum?" I snarl, still confused by words and their meaning. Was he teasing me?

But Jeremy assured me it was a term of love and affection. "Would you prefer pussums?"

"Pussums? Sounds like pussy." I'm getting my sense of humor back.

"I wouldn't mind." Poor Jeremy, I thought. He must be sex starved after my weeks of being ravaged by microbial beasts. But sex was the farthest thing from my mind. Not even fantasies of Jack could get my libido going. I then remembered our best-laid plans of mice and men. To meet up with Jack.

I close my eyes, even the dimmest room lights still blaze like a torch. "I'm just happy to be out of the woods."

"The woods here are coniferous forests. They cover over half the land in Sweden." It was Jeremy's idea of a joke, fire off a randomized factoid. I love that. We grin.

"And Jack?" I ask. Our plans to do some exploring together were no longer viable.

"He'll call from Gothenburg," Jeremy said sullenly. There's a chill in the air. I didn't wonder why.

25

Jumping Jack

When Jack first ran into Mai, he thought she might be a hotel conference groupie. Sometimes women with dubious credentials showed up at conferences looking for a hook-up, usually paid. But Jack never paid for sex. He saw that as a hit to his manhood and demeaning to women.

Jack rolled a big suitcase, larger than his usual minimalist carry on. With winter approaching, he'd need heavier gear once he joined Jo and Jeremy for Nordic adventures to come. Jack also packed a weighty stack of annotated articles. Old-school when it came to reading printed material, he liked to scribble his thoughts, highlight in different colors, and draw diagrams for perspective. He limited his carry-on luggage to a laptop, phone, and encrypted reader. He didn't share his newest research freely.

Bundled up in a winter coat, Mai paused to inspect a large mechanical robot at the hotel's entrance. It was created by a Gothenburg film studio. Although she glanced at it on occasion, she hadn't looked at it closely before. She was in no hurry to text Hong. He didn't expect her to join him until tomorrow. As an organizer, a free hotel room was part of the bargain for the duration of the conference and Mai would share his room. Although she wasn't officially registered, he printed her a badge that allowed free-reign to all the lectures and break-out sessions.

Jack literally ran into Mai as he quickly ascended the steps of the Riverside Hotel. He hadn't noticed her standing immobile at the top of the stairs. Always in a hurry, Jack had plowed his way forward and nearly knocked her into the huge robot.

"Oh my! I'm so sorry, did I hurt you?" Jack apologized.

At first Mai thought she heard Hong's voice calling her "Mai" with his familiar quirky American accent. The man grabbed her arm firmly to steady her. When she looked up, she was not only surprised, but pleased with what she saw. Like a low voltage electric shock, he not only knocked her off balance, but he caused her to lose her self-composure. With the good looks of a handsome American actor, she wondered if he was someone famous.

"No. I was captivated with that." Mai gestured towards the robot.

"Are you interested in AI?" Jack easily stuck up casual conversations. Having grown up in Rhode Island, people often chatted with strangers, more so than other states in the US. With barely a million people in the tiny state, almost everyone was either related or knew someone in common. He was curious to see what she knew about geeky science.

Mai reflected for a moment before answering his question. Yes, he was American but not the ordinary variety. With all the brilliant scientists checking in at this hotel, he was certainly a cut above the rest. Maybe he was a scientist worth knowing.

"I believe that Artificial Intelligence will transform the future of humanity." Mai knew she sounded pretentious, but she wanted to draw him in.

Jack thought this woman might be quite an opportunity. "In the next twenty years, AI will bring tremendous opportunities." He carried on with the conversation, using the same stilted tone. If this was the prelude to an overture, it was worth pursuing.

Mai smiled. Looking back and forth between the mechanical robot and the beautifully designed male specimen, she thought the latter more desirable. Mai appreciated well-built machines with gadgets and other elaborate apparatus. She kept nodding, encouraging him to keep talking.

"AI will have quite an impact on society. On wealth and power." Jack would say anything at this point to keep Mai's attention. "Could he be a killer robot?" Jack asked.

"Only if I can't control him." Mai gave Jack a sly smile. "But AI will be usurped by biology." Mai was thinking how designer babies might leap-frog Artificial Intelligence. Or perhaps the two could be merged? She took hold of the robot's right hand and caressed it as if it were real.

There was something about her intimate connection with the robot that struck Jack as eerie and strange. He pointed to the small banner suspended along the metal of the robot's left arm. It touted the offerings at the Cuckoo's Nest restaurant.

"Food, drinks, and beautiful minds." Mai read aloud the message.

"Which of the three would you like?" Jack hoped she wanted them all and more.

"Beautiful minds, of course."

"But you already have one." He was mesmerized by the machinations of her mind. "I'm Jack."

"I'm Mai."

A cold wind blew up from the river, the Göta älv, forcing them to retreat to the hotel lobby.

"Would you join me for a night cap? That is, if you don't already have plans for this evening." Jack bit his lip, he hoped he hadn't overstepped a boundary. He knew that the term "night cap" could be misconstrued. In the urban dictionary it's a veiled euphemism for sex. Translated it would be something like, 'am I getting laid tonight or not, lady?' But it was too late to take back his words, even though he mentally winced.

Mai didn't say no to what he offered. She grinned and nodded yes, although she wasn't familiar with the words "night cap". She thought perhaps it was a fancy cocktail.

Jack was seldom this forward with women, but while in Sweden, where attitudes about sex were probably the most liberal in the world, he hoped his approach would be fine. But this particular lady was an exotic import. If the opportunity would arise, Jack was not one to be bashful. And as the saying goes in Las Vegas, he paraphrased, "What happens in Gothenburg stays in Gothenburg."

❂❂❂

Jack queued at the front desk as Mai wandered into the hotel lounge full of science-themed artifacts and mementos. Mai always found something new there, ever since the time she first met Hong at the lounge bar. Sitting together at the bar, it was all about the chalk-marked mathematical equations. Now it would be Artificial Intelligence. Mai was attracted to men and science, the two seemed intrinsically linked in her mind.

Room key in hand, Jack returned to the lounge where he found Mai perusing a scientific wall display on graphene research, an area where Gothenburg excelled. Many thought graphene was the miracle material of the 21st century.

"Exciting." Jack snuck up behind her. "It's a new carbon material 300 times stronger than steel, but ultra-thin and light." Jack's grin grew larger.

Mai turned around and tapped him on his chest. "And harder than diamond."

Mai never shied away from people being suggestive. Jack in some ways reminded her of a past fling. There was something about his eyes, the flecks of gold and green and brown. But Jack was taller, stronger, more muscular. Mai could recognize the mutual attraction growing.

Jack set his luggage next to a comfortable looking sofa. "What would you like to drink?"

"White wine. A chardonnay, please?"

"Mai, have a seat here," Jack said with a wink and a smile. He pointed to the sofa, then tapped his suitcase and carry-on luggage. "Keep an eye on these for me, please?"

Mai nodded 'yes' with a demure grin. She was wary as she looked around the lounge, making sure Hong wasn't there.

Jack returned from the bar with a local Swedish brew in one hand and Mai's chardonnay in the other. He handed Mai her wine and cozied up next to her.

"Here for the conference?" Jack asked to which Mai nodded 'yes'. They talked about their mutual interest in all-things "genomics", the promises of gene editing and cutting-edge technology. They avoided any discussion of the perils. Their animation increased along with a second round of drinks. They had so much to talk about. But neither thought it would end there.

Jack glanced at his luggage more than once as the lounge fill up with conference attendees and local clientele.

"I'll give you a choice, you can either wait here in the lounge or come up with me while I drop off my stuff. I'm harmless, I promise." Few women could resist his alluring charm, his grin invited trust, his broad shoulders were, well, broad.

The two retreated to the foyer next to the doors of the elevator. Caged birds began to tweet wildly. Jack startled at their noisy greeting. They both laughed at how the birds caught him unaware.

"Oh, they're motion activated. I thought they were real." Jack felt like an idiot.

Mai chirped back, "No, they aren't. But I am."

Once in his room, Jack flung open the mini-bar. "Help yourself to anything you'd like. I really need a quick shower. Gotta freshen up after all that traveling."

While Jack soaked in a hot steamy rain, Mai poured herself another glass of white wine. She pulled her pink polka-dot nightie from her black leather sling bag, then disrobed and slipped the lingerie on. Mei scanned the familiar wallpaper—the double helix spirals of DNA, the carbon atoms, the mathematical equations—and smiled at the face of Albert Einstein; his lascivious eyes peered down at her. Albert's reputed affairs and the admiring women who lavished gifts on him reminded Mai of her own raucous and unruly love life. She had yet to decide how Jack might factor into her current string of conquests, but for now, lust would simply do.

26

Mai in the Middle

The next morning, robotic birds chirped in their cage as Hong waited for the elevator to arrive. To Hong's surprise, Mai stepped out with her black leather bag slung across her shoulder. But what really startled him was the familiar face of Jack, gentleman that he is, waiting for two older women to exit. Jack greeted Hong with a grin as he stretched his long arm across Mai's shoulder. He presented her as if they were a couple.

Mai and Hong gazed at each other wide-eyed, shocked as well as confused. Jack was too proud of his conquest to notice. His beaming smile was irrepressible. It was painfully obvious to Hong what Jack and Mai had been up to.

Hong shifted his gaze to the bright yellow ribbon attached to the zipper handle of Mai's black bag. He imagined her polka-dot, baby-doll nightie would be nestled inside. Hong felt a stinging pang that went beyond jealousy and a surge of anger he could hardly contain.

Hong needed his self-control to kick in and, at least for the time being, he knew he'd better not reveal the feelings that began to consume him. "Just bottle it up and stick in the cork," he told himself.

Jack grabbed Hong's arm so he couldn't get away. "Hong, I'm so glad we've run into you. I flew in late last night." He paused. "I want you to meet my new friend, Mai." Mai and Hong locked eyes and nodded to each other with blank forced smiles.

Neither one flinched or showed any recognition of the other, but Hong lacked his usual impish grin and playful humor.

Mai's restraint was there when she needed it. She could be cool as a cucumber, especially when she felt close to being pickled. She was surprised that Hong didn't let on that he knew her. He showed not the slightest flicker of a connection, intimate or otherwise. But unlike Mai, he was professionally trained at the art of deception. Hong's most valuable asset was his ability to conceal his other self. No one in his various groups of lab colleagues, acquaintances, college students, not even his close friend Jack, had any inkling of his double life. And he had plenty of practice hiding his secrets from Jack.

"Hey, come to breakfast with us." Jack, still clutching Hong's arm, nearly dragged him to the buffet area.

Jack piled a healthy assortment of fruits and vegetables on his plate, then led the way to stools along a high-topped table where he sandwiched Mai in the middle.

Hong stuck with a hunk of grainy bread and a plate of lunchmeats and cheeses, a common Scandinavian choice. One look at the traditional pickled herring made him want to retch. He knew the Swedes seemed to love the stuff.

Mai sipped strong coffee and nibbled on her favorite food, the Swedish pastries she could never resist. But she ate nothing else. She tried more than once to get away, but Jack insisted she stay while he woofed down multiple bowls of bran flakes.

"Wait here." Jack ordered Mai and Hong. Full of mischief, he delivered them each a glass of green kale ginger juice. Mai sipped his offering with a grimace, but Hong flat out rejected it.

"Try the 'fruits of the forest'." Jack repeated the alliterative name twice. He insisted Mai taste the mix of berries and yogurt from his spoon.

Jack's phone pinged with a text, "Meet us in Tesla meeting room. Panel prep at 9:30." Jack bolted upright as if he'd been shocked by a Tesla Coil. He hadn't organized his notes and he needed a shower.

"Let's meet here for lunch before the opening session. I'm in room 323 if you need me. Gotta get my stuff together for this meeting. "Where is Tesla?"

"He's dead. Died in New York in 1943, in his hotel room. He was 86, so I guess you could say he 86'd it." Hong joked, Jack laughed, but Mai didn't have a clue as to what was so funny.

Hong was always razor sharp with his wit. And for the time being, he hid his hot temper boiling below his cool exterior. He knew all the techniques for hiding emotions. And as a highly-skilled operative, he tended to stay in character. The comedian, the jokester, he had perfected his cover and rarely stopped the laughs for long.

Once Jack left the table, Hong grabbed Mai's hand, making sure she didn't try to flee. Her hand was shaking, she seemed agitated. But Hong was not the focus of her attention.

Mai averted her eyes, not just away from Hong, but from a group of Chinese scientists at a nearby table. One in particular she easily recognized, her x-boss Yi Lo, director of her lab at World Genomics. They had worked together in what was affectionately called "Nanoland". They also played together, by Yi Lo's rules, in his heavily fortified office. It was a *quid pro quo* arrangement that ultimately opened the door to Mai's fellowship in Copenhagen, just two years ago.

Mai hoped Yi Lo couldn't possibly recognize her since her transformation. Her cosmetic surgeons did artful work, skillfully re-designing her with full-chested curves and more rounded eyes. Less Chinese, more ethnically mixed, she was no longer the Mei Wong he would have remembered. But still, the presence of Yi Lo at this conference put her on edge. And sometimes, something as defining as a voice could be the one distinguishing characteristic that identifies you. Mai hoped he hadn't overheard her talking.

In a hurry to leave, Mai grabbed her coat and purse, but Hong seized hold of her arm. With a solid grip, he nearly frog-marched her to the elevator. As he escorted her to his room, she knew an interrogation was in short order.

"You fucked him, didn't you!" She couldn't look him in the eye. "He's my best friend." Hong harangued her.

Hong bubbled up inside like an effervescent mix of baking soda and vinegar. A bolus of sour vomit came up in his throat, but he forced it back down and swallowed it. His heart pounded fast and furious making him dizzy. Such were the side-effects brought on by this 'double, double toil and trouble' that no ant-acid could quell. Only a chemist could concoct the amalgamated mess that brewed in Hong's stomach.

Hong pulled Mai against him. He sniffed her like a dog from top to bottom. "I can smell him on you. I know his stench. And yours!" Hong's voice cracked. His ire was now beyond control.

Hong pushed Mai hard onto the bed. He would treat her like the vile, repugnant animal she'd become in his eyes.

"You deserve everything you get." Hong threatened. Jumping on top, he straddled her, wringing her neck like a chicken for dinner. Hong seethed with jealousy, he boiled with rage, his eyes bugged out, his complexion reddened, he felt capable of killing her with his bare hands. But Hong regained his self-control, he backed off, he couldn't kill the woman he thought he loved.

Sometimes you must kill the people you love, Hong thought. He knew this directive might someday dictate his decisions. His actions. But not now. After all, it was only infidelity, nothing treasonous. She betrayed his affection, but she didn't pose a threat to his country. Jack, on the other hand, was duplicitous. He betrayed their friendship. Hong knew Jack's genetic weapons were aimed to eliminate his heritage, the ethnic Chinese.

Hong had bitter thoughts about Jack. As a close friend, he knew Jack bragged about his sexual conquests. He thought Jack was probably gloating to his friends right now. Hong punctuated his thoughts, poking his finger hard against Mai's chest.

"I'm so sorry Hong, you know how much I love you. I didn't mean to hurt you. It was just a mistake." Mai cried tears of fear. She needed to convince Hong that she loved him, since he was still needed in her business scheme. There was a frightening side of Hong, something she'd never seen before and it scared her. She wondered just how far he'd go to hurt her in his frenzied rage.

"How could I know he was your friend? You never men-tioned him before." Mai tried to rationalize her fling as somehow Hong's fault. "He means nothing to me, Hong. It was just sex, after all. I don't know how it happened, it was so fast and very stupid of me."

"Who Jack fucks isn't my concern. But *you*, on the other hand, how could you have sex with my best friend?" Hong grabbed Mai again and threw her like a rag doll on to the floor.

Hong had shared nothing with Mai. There was nothing she needed to know. He wisely kept his personal life to himself. But he failed miserably when it came to vetting Mai. He started to realize how little he knew about her. She not only duped him, she exploited his weakness, his vulnerability. Sexual entrapment snared him every time. Not only Comrade 9, but now he'd fallen into what looked like a "honey trap". And part of his anger was because he failed to recognize the signs.

He asked aloud, "How could I be so foolish?" But Mai laid still and said nothing.

"Just who are you, Mai?" Hong didn't wait for an answer. He stood up and prodded her with his foot.

"Tell me now," he demanded, but still Mai kept silent. Her silence fueled his anger, but it also kicked in his training.

Hong had other methods, not just harsh words. Techniques that that would bring results. With his mastery of martial arts, he could extract information from anyone. Even Mai's deepest secrets would flow like a faucet. He could use the seventeen pressure points: those which inflict pain, those that give pleasure, and those that can kill. All were handy tools of his trade.

Hong no longer respected his own boundaries or this woman who betrayed him. He kneeled on the rug next to her. With his hands he gently lifted her face towards him, bringing her lips close to his. With his fingers he applied just the right nerve pressure to the back of Mai's neck.

Mai writhed and squirmed with pain. She gasped and gurgled, unable to flee, unable to scream, she felt a tantric mix of eroticism and near death. Mai almost passed out, but aroused she took Hong's hysterical bullying as it morphed into vicious desire. What frightened Mai also excited her. Jack and Hong were two best friends and now all three were connected by sex.

Hong stood up and gave a swift kick to Mai's limpid body. Having never hit, yet alone kicked a woman before, his range of emotions spiraled, as did Mai's black sling purse. Twirling it around his head, Hong let the purse loose. It smacked against the wall under the watchful eyes of Albert Einstein, spilling the contents on the floor, a litter of lipsticks, eye makeup, perfume. But what incensed Hong most was the wrinkled pink polka-dot nightie and assorted multicolored condoms.

Hong turned away from Mai and began to cry, partly from his own frustration. His constraint finally broke, he was not devoid of emotion, he never was. His stomach churned like an acid fermenter. Rushing across the room, barely making it to the toilet, he spewed chunks of his breakfast, curdled cheese and chunks of toast and sausage meats. Besides feeling physically sick, Hong felt bad for what he had done.

With Hong indisposed, Mai scrambled to stuff her belongings into her purse. She donned her coat and escaped the hotel room, making her getaway down three flights of stairs. She sprinted quickly past the lobby desk, out the front revolving door. She stopped briefly at the mechanical man who told her to get the hell out of town.

27

In Orbit

Hong watched as his regurgitated breakfast swirled around the white enamel toilet bowl. He wasn't surprised that Mai fled the hotel, she had every reason to. The room's digital clock glowed red at 9:13 AM. So much happened in such a short amount of time. Hong's anger, now redirected, shifted to Jack. His volcanic temper was set to vent again. His next stop was room 323.

Hong knocked impatiently, "Hey, it's me. Open up," he demanded.

Jack, in his usual cavalier fashion, pulled open the door to expose himself clad in nothing but a white terry cloth towel. A thick icing of cream decorated his face. Half-shaven, he held a razor in his hand.

"Come on in, I've gotta finish up." Jack retreated to the bathroom.

Jack's room was a mess, his clothes strewn about, the bed beyond being slept-in, the sheets were a jumble, twin duvet covers lay on the floor. It was evident that more than sleeping had occurred.

Hong sniffed the pillowcases, he could smell Mai's familiar perfume. Random strands of her hair, smears of her purple-red lipstick, specks of black mascara, and streaks of pink-rose rouge decorated the white cotton. On the sheets, a dried crust flaked as Hong scratched with his fingernails. The familiar scents of Mai and Jack made him fume like an incendiary bomb ready to explode.

"So, what do you think of my Mai?" Jack peeked out from the bathroom, displaying his most impish smile. But Hong was already standing at the door. Throwing a direct punch, he nearly launched Jack into orbit around the moon.

When Jack came to, two hotel maids hovered over him. "Are you OK? Should we call the front desk? An ambulance?"

Jack assured them, "I'm fine. I slipped. Wet floor." His mind in a muddle, Jack was confused. Why would Hong lay him out? He hadn't picked up any animus, no ill will. He was absolutely flummoxed over what happened.

Neither maid wanted to cause a panic by calling the front desk. Distracted by his enticing bare butt as he lay on the floor, they were highly amused. They had seen similar and worse before. One maid handed him a towel.

"What time is it?" he asked, covering himself and picking himself up.

"9:49", said one.

"Should we leave?" asked the other.

Jack nodded 'yes' with a sheepish grin.

Once again on his own, he checked the time. Surprised at how long he'd been out, he sent a text to the panel group: "Minor Emergency. Unable to attend."

Next, he texted Hong a series of, "?????!!!!!" but Hong didn't reply. He called Hong's room, but got no answer.

He called the front desk and asked, "Could you please ring the room for a Mai, M-A-I. I don't know her surname."

"Sorry, there's no one registered by that name."

"Anyone with the first name, Mai?" Jack asked again, he had trouble focusing.

"No, nothing for M-A-I. There's no one with that name."

The convention brought in academics and scientists from all over the world. But was Mai an illusion? Eerie, the way she disappeared. It was as if she never existed. But what's gotten into Hong? Why did he blind-side me? Maybe I have a slight concussion? Feeling woozy and out of time, Jack put the blame on Hong's sucker punch, jet lag, and a marathon night with Mai. Perhaps he needed to sleep it off.

Jack dozed for a while. A light snow fell. He bundled up in this puffer jacket and wool cap before he ambled over to the convention center next door.

At the conference registration desk, he asked two women, "Do you know Hong Min Chan?"

Simultaneously they shook their heads 'yes', but from their expressions, neither looked pleased.

Hesitant, Jack asked, "Is he around?" He wondered what Hong had done to upset them.

With an irritated frown, a bookish woman with owl-like glasses replied "No, he should be here working with us." Her name tag read, "Welcome, My Name is Amanda." Not exactly the welcome you would expect, Jack thought.

Jack scratched his wool cap. Even more bewildered, he asked, "Do you know where I can find him?"

"No, but if you run into him, tell him to get his ass over here." Graduate fellow, Olivia, swore with glee.

"Olivia, how improved your English is," Amanda quipped. "There should be three of us doing the badges," she said to Jack.

"Hong's usually reliable." Olivia moderated her criticism. "Perhaps you can find him? Here's his address. It's not far." She showed him on her phone's GPS. "A quick walk."

Jack walked briskly down the road. It took less than ten-minutes to reach the unimpressive block of flats. But he had no luck when he rang the door buzzer. Frustrated, Jack called Hong's cell again and texted to no avail.

Back at the hotel, the caged birds chirped as he waited by the elevator. Mulling over the events of last night, the mystifying Mai and the baffling behavior of Hong who for no apparent reason clobbered him, he decided that nothing made any sense. The thump to his jaw had left him disoriented, his head still ached. "Damn Hong. Why?" Jack asked himself.

He walked down the long hallway and knocked again at Hong's room. No answer. Listening for any signs of life, he heard nothing. Jack thought to himself, "Something stinks and it's not that awful pickled herring from breakfast." He suspected that Mai had something to do with it.

Jack returned to his hotel room exhausted and confused. The maids had cleaned his room and changed the bed linens, erasing Mai's make-up—the purple-red, the dusky rose, and the dark black streaks that looked like charcoal. The residues and scents from their tryst would be laundered so that Mai physically disappeared, literally without a trace. Jack had no way of contacting her. Too hurried that morning, he'd forgotten to get her cell number. But he thought for sure she'd be at the conference.

Jack dozed again and woke up hours later having missed the opening session of the conference. Ravenous, he ordered room service. After eating some fresh baked cod, his braincells began to fire. He began to dissect just what might have happened. Why did Hong slug him? It must have been about Mai. She had some connection with Hong. Was she close to him? The attack strongly suggested this was the answer. And just who was Mai?

Jack returned to the registration desk where he told Amanda and Olivia, "Hong is still missing. He's not at his apartment and he's not in his room. I wonder if something has happened to him?" With Jack's suggestion, they started to become concerned.

"Oh my, I hope he's alright. I didn't think he was deserting us," Olivia said. "That wouldn't be like him."

"Perhaps he is too ill to have called us?" Amanda wondered aloud. She frowned with guilt for having accused Hong of shirking his duties. "Should we look in his hotel room?"

"Yes, we need to check that he didn't pass out. Or something worse." Jack fueled their fears. He needed answers, the what and why for Hong's stunning assault.

Together they tried to convince the hotel manager to give them access to Hong's room.

"He may have had a medical emergency." Amanda uttered her plea. She was adamant that Hong's life might be at risk.

Despite the manager's objections, he escorted them to Hong's room. He unlocked the door with a key card and opened the door a few inches. "Is anyone here?" he asked in English and Swedish. Repeating himself a second time.

When no one answered, he led the way in, checking the bathroom and shower to make sure Hong hadn't slipped. "There's no one in here." He announced to the others. "Just his toothbrush, paste, some soaps and shampoo."

Jack panned the room. There were a few clothes and a duffle bag, but no visible cell phone or other electronic devices. Everything was in order, except for a transparent tube of lipstick, a dark purple-red, that lie next to the trash bin under the desk. Amanda and

Olivia were busy chatting with the manager and didn't seem to notice as Jack picked it up. He dropped the tube into his pocket.

Jack asked, "Does Hong have a girlfriend? Is there a conference attendee with 'Mai' as the first name?"

"I made a conference badge for Hong's friend, Mai Tran. I've seen them together. I think they are *särbo*." Olivia translated before Jack could ask. "*Särbo* means just dating."

"I think they're *'sambo'*," Amanda countered. "Living together." Neither of them was too sure if they were merely seeing each other or cohabitating. The Swedes had different terms for so-called "partners". But Jack thought Olivia had it right, they were dating. He knew Hong had no steady relationships.

Jack was reeling at the twin disappearance. Whether *särbo* or *sambo* he didn't really care, but he knew Mai had been in Hong's room. And what was their relationship? And where were they now? He wondered if they'd gone off together. Hong and Mai were on Jack's list of missing persons.

Jack's next question for Amanda and Olivia was, "Who is Mai Tran? A scientist?"

Olivia shrugged and said, "She's not on the registration list, Hong wanted the badge as a favor. I have no idea why, maybe she missed the registration deadline, that was what I guessed at the time."

Neither of the women had ever spoken with Mai. Beyond seeing her briefly, she was a mystery to them too.

In all the years that Jack knew Hong, nothing ever provoked the hostility and rancor he now had experienced first-hand. Or was it first-fist? Hong's knuckle marks showed the precise point of contact on his left jaw. Jack peered into his lit-up shaving mirror. He rolled a bottle of cold beer over the bruised imprint, a bit too belated to do any good.

Unusual for Jack, he ran a bath. He hoped it would relax his mind, which was twirling from a barrage of turbulent emotions. He needed an explanation for all the weird stuff that surrounded him. As he soaked, he drifted to memories about growing up in Rhode Island with his buddy Hong and the secrets that they shared. Both were science geeks. As kids, they would hang out in Jack's basement lab where they toyed with chemistry sets and microscopes.

In college, they progressed to designing harmless but bizarre bacterial creations, like E.coli that smelled like wintergreen mint. Years later, Jack did research in microbiology while Hong managed the lab animal colony on the university campus.

Jack remembered the day he asked Hong, "Can you believe what they did?"

"Foolhardy, but fun, fun, fun!" Hong had seen the news. "That so-called 'stupid' experiment." A university in the Netherlands created a dangerous strain of bird flu. The mutated flu virus was lethal and could be transmitted in the air from human to human. Other universities soon followed suit.

Jack and Hong, in their reckless days as DNA hackers, tried to replicate the experiment by infecting ferrets in Hong's lab. Luckily, they didn't succeed and their rogue project in genetic manipulation came to an end.

Jack cycled back in his mind to Hong's ballistic blow. Jack and Hong shared a lot with each other, but never women, at least not to their knowledge. But he wondered if there was another reason for Hong's insane assault. He'd never seen such an unbridled emotion come from Hong.

Where are they now? Jack asked himself. Did they flee somewhere together? And who is Mai Tran? She's not part of the conference. A sex worker? No, she demanded no money. Or was she just a lusty woman looking for a fling? For Jack, it wouldn't be the first time he had been flung.

Jack's thoughts continued to cycle, always returning to the same conclusion. Hong and Mai must be lovers. Why else would Hong sucker-punch me?

"It's a triangle!" Jack thought he got it. A stupid love triangle had violated his long-term friendship.

28

Spider Web

"Hong, you idiot!" He berated himself. "Man, did I screw up this time."

Despite his training, his loyalty, his devotion to the Chinese state, his weakness was singular, Mai Tran. He couldn't resist her compelling ways, she sucked him in, both emotionally and physically. She drained him dry. He had no resistance to her charm.

"Honey trapped," Hong said, a little too loud. He hoped his neighbors weren't around to hear him chastise himself. "Idiot." He thumped his fist against his desk, then opened the desk drawer and pulled out the black lace veil Mai wore when they were together last.

Hong cried real tears. He hadn't realized how entrapped he was in her black-widow spider web. He never saw her as a threat. He was bemused by how his emotions had clouded his judgement.

Deluded by his foolish pipedream, he shook his head and sighed with emotion thinking he'd really let his guard down. *Afterall, we were lovers.*

But then his rational side took over, underscoring the reality of his situation. *Damn, I might have jeopardized my entire career.*

Hong thought about his diverse expertise, what a spymaster he'd become. He was a Jack of-all-trades and a master of some.

"Very punny, my friend," Hong said and laughed to himself. He never completely abandoned his jokester persona.

He thought about what else he had to offer. An expert in distraction and diversion tactics, but his funny guy facade was his best disguise. He knew he could be incredibly convincing. He used his humor as part of his masquerade—it was a smokescreen that concealed his innermost feelings and thoughts.

Hong tried his best to convince himself that he was still a high-value operative. Hong thought that, surely, they'd want to keep him. *I need to be confident. I will overcome this error.*

But his current performance suggested otherwise. He knew deep down he was in deep shit. He should have known better.

Hong thought about Mai and their designer baby business. Could their "Baby Hacker" scheme come back and take a hatchet to his career?

He told himself, it was just a fanciful dream, like Mai's fascination with anime characters. She hadn't delivered any promised money to him. He didn't expect to be paid, nor did he care. It was just part of a game they played. And Mai played him. Fulfilling his raunchiest desires, she surpassed the sexiest of anime characters they watched together on late night u-tube. Only she was no fantasy, she was the real deal. Or so he thought.

"Mai's a con artist, stupid," he beat himself up for missing the obvious signs. After all, he wore his own mask well. So, of course, she could deceive with her own mask. In retrospect, it was easy to see from her designer baby scam that she was a full-time fraud.

There were other unmissable clues. Physically, her enlarged breasts could not be originals, they were scarred from stitched alterations. Mai's oddly rounded eyes? He dismissed the small scars as wrinkles. She concealed the surgical incision lines with her cleverly applied cosmetics.

Not just a con, but an absolute fake. The more Hong mulled, the angrier he became. All his illusions were smashed. His double life might soon to be shattered.

"Two-faced bitch! Narcissist! She only cares for herself."
Hong's heart thumped fast, pounding him hard, punishing him
for not seeing through her ruse.

He wondered, just who is Mai Tran? He had to find out.
Duped, he didn't want to be taken as a fool. "I'll bet she's not
even Vietnamese." He suspected all along that might be a lie.
Ethnically mixed? Well, that was debatable. She had cosmetic
changes, even surgeries, but her DNA would tell no lies. The
evidence is always in the DNA.

He panned his apartment, collected a comb with a tangle of
hair strands and a wine glass with tell-tale lipstick stains. He
plastic-bagged those remnants, then separately bagged the un-
washed black lace spider web he found in the desk drawer. He
pictured her prancing before him two days earlier, modeling the
gift he bought her. How could he not recognize such a duplicitous spider?

But it was the image of her in the pink polka-dot nightie, the
same nightgown that fell from her sling purse, that made him
seething mad. She would have used the same seductive ploy to
tantalize Jack, arching her back in her pink pussycat pose, then
displaying her rump in the air like a cat in heat. He knew her
lascivious antics were shared with his former best friend. But
now it only aroused his ire.

"Fucking whore!"

As any good intelligence agent can tell you: *Know your enemy and know yourself.* Hong knew this precept well.

Hong was trained to see the enemy. He knew he was a valuable hybrid, more American than Chinese, but still ethnically
mixed. He thought he was a cut above the Chinese scientists,
who were only information gatherers coopted by MSS. They had
only rudimentary skills and couldn't tell what was happening
around them.

"I have the trade craft that they lack," Hong practiced his
defense, should he need it.

Hong's evidence kit was ready and secured for pickup. If it
didn't reveal Mai's real identify, the DNA would at least verify
her ethnicity. As for the real Mai Tran, she couldn't possibly

exist. Hong thought that she was as phony as they come. The only way he could save his ass…report her as a suspicious person."

Hong's current handler, Chen, was an attaché with the Chinese consulate in Gothenburg. He could trigger an investigation into the identity of Mai Tran. Hong used his encrypted phone to call him.

"A courier will pick up the package," Chen said and sent a courier who arrived in record time. She asked Hong to sign a blank label on the evidence package. In return she gave him a hand-written note from Chen.

"Meet me at the safe house tomorrow."

29

Re-do

After everything that transpired with Jack and Hong, Mai was scared that something terrible might befall her. Frightened of Hong's displayed violence, she feared he would beat her badly, maybe even kill her. The surprising anger he vented in his hotel room might have been only a precursor to a deadly volcanic eruption. On the seismic scale, he seemed ready to blow in pyroclastic proportions.

During her hasty retreat from the hotel, Mai boarded the bus in front of the convention center. Packed with students, she disappeared among their winter hats and coats. She was bound for the city center.

Lucky for Mai, Hong had never been to her apartment. They always met at Hong's apartment or at the science center. When he asked to see where she lived, Mai complained that her fictitious flat mate leased the flat. "I sleep on a cot in an alcove. There's no privacy." The lie squared with the fact that it's not uncommon to share small quarters in Sweden. With high rents and a limited supply of apartments, it was part of the norm for students and young people to sub-rent a bed.

❤❤❤❤❤

Back at Lars' flat, Mai paused to reflect on the morning at the hotel's breakfast bar. Mai was more than uncomfortable, she felt mildly tortured. Not only had she been wedged in tight with Jack on her left bantering to Hong on her right, she felt Hong's wrath as he poked her with his sharp elbow. She winced but kept silent.

Even more disconcerting was that group of Chinese scientists who sat at a nearby table. One of the men, Yi Lo, looked exactly as Mai remembered him, only he wore a stylish suit instead of a white lab coat. He looked almost trendy with his spiky haircut. Perhaps, Mai thought, he's on the look-out for western women.

But Mai couldn't help thinking "fat chance of that", she loved that English expression. Yi Lo had little to offer when it came to looks and sex appeal. Director of the World Genomics lab, he sloppily ate Swedish pastries, fruit, and yogurt. His manners would put any woman off.

She avoided looking in Yi Lo's direction. In her past iteration, she was his lab assistant, Mei Wong. Ultimately, she manipulated him for perks in the lab and for access to life in the West. Had it not been for the extra privileges, courses in Hong Kong and her fellowship in Copenhagen, she would never have let him near her. But it was a *quid pro quo* arrangement where she got what she wanted.

Mai tried to listen to the group's chatter, but she only picked up small clips that weren't drowned out by Jack's weird jokes and Hong's forced laughter. She hoped Yi Lo didn't recognize her—so transformed she barely resembled her past self. "No, I don't think so," Mai thought, but she wasn't convinced. "Maybe he heard me talking?" Mai worried that her cover might have been totally blown.

Mai knew her safety in Lar's condo wouldn't last long. She called him on his mobile phone.

"Lars, I'm in trouble." Without any explanation of the details, she pleaded with him, "Please help me, I must escape." Her voice quavered, he'd never heard her so frightened and vulnerable.

"You have a problem? What kind of trouble is it?"

"It's me. The real me. It's who I am." Mai whimpered a slow moan and cried, something she seldom did, shedding real tears. Not the forced tears she would feign to help get whatever she wanted. To Mai it was stunningly obvious that without Lars, she had no plan. Where could she run to next? Who? Lars was her only way out, unless she wanted to return to her dangerous game and possible poverty.

"Tell me more." Lars wasn't surprised that her enigmatic real identity was compromised. And Mai confirmed his suspicions.

Mai confided in him, "I'm a most wanted woman." She wondered how much she should tell him. "I think the police will come after me." She questioned herself, do I need to tell Lars everything?

But Lars already knew and uttered one word, "Stockholm." Lars heard Mai gasp, partly from surprise. "It's Stockholm, isn't it?" he repeated. She coughed, sniffed, and blew her nose, then heaved a sigh of relief that she wouldn't have to lie or make up new stories.

Mai worked out that Lars knew what transpired. Gasping again, she was convinced he knew about the murder of Vladimir, the vicious Russian thug. She placated herself with calming thoughts that Lars would understand. She was certain that he loved her. He would protect her.

Lars instructed, "We'll meet at the condo, I'll take a flight. I have an escape plan. Get ready. Pack very little. Dye your hair, a dark brown. We're going dark." And he meant it. Literally.

"You'll travel as my wife."

When Lars left his clinic in Stockholm, he told his assistant he'd be away on business in Copenhagen for the next week. "Don't call me unless there's a dire emergency. Just forward any important e-mails." His knew his office was in capable hands. Between his surgical associates and staff, they could cope with his absence.

At his comfortable but sterile home, he descended to his basement office where he kept his financial records and a safe with a considerable amount of cash. He had some US dollars, but most of the cash was in Euros and Kroner. Lars always planned for the worst, in the event of power outages, bank closings, or various stages of social or political unrest, cash would be king.

In the safe, he also kept his Swedish passport and that of his wife. She told him that morning she wouldn't be home until late evening. She'd be with friends and donors at a fund-raising dinner for a private art museum.

Lars posted a note in their spacious kitchen: "Clients in Copenhagen need me for the next few days. Don't worry. I'll call when I can." She didn't worry, usually she had some event to attend or was involved in a foundation project, mostly for the arts and poetry.

He checked on-line his multiple millions in funds deposited in offshore accounts. Lars' bank accounts and business shells funneled his dubiously acquired money. He made one last transfer of euros from a temporary holding, a large transfer from one of Sven's foreign accounts.

"Ah, Sven, thank you. You are my Ethereal Angel." Lars said, relieved that the transaction had gone through.

He printed copies of account numbers and other vital information. To secure his home computer, he changed his access password. Lars packed a small carry-on case with just the essentials.

As he closed the front door, he made a sweeping gesture, waving goodbye to his home, his boring wife, his mundane life. "Where ever life takes me, it will be an exciting journey. I'll re-invent my future. Re-create my perfectly designed woman."

Lars headed to Gothenburg on a flight out of Stockholm's Arlanda airport.

"Here are your eyeglasses." Lars slipped the glasses across Mai's nose, she grimaced from the distortion.

"These have graduated lenses, look down to see better. Here." Lars pointed to the lower area on the lens. "You'll only wear them when needed."

"But I don't look like your wife, I'm much younger," Mai complained. Removing the glasses, she frowned as she inspected the matronly style of the frame.

"I can age you with creative cosmetics. My surgeries don't always have perfect outcomes. Cosmeticians must airbrush the final look. In my work, I use cosmetics to cover any flaws."

"But what does your wife look like? Do you have a photo?" Mai asked.

"Don't worry, Mai. Here are our passports." Lars opened his leather valise; he seldom went anywhere without it. Before he could hand the passport to Mai, she snatched them both, flipping to the photo page.

"You look younger here," Mai said and gave him back his passport. Then, she closely examined the other passport. She pointed to the name Åsa.

"Your wife's name? Assa? I am Assa?" Mai mispronounced many Swedish words and names. Her language skills in Swedish were pretty rudimentary and most Swedes spoke English to some degree.

"Not Assa, my wife is not an ass." Lars laughed at Mai's corrupted attempt. "You pronounce your new name as "aw-suh". Lars repeated, "aw-suh". Back and forth they practiced until Mai got it right.

Mai's mind swirled with more questions. "Won't Åsa miss her passport? Will she look for it?" Mai wasn't sure if the plan would work. Her look of consternation amused Lars, but he was too excited to worry about what lie ahead. Escaping the past and leaving your troubles behind wouldn't be easy, but what was the alternative?

"My wife thinks I'm on a business trip for the next week. She won't realize her passport is missing. She rarely travels without telling me."

"At least my hair is a similar color. I chose well, yes?"

"Yes, your hair color is good. Height is close enough. We can age your face with lines and a paler skin tone."

"Once we escape to another country, we'll buy passports in new names." Lars assured her.

"But could we be caught if we travel by plane?" Mai figured she would somehow be flagged. And her connection to Lars might have already been exposed. She'd been evading the law long enough to be aware of the pitfalls.

"For now, trust me." Lars opened his cosmetic case and laid out his contour pallet.

30

Is it Safe?

Hong knew he wouldn't be coming back to his apartment again. He cleaned up whatever remnants he could find of Mai Tran—a sweater, eye-liner, face cream, and hand-drawn sketches of her anime favorites. He scoured the shower, plucked a mix of his and Mai's hair from the shower drain, changed the sheets and pillow-cases, and tossed the dirty linens into a trash bag. He hoped that anything with DNA was bagged for destruction.

He packed only the essentials for himself. Everything electronic, his laptop, his chargers, were co-mingled with his personal belongings. Hong had no idea how long he would stay at the safe house.

The safe house was an apartment leased by the Chinese Consulate in Gothenburg. When Hong arrived, a very large guy let him in and brought him through to a modest kitchen. A rail-thin Chen sat at a white wooden table.

"I'm your current contact," Chen said.

The two men in the safe house bore no resemblance to each other, neither their body shapes nor their dispositions. Except for their ethnicity, they could have been the comedy team of Laurel and Hardy. Hong couldn't suppress his joking thought about the two men he'd just met.

"Are you Oliver?" Hong asked the rotund one, but the humor was lost on him. Chen on the other hand winced at the reference. He'd studied American culture and their comedian icons.

Chen was not pleased to see, on his first impression, that his new operative was an airhead.

"I'm Lu." The plump elder guy said without losing the constant smile that spread across his broad face. Hong thought he recognized the same deception training, use a big grin as a mask to hide behind.

Chen didn't crack a smile. He was solemn and highly organized as expected of a manager of spies. Older than Hong, he matched his perfunctory voice that Hong was accustomed to from early phone conversations.

"Sit down." Chen turned on his recorder.

To Hong, the safe house seemed anything but safe. He thought it more like a steak house the way he was being grilled, like a well-done slab of filet mignon.

When Chen told him, "Mai Tran's DNA is an identical match to the Chinese terrorist, Mei Wong," Hong was shocked. "And your DNA was intermingled with hers."

"Damn woman. I never suspected she had terrorist ties. Believe me, Chen, she hid her real identity like a..." Hong couldn't finish his sentence.

Chen skewered Hong. "Why didn't you suspect her? It's what the Russians call *kompromat*. She was the bird of prey and you were a piece of dead meat!" Chen delivered the first in a series of relentless slaps across Hong's face.

Hong tasted the salty blood trickling from his nose. It had the metallic flavor of an iron-rich piece of meat. He mumbled, "Dead meat." Knowing he was destined to become just that.

"She's a seductress, you fool," Chen admonished. "Sexpionage, idiot!" Frustrated, he tried to calm himself down.

"You were set up. The old KGB were notorious for that. Didn't you learn that in your training? Swallows and ravens? She's a swallow. If you were gay, a raven would have seduced you." He ramped up the attack yet again.

"Sexpionage? How could I be so stupid. A basic honey trap and I..." Hong faltered. His hang-dog look said everything. He cringed as he remembered Comrade 9. Was 9 a raven in MSS training? Was Comrade 9 actually testing him for vulnerability?

146

Hong wanted to retreat and simply disappear, but there was no escaping Chen's wrath.

"Did she compromise your data? Were you sloppy with your surveillance? She could have been working for the Americans. Or the Russians." Chen got angrier as he accused Hong of shoddy, compromising activities and absolute recklessness. Each time his voice rose, he slapped Hong again, only harder.

"She doesn't know I'm an agent," Hong nearly whispered. "She had no access to data."

Chen paced the small kitchen, a room with hidden cameras. He knew everything in the safe room was recorded and transmitted. Safe but not private, fully monitored, no secrets were withheld from the MSS.

"Hong, we know she assassinated a Russian tourist. Did she have any reason for targeting him? Think about it."

Hong shook his head, he didn't know. Confused, he wondered how Mai could possibly be Mei Wong, a known bioterrorist. "Maybe she has a split personality?" he questioned aloud.

"Don't be so stupid," Chen warned. "He was Russian. Assassination comes right out of their playbook." She was good enough to fool a paranoid Russian to take her bioweapon. Somehow, she gave him Tiger Flu and death."

Hong's thoughts drifted as he took in what Chen said. Hong knew that bioweapons were a dangerous threat when it came to killing people on a global scale. Despite Hong's small-time role as an information gatherer, sensitive conferences like the one in Gothenburg attracted the attention of many intelligence agencies. FSB, FBI, CIA, MI-6, and others littered international venues with tiny bugs, cameras, and other gadgetry, as did China's MSS. All spy agencies used the same crafts, whether cell-phone spoofing or surveillance video, they played the same game, only the players were different. Their techniques, too numerous to count. Their rules, non-existent.

Hong hadn't thought much about Russian intelligence, the FSB. But he knew they kept their auspicious eye on high-profile people, especially Americans and Chinese, like the scientific delegates at the conference in Gothenburg. All major powers knew that gene editing tools were potential weapons that could one day be turned against them. Or tools that they could, in turn, use against others.

Chen poked Hong hard and returned him to the present. "You never questioned her motives? What did she want from you?"

Hong tried to clear his mind, but his emotions kept getting in the way.

"I don't know. I thought she was Mai Tran. Not Mei Wong. How did MSS find out who she was?" Hong's voice cracked as he shook his head.

"She worked at World Genomics, so we had her DNA on file."

"So, from her DNA?" Hong's mind was still reeling over the revelation.

"Not just her DNA. In Stockholm, our embassy obtained video from the hotel where the Russian tourist died. They found images of Mei Wong." Hong was surprised at Chen's candor.

Chen cued up a news item from a Stockholm TV station that showed a clip of the woman. The news reporter said, "...the Swedish forensic police unit confirmed a match for the woman who murdered a Russian tourist..."

"But the Swedes never disclosed the real story," Chen said, "whatever the reason."

"Which is?" He asked, "What reason?" Hong wondered how she murdered the Russian.

"It would scare the public if they knew." Chen titillated Hong. "Mei Wong's mutant strain of Tiger Flu was her assassination weapon. She used it to kill the Russian."

"How do you know about the Swedish forensics?" Hong grimaced, scrunching his eyebrows.

"The autopsy report, fool. Don't ask how. But if I tell you, I'll have to kill you." Chen threatened. He knew it was an over-used expression. Chen wanted a sinister joke to unbalance this clown.

Chen looked at Hong's expressions with amusement. "You know I'm only kidding, don't you, Hong?"

Chen laughed. Hong laughed, but he didn't think it was funny.

"Hong, what do you know about this woman?"

Hong revealed what he thought he should. "She was my girl-friend, Mai Tran."

"What else?"

Hong's left eye began to twitch. He never felt so naked. He promised Chen he'd divulge everything he knew about Mai Tran or Mei Wong or whoever she was.

"She has a Swedish friend, a man who set up a business with her." Hong didn't mention his own role in their designer baby scam. After all, Hong received no money that would incriminate him. No money meant no bank trail to trace.

"We know who he is," Chen said." Hong was behind the eight ball and he knew it, MSS was way ahead of him. He was sweating in the hellish hot seat he'd sat himself in.

With the demeanor of a typical bureaucrat, Chen recorded and documented everything.

"When did you suspect she wasn't who she said she was?" Chen asked.

"Only when I contacted you. That morning I found her with Jack Ashbell, she exposed herself as the duplicitous bitch that she is." Hong gave a plaintive look to convince Chen he'd been duped by a beautiful woman. "I was blinded by my infatuation." Hong knew he'd been compromised but hoped he could somehow redeem himself. "She had sex with my best friend." Hong purposely displayed his raw emotion, to excuse his major balls-up.

Chen gestured for Hong to go on.

"She gave Jack and I a double whammy," Hong grumbled the American idiom, meaning not one but two big blows. "and she's Mei Wong." Hong slapped his palm against his forehead. "Right in front of my face. I couldn't see beyond the tip of my nose." He chastised himself. "What an idiot I've been."

"Tell me about Jack Ashbell."

"I've known Jack since we were kids."

"Start there."

Hong told Chen his story. "Mad magazine. It got me fascinated with the world of spies since I was a kid. Jack and I loved the wordless cartoon, Spy vs. Spy, in Mad magazine. It captured our imagination for years. We devoured the magazine from cover to cover." Hong's verbal diarrhea ran on.

"I've been briefed on Spy vs. Spy. It is meant to be funny," Chen said deadpan.

"We thought it was hysterical. Really audacious." Hong remembered with a smile. "The sinister duo had long pointy noses,

Black Spy and White Spy. Always trying to outwit each other with their espionage hijinks."

"So, that's where you learned about espionage. In a comic book?" Chen shook his head in disapproval.

"My parents wouldn't buy anything that wasn't a textbook for me. So, I read Jack's wrinkled, torn, finger-marked ones."

"Sounds like you often got Jack's sloppy seconds," Chen quipped.

Hong took the cruel jibe in stride. He needed Chen for his salvation.

Chen questioned Hong, "Maybe Jack is your counterspy? Could he be working for FBI or CIA?"

"Perhaps. He's a microbiologist. You know about our rogue experiments, our attempts at creating pandemic bird flu. Lethal. Contagious in humans." Hong tried to redeem himself somehow.

"Yes, I know that." Chen snapped back.

Then Hong had a flash of inspiration. "Well, Jack says there are new bioweapons that can target and kill people. Not just individuals, but these new genetic weapons can target and wipe out an entire ethnic population." Hong hoped he'd capture Chen's imagination.

Chen grimaced. He wasn't sure if he heard Hong right. He didn't know enough about genetic weapons or what Hong implied. "So, what are you getting at?" Chen asked.

"Genetic weapons could target China. The Han Chinese," Hong said, making it explicitly clear to Chen that the threat was real and personal.

Chen puckered his brow and stroked his chin. "I'll pass that information on."

Hong slept very little that night, obsessed with the question, "Will there come a time when I'm deemed worthless?" He realized he was only a low-level asset, expendable if he wasn't useful in some way.

But Hong thought to himself, "Maybe Jack will save me. What an irony."

31

A Perfect Disguise

Lars shredded Mai's French passport and burned the remains. "Sit down. This make-up will disguise you, age you. Mimic the appearance of my wife. After all, I'm more than a cosmetic surgeon who wields a scalpel. Sometimes I'm a make-up artist. I use foundations to conceal flaws and enhance traits on many women. And a few men too."

"Please remake me. Disguise me. I'll be anyone you want. Just not me." Mai no longer cared about Mai or Mei. She just wanted to avoid capture. "Re-invent me, Lars. I'll do anything for you," she said with a note of desperation in her voice.

Lars thought about Mai's offer in broader, permanent terms. He wanted to possess her and now she could be his alone. "This is a temporary cover. Perhaps in the future, we'll both be changed."

"How? Where?" For Mai, re-invention was always possible. It fit the pattern for her survival over the years.

"Not here in Sweden, but I have contacts elsewhere." Lars thought of their special bond. "What have you always wanted Mai? Or should I say Mei?" Lars taunted her.

"Not a more perfect me, but a perfect disguise. Hide me."

As Lars worked on her transformation, he thought about who was out to find them. The law would certainly pursue them. Lars reckoned the Swedish police already spotted them on CCTV, somewhere in Gothenburg. There could be any number of sightings where he and Mai were together—near his apartment, at hotels, even on the harbor. But Mai's head was covered, wasn't it? What about Sven's security cameras on his yacht? And Lars worried about Hong, their lab accomplice. Just how much did he know? How much would he tell? Lars didn't want to face the prospect of long-term jail.

"I've transferred many millions," Lars said to soothe Mai's worries. He could keep her for the rest of his life.

"How many millions?" Mai asked.

"Too many to count. We must disappear. Let's go now, on my boat. I have an escape route. No one will know, we'll disappear. People won't know where to look. Eventually, they'll forget about you and me."

"How could they ever forget about me?" Her ego demanded that she be pursued, but never caught. It was the cat and mouse game that thrilled her. The tiger, escaped from her cage. Come and find me if you can. But torn between the excitement of being on the run or the fear of being caught, Mai preferred to run. She was a survivalist, no matter how austere the conditions, she'd never be a prisoner. She had a notion that Lars was too possessive. He had fantasies of keeping her in an emotional jail of his own making.

Mai had other growing concerns. It was China, the PLA and MSS, that petrified her most. The anticipated torture. The endless interrogations, until they had no more to extract. They would execute her for her transgressions, in particular for her part in a bioterror plot that caused difficulties for China. It was widely known that the mutated virus in Tiger flu originated in a Chinese lab.

Lars called his usual limo service. With a bundled-up Mai, they arrived at the marina where they boarded Lars' yacht.

Mai was unimpressed with Lars' barely adequate staterooms on the lower deck. When she compared it to Sven's yacht, well, there was no comparison. But if this was part of the escape plan, at least they might not be obvious. The 50-foot yacht would blend in with the others.

But the disappointment on Mai's face did not go unnoticed by Lars. He knew she had no choice. At the moment, he was her only salvation. She had nowhere else to go. He controlled her immediate future. And her life.

In what sufficed as a master bedroom, Mai browsed through a cupboard with an assortment of women's clothing. Mostly casual things Lars' wife Åsa kept for when the sea was cold and treacherous. Mai's choice of what to wear screamed function over fashion in his wife's wardrobe.

In the closed cockpit on the upper deck, Lars navigated with high tech touch screens and a joystick. Although it wasn't the scale of Sven's super-yacht, it was upgraded for ease. It was Lars' small indulgence, but as most things in his life it was never enough. A bigger and better boat, a younger and prettier woman might fulfill his needs. Lars wanted to express himself as the man he aspired to be. Despite the accoutrements he collected on his road to riches, enjoyment and satisfaction mostly eluded him.

With Mai as his captive, he'd have what was missing. That final piece of the jig saw puzzle that would complete him. Along with the freedom of being at sea, Mai elevated his drive. His libido would hopefully rejuvenate. Mai could inspire his lost eroticism. Lars thought of Mai in her most provocative pose, sprawled out in his own private boudoir. She promised she would do anything for him, and he would insist upon that promise. In his mind he would consume her, devour her, she could not escape him and would be his forever.

Lars held the joystick pointing North-West without straying far from the coastline. As his grip tightened, his mind swirled with the endless possibilities. He'd be born anew, a young and virile man with the stamina of a bear. But Lars' fantasies dissipated as Mai emerged, still fully made-up as an older woman, wearing one of Åsa's oversized light gray sweatshirts and pants to match. A scruffy, moth-eaten wool cap covered her mousy brown hair. She was a perfect imitation of his wife in Stockholm.

The sea was unusually calm as Lars cast anchor for the night. Once in the stateroom, he removed Mai's make-up with greasy cold cream, liberating himself from the woman he left behind. Then Lars pulled off her clothes. A dark blue bruise on her left hip and butt cheek caught his attention.

"Who did that to you?" he asked. He'd seen signs of abuse on Mai before but this one was fresh. "Who, Mai?"

"No one. I tripped and fell," Mai said nonchalant, but Lars knew better. He stripped down, showered with her, washed her hair, scrubbed every inch of her body so that no trace of her past lives remained. She didn't complain. It was a ritual he felt necessary. A therapeutic purgative and a thorough cleansing so that each would emerge regenerated and renewed.

He laid her out across the bed as if she were an empty canvass, then applied his first brush strokes. He painted her with smoky eyes and concealer to erase the tell-tale scars that removed her epicanthic folds. Her lips he painted ruby red, her cheeks he highlighted with shades of dusky pink rouge. With tinted foundation, he obscured the scars on her breasts. With body makeup, he hid the deep blue bruise.

Lars repeated, over and over, "You are my Designer Baby."

It was a transient re-invention of someone new. For now, the process excited him. Later, he'd take a scalpel to her, re-design and create his own designer baby with traits only he could want. She would be unrecognizable but lovely to him as his own exotic creation, his distorted idea of perfection with changes so drastic, so shocking, she could never be anyone elses but his.

Lars felt so alive, so potent, so fulfilled by his power to re-create the woman of his dreams. He embellished her with drawings and added hues of color until exhaustion overcame him. His artistic frenzy was followed by sleep so deep, so dense, so overwhelming, he couldn't resist the downward spiraling vortex that sucked him into the sea's abyss.

Lars awakened to the boat rocking, water slapping against the hull and Mai squirming next to him. She slathered her face in cold cream and rubbed-off with cotton the remains of Lars' fanciful, wet and wonderful dream.

⟨▷◁▷◁⟩

Hours passed by as Lars navigated in the cockpit, breaking only for coffee and snacks.

"Are we there yet?" Mai complained like a child.

Early the next morning, they arrived. "We're here. Bergen, Norway," Lars announced as he joined her in the bedroom.

"Where's the sunny island you promised me?" Mai grumbled. Frowning and pouting usually worked with Lars.

"We need to escape from Scandinavia first, to somewhere no one can find us. We'll get to the island eventually."

Fueled by coffee and packaged biscuits, they retreated to the bedroom to prepare to disembark. Lars reapplied Mai's cosmetics, re-inventing her matronly look, and handed her the dark rimmed eyeglasses. She dressed in a bulky dark velour jumpsuit. Lars then wrapped her in a down-filled beige puffer coat. She looked passable as Åsa, plumped up to perfection.

"Must I wear these glasses? Everything is blurry." Mai continued her whining and complaining.

"Yes. You must stop this!" Lars gave her a firm shake, reprimanding her to focus her attention. "Say nothing unless asked. Simple answers only. Keep this wool hat on." He lifted her glasses, stared closely at her eyes and smiled, partly to encourage her, but mostly because he approved of the Åsa impersonation he had fashioned. Mai turned around to see herself in the full-length mirror. She laughed at her transformation, even Mai thought it a clever ruse.

"The proof is in the pudding and the eating is yet to come," Lars said, but the meaning was lost on Mai.

32

Love Triangle

Jack picked up the restaurant menu that lay on his hotel room desk.

He read to himself, "A meeting place for visionaries and dreamers, creators and contrary thinkers, innovators and people of possibilities, and for anyone who wants to meet them." Jack saw the appeal to academics and scientists and their elitist egos. So many considered themselves bestowed with beautiful minds. And love, self or otherwise, was always in the O2. The conference hall and the adjacent university made the science and innovation theme a good marketing ploy.

But his mind drifted back to Mai's beautiful body.

"A love triangle." Jack audibly mused to himself. He thought about the geometric shape. With all the allusions to math and science, the hotel catered to thinkers of like persuasion. And clients like Jack were easily persuaded.

"So, it's the triangle." Jack thought it significant. "And every triangle has three sides. Me, Hong, and Mai." Jack patted his face and winced from the pain. The bump on his jaw was huge.

Jack considered the triangle, it's three angles. Three people with three different angles. He talked to himself, as he figured the angles. "Mine, a fortuitous moment of passion. Hong, his potential love everlasting. And Mai? What was her angle? What was in this relationship for her? And who is she?"

Jack had an inkling. His mind reverted to a story of Mei Wong and the drunken conversation with Jo. Jack began to wonder. Could the mysterious Mai Tran be the infamous Mei Wong? Or was it all just too far-fetched? He went over what he remembered, that she was last seen on CCTV camera screens in Paris before dropping off the radar. There were no more sightings—nothing picked up by facial recognition software despite all the efforts to find her. Wong disappeared and Tran appears in a hotel in Gothenburg.

As Jo put it, in the deck of cards of notorious terrorists, Mei Wong was the queen of spades, right next to her king—nihilist professor and co-conspirator, Kahliy. But Jack questioned himself, "Maybe I'm just speculating, connecting dots that are nothing but random points. But could Mai Tran be Mei Wong or is that just crazy?"

The recent disappearance of both Hong and Mai unsettled him. He thought it wasn't just coincidence, those two were somehow joined. And he had a creepy sense that something very bad was about to happen.

Jack texted Jo, "Let's talk."

His phone rang back, but instead of Jo, he heard Jeremy's voice. "I was going to call you. Something bad happened to Jo."

Jack flinched at the news of something untimely, wondering if she died. "Oh, my god, what the...? What happened?"

"Jo's recuperating. We're here at our hotel, near Stockholm's Arlanda airport." Jeremy then explained Jo's ordeal with spotted fever. "Long story short... once they ruled out contagious disease, they took her out of isolation. Gave her a load of antibiotics. Drops for her purple zombie eyes. She's slowly improving. If untreated, this *Rickettsia* strain has a death rate of 35%."

"Yikes, that was a close call. I know how bad spotted fever is. I studied *Rickettsia* during my graduate work." Jack felt like another blow struck him on the head.

"Jack, how are things with you?" Jeremy gave him an opening.

"Jeremy, hear me out on this. I've got a problem. I met this really hot woman."

"And that's a problem?"

"Mai was here for the conference. We barely met each other and she spent the night in my room."

"Well, what could be a problem with that?" Jeremy couldn't contain his amusement.

"I'm listening, Jack," I say from my bed. The phone was on speaker mode.

"Jo, so glad you're alive! That must've been absolute hell for you." I can hear Jack's embarrassment at having been exposed.

"Jack, back to your story, this should be interesting. How could a quick roll in the hay be a problem?" Jeremy says and silently gloats.

"The next morning, we ran into my friend Hong."

"Your lab buddy from Rhode Island?" I ask. Jack talked about Hong, but Jeremy and I never met him.

"Yep. It was really strange. Hong wasn't his usual fun self. Said he'd been really busy, ya know, with the conference and all the organizing. But he seemed angry, kept glancing at Mai. Hong is Chinese-American and Mai says she's Eurasian. They look so similar they could be brother and sister."

"And the point of this is?" Jeremy asks.

Jack hesitates and says, "Hong came to my room later that morning and laid me out cold with one solid punch."

"What the fuck," we say in unison, shocked at Hong's unexpected assault. And I'm thinking, so when does your best friend, for no apparent reason, lay you out flat on the ground?

"When I finally came to, I tried to find Mai but I didn't know her last name. There was no one named Mai on the hotel guest list. I tried to find Hong in the conference center. Two women who worked with him said they made a conference badge for his girlfriend, Mai Tran. Gratis."

"Whoa, slow down. So, where are Hong and Mai now?" Jeremy asks.

"No one's seen either one. But here's the kicker. Mai Tran must be late 20's, maybe 30. Smart. Academic. But you know what was really odd about her?"

"Besides everything?" Jeremy asks, droll with his customary sarcasm.

"*Beyond* everything. Her boobs were way too firm to be natural. Not the soft and pliable type. And very big." Jack hesitates and adds, "I'm speaking as a scientist."

"More than a mouthful?" Jeremy jokes, "Sorry, my bad." He grins at me as I roll my eyes. Still a bit delirious, I'm not sure if Jack is just boasting about his conquest. It's a good thing Jack can't see our smiles and silent laughter. Jeremy whispers in my ear, "Jack seems embarrassed."

"I'm sure they're implants. I could see scars."

"Fake tits?" Jeremy asks. He shrugs his shoulders. "And the point is?"

"I think she's fake in another way. Jo, you told me your story about Mei Wong," Jack hesitates and says "Oh, you made me promise not to tell on you." Jack caught himself as he outed me to Jeremy.

"What? Jo, why did you do that? Silly woman." Jeremy wags his finger at me. I knew I was in deep doodoo.

"Mei Wong is here in Sweden. And, well, I think I screwed her.' Jack pauses. "One other thing. She used my hairbrush."

"Hold on to it. For DNA." Jeremy had a plan.

Needless to say, we are no longer amused.

Once off the phone call with Jack, Jeremy fumes at me, "What a big mouth you have, Jo. You told Jack!"

"Sorry…" I begin but Jeremy cuts me off.

"Somehow, this time it may work to our advantage," Jeremy says. He walks towards the window and makes a phone call.

I can hear truncated clips of Jeremy talking with DHS Max about "Tiger Girl". They came up with that sexist euphemism ages ago despite my objections.

Max heads up Operation Tiger Girl, the mission to find Mei Wong's whereabouts. He can set things in motion at a moment's notice, contact the FBI, Interpol, CIA. Whoever he needs. I don't know how inclusive the group is nor how they operate. But Max has his sources at home and abroad.

When Jeremy gets off the call, he loads his necessities in his carry-on backpack. "You sit tight. There's great food here. Order room service. If you're feeling up to it, go to the restaurant. They have your favorite seafoods."

I've lost over 10 pounds this past month. Even the smell of food would bring on bouts of stomach unrest. A few bites would leave me with agonizing pain. For the last few days, cinnamon toast passed the olfactory test and I thought I might live to eat another day. And now, just talking about food makes me hungry.

"You've got your drugs," Jeremy says as he sorts through the myriad of pills and eye drops, "make sure you take these." He jots down a list of meds and instructions for me to follow.

"Don't tell anyone where I'm going. Understand, loosey lips?" He wouldn't let up on scolding me for my sins.

"OK, so now I'm Lucy. Got some 'splainin to do?" I ask, trying to make light of it.

"That too. But what I meant is 'Loose lips sink ships'." Jeremy refers to the adage on American WWII posters. In other words, don't compromise national security.

"So, no loosey Lucy." I give Jeremy a wimpy grin. The look on Jeremy's face suggests future forgiveness is possible.

"Go see Jack, the jackass," I say and we chuckle.

Jeremy presses the end of my nose as if it were a door bell. "I'll be off the grid. No communication. No calls unless a dire emergency. If I need you, I'll call. Not vice versa. Love you."

33

Muddled Mind

Jeremy's left for Gothenburg. As I lay in bed, our phone call with Jack repeats over and over in my muddled mind. What happened to him both amuses and annoys me. What really blows my baffled brain is the coincidence of him hooking up with Mei Wong. Now how likely is that? I'm not a believer in happenstance. It's more than just the revelation and disbelief, jealousy overwhelms me. How could he cheat on me? I feel slighted for no good reason. Even though he wasn't mine, just an infatuation. And a stupid one at that.

I'm equally fixated on Mei Wong—murderer, terrorist, scam artist, and user of men. My enemy and nemesis. She plots a terrorist attack against America, yet loves all things western—the culture, the fashion, and especially money. An arch capitalist born a poor communist. What a contradiction. She's on the run and must be found, no matter what.

Jeremy and Jack, the most unlikely of partners, are on the hunt for Tiger Girl. And how many others are following her tracks? The spooks, the spies, the police? All the acronyms of intelligence, Interpol and Europol, and likely the Scandinavian police have clues as to her whereabouts.

It was in Paris that Mei Wong was last sighted. It's been over a year since CCTV images of her abruptly came to an end. As if she dropped off the face of the earth, or at least that part of the planet that blankets its streets with surveillance cameras. Jeremy and I thought all along that Tiger Girl assumed another identity. The only way she could travel unhindered was to foil the algorithms of facial recognition software. How else could she manage to evade all those agencies?

Jeremy and I had tracked down Mei Wong once before. Now we're on the track of Tiger Girl, reinvented as Mai Tran. She hid in plain sight. Like a veiled chameleon she morphed, changing her colors to blend in with her surroundings.

I recall the story of Tiger Girl's exploits. She delivered her 19 Tiger Flu pastilles to her terrorist lover in Copenhagen at the Bella Hotel, where she later murdered her second Tiger Flu victim, Albert. The American scientist was her second "proof of concept". The sucker fell for her "Honey Sweetie" candy—the tiger bioweapon that festered with a fiery fever and devoured his brain.

I wonder, why would Mei Wong come back to Scandinavia? It seems so risky. But when you think about it, sometimes the best place to hide is where no one would expect to find you. And now Jack, of all people, not only finds her, but does so in such a surprising way. Was Jack a part of Tiger Girl's plan? How? Lucky for Jack she didn't tempt him with a Honey Sweetie.

Forget Jack, what does this Hong have to do with it? Where does he fit in? Hong and Jack shared friendship and an interest in genetics. Does that mean anything?

A quagmire of questions and no answers. But my brain is a jumbled mess. I lose focus. My thoughts are adrift like a ship lost at sea, and I'm unable to anchor. I hope I'll soon make landfall.

⬤⬤⬤

After those days on drips and extra doses of drugs, the spotted fever and its massive black continents diminished to blotchy red islands. I pull down the duvet and grasp my thigh, my white fingerprints leave an imprint before the red splotches return. I hope like hell that I'm not left with indelible marks, that the patchwork quilt fades over time. But the doctors aren't optimistic.

I manage to muster the energy to make it to the bathroom. At least I'm no longer expelling noxious substances from every orifice. What a relief. The mix of antibiotic belly aches and exploding dead sausage-shaped micro-beasts really left me reeling. There's nothing like harboring an army of vicious warriors fighting against chemicals—they wreak havoc with your digestive system.

I peer into the shaving mirror grateful the red spots have at least spared my face. But I look older than my age, and the magnification doesn't help much to dispel my dismay. What could any man see in me? My self-doubt more than doubles.

Then somewhere in the dense mist of my mind, Jack's face appears. I knew he was a charmer, he certainly had me enamored. But a womanizer? How could he be such an opportunist? Who'd have known? I had a fantasy that we were a merge of two minds, like the mingling of two flames and other romantic and mystical crap that people subscribe too. I shudder at those cornball dreams. I know sheer lust when I see it.

I return to my bed and briefly sleep, awakened by a bizarre dream of Jack's comeuppance. In the dream Jack, the Lothario, meets his match. Mei Wong, a wanton woman and modern-day Mata Hari, assassinates him with her Tiger Babies. Unscrupulous seducers, both of them, get what they deserve. Then Mei Wong is arrested and brought to justice, her legacy is finally put to rest.

Maybe the dream was a symbolic purge, to rid of Jack in my still fevered brain. But then I worry that something bad might happen to my guys. Where are Jeremy and Jack now? Will they find Mei Wong?

There's a wall mirror in the bedroom where a warm golden light makes my face look rested and youthful. I comb and style my hair, apply lipstick, a few cosmetics, and dress in my best lace tunic and leggings. Time to stop dreaming and return to the real world.

In the dining room I order my favorite baked salmon with Dijon mustard sauce.

34

Wet Work

Hong knew he wasn't safe despite staying in a so-called safehouse, he couldn't resist a slight chuckle. He could hear Chen's muffled voice talking to someone, presumably the MSS, but as far as he knew they could be planning his execution. Then everything went silent. He imagined the worst. He thought they probably decided what to do with him, now that he screwed up.

Hong didn't trust Chen. He could be primed to turn the wet work hose on him. Chen threw open the door to the kitchen where Hong took shelter. Hong cowered, but thought he must try to convince Chen that he was truly penitent.

"What is it? What does China want from me? I'll do anything. My loyalty and dedication are beyond reproach. I'm a true soldier." He begged for clemency, choking up, he tried to contain his tears, scared shitless of what MSS would do to him. "Will I be punished?"

"You should be, but lucky for you, you have something they want," Chen said.

"My training with MSS? All the years I spent as a sleeper? Is that what they want?"

"Haven't you connected the dots that have saved your sorry ass?"

"Yes, I reported to you. Jack and I infected ferrets with mutated flu viruses. Highly contagious. Very risky. Capable of unleashing a deadly global pandemic. But I can't think why China would create bioweapons that could come back and bite them in the ass?" Hong kept on talking. "It's ludicrous to think they'd run the risk of self-annihilation."

Chen shook his head, frustrated with Hong. "See, you're so stupid. It's not your playing around with rodents. Plenty of idiots like you two guys try to create bioweapons in their basements. So do other rogue terrorists and nation states in their secret labs. Not to mention all the legitimate labs in the U.S, China, Russia, elsewhere. Don't they? We Chinese are working to defend against that. Look at the terrorist Uighurs, we are fixing that problem," Chen told Hong.

Hong hesitated and said, "Yup. Aha." He pulled at the long bristles sprouting from his chin. He'd been allotted no time for shaving and personal primping. Hong still didn't know quite what Chen was getting at.

"Hong, what did you tell me about Jack? What's he talking about now? What's he working on?" Chen was exasperated.

"Targeted genetic weapons. Ethnic genocide." Hong finally got it. Jack in the end might indeed save him. "We need to watch Jack closely."

"And we will. Don't you worry about that. There are scientists in China researching futuristic bioweapons. Targeted genetic weapons are designed to kill people of a particular race. Highly selective, they kill certain races and leave others unharmed. But obviously, you were unaware of the technology until Jack told you."

Hong had no reply. So, he asked again, "How can I help the People's Republic of China? I have other skills."

"They want you in their biotoxins and biopoisons unit, for 'wet work'. What do you know about biotoxins?" Chen asked.

Hong was surprised. "They want me to be an assassin?" He knew what wet work meant. "Yes, I can do that. Biotoxins can be eaten. Or they can be injected. Some can be inhaled. But most can be found in the blood, they're detectable," Hong said scratching his head.

"Hong, how about a biotoxin like Ricin? Could you change its DNA so that it *cannot be detected?*" Chen raised his eyebrows.

"Anything is possible," Hong wondered aloud, "if you can think the unthinkable, it may be possible."

Hong sat quietly for a while, he had plenty of ideas. "I could make it undetectable with gene editing. Make it a stealth killer. For an assassination, you could spike someone's favorite hamburger. The victim will get a bellyache, feel nauseated, throw up." Hong worked through the scenario. "If no evidence of bio-toxins are found in the blood and food poisoning is also ruled out, then…"

"So far, so good." Chen said and smiled. "Then what?"

"The next day, there's more symptoms. Our hamburger-eating victim is very dehydrated, soon his kidneys and liver shut down."

"So, he won't last long." Chen pursed his lips. "Hmmm."

"Do you remember what happened to that guy in London?' Hong asked. "That Bulgarian dissident?"

"Remind me."

"An assassin used an umbrella tip to fire a tiny pellet of Ricin into his leg. The Ricin was detected in his blood. But what if….?"

"But if the Ricin is undetectable, there's no evidence of murder," Chen completed Hong's thoughts. "Nothing shows up in the blood, there's no smoking gun."

"Precisely. Add that to what Jack told you about genetic ethnic cleansing. We are talking about mass killings, not just individuals."

"Genetic bombs that leave no detectable trace. Stealth bioweapons." Hong said, "I could do that."

Chen paused and licked his lips. "That hamburger makes me hungry."

Chen fried up some ground meat patties and laid them out on bread rolls. Hong ate as if it were his last meal. He hoped it wasn't. He didn't trust Chen nor the directives from MSS. Hong acted like he'd never tasted anything so delicious before. He let out small grunts of appreciation.

"What else do you know about assassination tools?" Chen asked. "You need that knowledge to work in wet work."

Hong paused to think. He belched before answering. "Other bio-materials. Also, radioactive agents. Polonium 210, the

British called it 'Vlad's tea'. In England, two guys from Russia's FSB killed a defector, a former officer, by dosing his tea. A slow death by radiation poisoning. A Spy vs Spy antic."

"Spy versus Spy?" Chen raised his eyebrows. "Ah, Mad magazine." He nodded in recognition.

Hong went on, "Of course, there's Novichok, the nerve poison used in Salisbury, England. Those two Russian GRU agents." Chen nodded that he knew. Any Chinese MSS agent would be hard pressed not to know the intimate details of the attack by the GRU, Russia's military intelligence service.

"Hong, I like your gene-edited biotoxins. If they are extremely hard to detect, no one will know how or why someone dies. It would be easy to blame the death on something else, like a heart attack or kidney failure."

"A virtually undetectable Ricin would be excellent as a new assassination weapon. Whether it's in somebody's hamburger or in the water supply of cities. And it's much cheaper than most weapons." Hong used his sales pitch. "It's a better, faster, less obvious way of eliminating enemies."

"Hong, why do you think you're still alive? Maybe you aren't dispensable after all. Lucky you." Chen made Hong squirm.

"Or I'd have been dead by now," Hong said under his breath. He wondered how long MSS would find him useful.

35

Cute Yakut

L ars paid his fees to the Bergen harbor master in Norwegian
Krone. He'd stashed a healthy supply of mixed currency
bills in his yacht's safe. They came in handy when traveling
among Scandinavian countries. Using cash in Norway was not a
problem.

Mai's perfect disguise passed a cursory inspection by the
harbor master as Lars' wife. Their Swedish passports weren't
necessary to travel between the Scandinavian countries. But Lars
knew he'd need to show passports once they left Norway to parts
unknown.

As they walked along the boardwalk and down the streets of
Bergen, Mai followed Lars like an obedient wife. He pointed out
some of the attractions, the old wharf, its traditional wooden
buildings and the steep climb up the Fløibanen, the funicular railway. He'd ascended the mountain of Floyen many times before,
often with his wife, to overlook the city and wharf below.

They walked briskly and arrived at a coffee house, one of
Lars' favorites. Bright flowers and flags invited them in.

"Ah, *Fika*. We will snack here. So many good waffles to
choose from in Norway. And I'll tell you our plan."

The waiter introduced himself as Willem. The bar was its
busiest in the evening, but it had just opened up for the afternoon
crowd wanting lunch or a *Fika* break. Willem and his partner,
Oscar, usually worked together on weekdays. They were a

fashionable couple who blended in with the array of avant-garde items that packed the lounge. It had a decidedly burlesque flavor.

Willem offered them a menu. "There are plenty of delicacies and coffees." He pointed to the chalked blackboards above the bar.

Lars ordered an assortment of pancakes. Thin and slightly crispy, they came with small cups of sour cream and jam.

"You might like the *hindebaer*, a raspberry jam." Lars slathered the waffles with jam and rolled one up to tempt Mai who could never resist sweets. She had a hard time keeping her eyes off the cafe's décor. It seemed to delight her even more that the pancakes. Mai never got enough of the liberal approach to life in Scandinavia. Having grown up in a closed Chinese society, she was taught that open-minded views in the west were corrupt.

Mai sampled each waffle variety. One was savory and stuffed with brie, another full of peanuts and caramel. Lars' shared from his plate and nibbled off Mai's. Perhaps her favorite was the waffle oozing with chocolate. She paired it with a café latte topped with a mountain of cream and drizzled with more chocolate. After a few more shots of espresso, she felt energized, hyped with sugar and fueled with enough caffeine to power a motor boat. Lars grinned at her appreciation for the finer things in life as she licked the jam and chocolate syrup from her fingers.

On a deep pink napkin, he drew a simple map with cross-hatched train tracks showing the route from Bergen to Voss. A single line followed to the Russian border.

"We'll meet with people who can help us cross the border to Russia." Lars told her more. "Later we'll sail off in a grand boat to our island paradise where people in the world of money live."

"People in the world of money?" Mai swooned. "My dream come true."

"In Russia I have friends, cosmetic surgeons." Lars said. "I will remake you, just a little nip and tuck." He brushed his long fingers across her face, exploring her cheekbones. "I'll change my appearance. Become younger, more handsome. My surgeon friends are very capable."

Mai stroked his heavily-lined and discolored face, wondering if such a transformation could be done.

"You'll easily blend in with the arctic nomads." Lars smiled. "A young girl. Yakut. And you'll have a new passport."

"A cute girl? What will my name be?" Mai would do anything to save herself from incarceration.

"Yakut. Nomadic people."

"How will people call me?" Mai asked. She was sure of one thing. "It must be a beautiful name."

Lars thought about what name to use for Mai's new identity. He then looked up a list of Yakut girl's names. "This one is best. Sardaana."

"Sardanna. Does it have a special meaning?"

"It's a beautiful flower, like you. A Siberian lily." Lars fawned over Mai whenever he could.

"I hope these lilies have a sweet aroma and don't smell of death." Mai said. She recalled the odor of pink and white Stargazer lilies in a Copenhagen hotel room and their noxious smell of rotting flesh. A flood of unpleasant memories surged through Mai.

Lars grimaced, not knowing where that macabre comment came from.

In Mai's typical fashion, she rose to her feet to explore the eclectic jungle, the up-side-down umbrellas, the multicolored sombreros, the hanging crystal lights, the incandescent lamps, the mix of modern art and Victorian furniture. The oil paintings got Mai's attention, in particular the tattooed nudes of the lounge proprietor, the robustly round and voluptuous Queen. Her King and co-owner didn't bare himself.

Willem collected the mostly empty plates, napkins, glasses, coffee cups and mugs while Lars watched Mai in her child-like trace. She circled the lounge more than once before disappearing through a door to the bathroom.

While he waited for Mai, Lars mused, thinking how he could re-invent her into a new woman. Her eyes would be rounder, her nose a bit wider, her lips.... he would keep them as they are. Her breasts, he would reduce in size, a bit smaller and not such a lure, they too easily attract other men. He would feed her rich foods to plump her up, she could easily afford a few extra pounds. He preferred a Rubenesque ass on a woman and more pear-shaped curves. But her mind, he must wash, sanitize, make her more caring, loving and emotional. Perhaps additional hormones would help.

Once the cosmetic changes are made and healed, he would begin her hormonal and dietary transformation. With needles he'll administer the hormones, the estrogen doses. With IVs he'll infuse designer chemicals, fattening boosters, and dietary supplements. He would design her as he sees fit.

While Lars mused about his cosmetic fantasies, Mai complained to the ladies' room mirror, "I look so hideously old." Mai removed her make-up and dumped the baggy sweatpants in the trash. She slipped on the tight winter leggings she had in the black knapsack she always carried with her.

Lars began to wonder why Mai was taking so long. When she finally emerged and sat down across from him, his jaw dropped. "What have you done? Why have you removed your make-up?"

Mai smiled with her pretty unadorned face. "This is the natural me. Don't you like it?" Lars stared at her naked face and rethought her next surgery. She might need some bone work to broaden her face. A break or two…he could crush her high cheekbones to flatten and widen her features.

"At the border, you must be my wife again," Lars said. He would redraw the wrinkles and lines and add mottled patches of red to resemble Åsa's complexion. Lars was annoyed at Mai but only for a while. It would be some time before they'd get to the Norway-Russia border.

"We can walk to the railway station. It's not too far," Lars said as he stroked her cheek.

36

Red Notice

The Stockholm police were the first to investigate the mysterious death of Vladimir Petrov.

Vlad Petrov carried two passports. When he checked into the hotel, he didn't use his Russian passport, he used the country of his mother's birth, Poland, to snag an EU passport. During the initial investigation into his death, the police found both passports in his room. When they looked into Vlad's past, the police also found loose ties to organized crime. He had friends in criminal gangs, the Russian mafia, in Moscow.

At the police station, two investigators rummaged through the bagged personal effects they'd collected in Vlad's hotel room.

The lead investigator asked his partner, "Could this be a mob-inspired hit by one of his enemies?"

"Judging by his contacts, he likely had a few." The investigators pondered Vlad's dubious connections.

"But the coroner says he died from natural causes. A bad case of the flu. Maybe he had weak lungs from all the smoking?"

"Yah, lots of cigarette butts." The young investigator displayed a bagful. "And that's not all that was going on. Look at these sex toys and hand cuffs." He wiggled a second bag with a curious glimmer in his eyes.

"Bondage. Kinky sex," the lead investigator said with a smirk. "Our Vlad liked the dark side of deviant play."

"The staff saw him take a blonde woman to his room. A sex worker. Quite a few frequent this hotel. Lots of sketchy foreigners stay there. Business men. Yah, sure," The young investigator said with a sarcastic snarl.

"I don't see any evidence of suspicious behavior here. But we should find the working girl. Let's get the hotel's security camera videos. I'll ask the captain to authorize."

〰〰〰

A police technologist found the images, although they were grainy and the woman's facial details were hidden under a mop of blonde curls. On the time-date stamp, the woman entered Vlad's hotel room with him and left on her own five days later. Vlad was found in a fevered coma the day after she left.

To help find the mystery woman with Vlad before his death, the police issued a bulletin for the local area. The BOLO or "be on the lookout" notice scrolled across the Stockholm news stations as the police captain make the announcement: "We ask the public to be on the look-out for a woman last seen with a tourist, Vladimir Petrov, prior to his death. She is medium height with blonde hair and dark eyes. She carries a small black backpack." The news station showed edited video highlights of a blonde woman leaving Vlad's room.

The captain continued: "After she left Petrov's room, the Russian national died from flu in the hospital. If anyone knows the identity or whereabouts of this woman, please contact the police at….."

Despite a few leads, many of them bogus, none led to Mai Tran. She disposed of the wig and no longer played the role of a blonde bombshell.

〰〰〰

It took months before Stockholm police received test results from Vladimir Petrov's postmortem. The death wasn't deemed suspicious, so detailed genetic analysis of the flu virus was a low priority. But, in a stroke of luck, Vlad's tissue samples were sent to a surveillance lab for seasonal influenza.

173

In the lab, technicians analyzed the types of flu strains that circulated that season. But in their daily routine, a lab tech came across an unusual sample.

"Woah! This sample comes from a police investigation. Interesting. This guy died, a Russian tourist. I remember a Stockholm news clip about it." The tech showed it to the lab director.

We'd better take a closer look at this strain," she told him. "Run the virus through whole genome sequencing."

"I'm surprised we didn't get this sooner. It's a severe flu strain that caused death," the tech said, he thought it odd.

"I'm not. They didn't suspect murder, they assumed it was an ordinary flu. His next of kin probably ordered cremation. I'll check with the morgue."

When the gene sequencing results came back, it wasn't an ordinary flu strain like H3N2.

"We've got a genetic profile. The Russian tourist died from H5N1, bird flu virus." The lab director couldn't hide the shrill alarm in her voice. "Our health department will keep it quiet until we know more. Bird flu sends up red flags. And the public will be alarmed. We don't want to cause panic."

"Is it the same H5N1 Tiger flu that killed two people last year?" A lab microbiologist asked.

"Yes, nearly identical. The victims were a woman who flew from Hong Kong to Seattle, and a man who travelled to Boston from Copenhagen." The lab director gulped, she could barely get out the words, "It's the weaponized H5N1 Tiger flu. This could be a serious."

She notified the Swedish National Police. They contacted Swedish Intelligence, SAPO, who in turn notified the FBI. Test results and samples were flown to European and US disease centers for confirmation.

It didn't take long for the FBI and SAPO forensics to nail the Stockholm woman's identity. DNA from her hair and saliva on a drinking glass confirmed her identity—the blonde prostitute was Mei Wong, the bioterrorist who murdered two people. Now there were three dead victims.

The police Commissioner at the Swedish Police headquarters was not happy.

"Interpol sent out a Red Notice alert months ago." The Commissioner chided the captain and his investigative team. "You missed the possibility that she was the same woman involved with the Copenhagen and Hong Kong murders." The investigation team were in for a harsh reprimand. "You didn't connect the dots. You were obsessed with your mob hit theory."

They should have known better. A Red Notice isn't an arrest warrant but it's the closest thing to it. They help national police forces find and arrest criminals. And globally, bioterrorist Mei Wong topped the list. She hadn't been sighted anywhere for nearly a year.

"Interpol notified us. This tiger flu Mei Wong is a most wanted woman," he fumed. "Why didn't you suspect her? How did you miss the possible connection?"

"But Vladimir Petrov's cause of death was recorded as ordinary flu. The coroner made the call." The police captain tried to absolve his department of blame.

"That's not what I asked you. How did you miss the connection with Mei Wong?" His face reddened as he scolded.

It was not a great moment for the homicide department.

On closer inspection, the department found out more about the mystery woman. Gothenburg's CCTV cameras picked up earlier images of her comings and goings, although her hair color varied wildly. She was often seen leaving and entering an apartment building owned by Lars Lindon and spotted at the Riverside hotel with an American scientist, Hong Min Chow. Two days ago, she visited the Riverside Hotel guest rooms of both Hong and his friend Jack Ashbell.

"This woman really gets around." The police commissioner told the captain.

"A few weeks ago, Mai Tran and Lars Lindon were seen leaving his apartment complex together. They boarded a yacht in the Gothenburg marina, a luxury yacht that belongs to Sven of the Ethereal Angels." The captain added that savory detail. "We will follow up."

When the Swedish police tried to contact Sven, he was away in The Netherlands on a European tour. Once they got hold of him, Sven outed Lars and Mai for scamming the Ethereal Angels with their designer baby scheme. He learned too late he'd been taken bigtime by his trusted friend. His bandmates were angry for having been duped, but it was Sven's big money investment that went missing.

The captain called the commissioner to report his team's findings. But he had something new to add. "Lars Lindon left with a woman on his 50-foot yacht. On video, the woman looks like his wife, Åsa. But Stockholm police found his wife at their home. She said Lars went to Copenhagen on business."

The police commissioner issued arrest warrants for Lars Lindon in all Scandinavian countries. The Swedish police gathered a rolling snowball of clues they shared with contacts in SAPO and FBI. By now, everyone knew that Mai Tran's DNA was a match with Mei Wong. The fact that she was the notorious Tiger Girl made them all wonder what else she might be up to next.

"With Tiger Flu as her murder weapon for Vladimir, how many more are on her hit list? Is she planning another terrorist attack? Does she have a newer, nastier bioweapon?" Such was the chatter among the agencies.

The FBI, CIA, SAPO, MSS and other "eye in the sky" agencies mobilized every available source, each trying to outwit and outmaneuver the other. The Russian FSB wasn't far behind in their search for Vladimir Petrov's murderer, the blonde assassin in the Stockholm hotel room. The Scandinavian Police forces worked closely together, despite their natural rivalries.

But in the end, whoever captured the prize would win the game. And Tiger Girl was the ultimate gold trophy.

Intelligence is as intelligence does. And the big eye in the sky agencies activated their digital and human intel to intercept Scandinavian police communications. The two with the most at stake, the US and China, were quickest off the mark. They'd already dispatched their agents.

The marathon race was on.

37

Marathon Race

Hong's stomach churned with the stress of the unknown. Even Chen's explanation of Hong's value in the wet work operations did little to quell Hong's nerves. He began to wish he hadn't eaten that greasy hamburger and hoped Chen hadn't laced it with Ricin or some other biotoxin.

Hong drifted in and out of slumber, each time he fixated on the consequences of his disappearance. People at the conference would be looking for him, especially Jack. He fell asleep, exhausted from worry.

Chen woke Hong by repeatedly tapping a purple passport on his head. "Do you like your new identity?" Chen flashed the cover of a diplomatic Chinese passport at him, then handed it to him.

Hong opened to the bio page and peered at his new stock photo. He grimaced at the name, "Li Wei. That's common enough." It was like being named Smith or Brown. The passport had enough visa stamps to make it appear old and the traveler well-seasoned, it's better not to look like a freshly minted fake. With diplomatic immunity, he could pass through borders without questions.

Chen looked at a text on his secure phone. He laughed and said, "Mei Wong, your girlfriend Mai Tran, has been spotted in Bergen."

❄✦❄

An SUV with diplomatic plates picked up Hong and Chen at the Gothenburg safe house to join a convoy of "diplomats" headed for Norway. On the nearly ten-hour journey, Hong had plenty of time to think about what might lie ahead.

Hong wasn't out of the woods, not yet, and he knew it. He was too slow, too vulnerable. Mei Wong compromised him. He knew he should've reported her early on with his suspicions. Abducting her would have been easy. MSS could have picked her up, she'd disappear into thin air. She could have been "vaporized"—a euphemism used during Hong's training—but now it's an international incident.

Hong hoped he wasn't bound for his own vaporization in a re-education camp in western China. The MSS magicians excelled in the art of vanishing acts.

It was the Norwegian police that picked up the reflection of Tiger Girl in a Bergen café window. She intentionally turned her head away, trying to avoid the CCTV camera outside the Bar Barrista. But her image was clear enough for the Norwegian Police to match her and Lars to the descriptions and photos shared by the Swedes.

With the minutes ticking away, too much time passed before the Norwegian Police realized who they had. They issued updated arrest warrants and asked the Swedish police to join them in the search. Unknown to them, other intelligence agency techies intercepted their messages. The long list of acronymic agents would soon be swarming like locusts all over Bergen.

Max texted Jeremy, "Fly to Bergen. Tiger Girl with Swedish man, Lars Lindon."

Jeremy had just landed at Gothenburg's airport where he met up with Jack. With no time to waste, a private plane made the quick hop to Bergen from Gothenburg. Jeremy and Jack were to join the other locusts.

As head of Operation Tiger Girl, Max had the biggest stake in finding Mei Wong. Max held a tight rein on designated operatives and affiliates from FBI, NSA, CDC. Even the CIA couldn't go rogue on him. He called the shots.

A private car waited for Jeremy and Jack at a small landing strip near Bergen. Jeremy was amazed at just how far Max's feelers extended. He seemed to have contacts and work miracles no matter where or what the situation. They were dropped off near the entrance to the funicular where dozens of tourists congregated for the famous attraction. It was just a minute walk to the Bar Barrista..

Jeremy asked the bartender, "Can you help us?" Willem nodded, curious at the demeanor of these two foreigners.

"Have you seen this woman?" Jack showed a head shot he cropped from his au naturel photo of Mai. He surreptitiously captured her sprawled across his bed. She'd been too busy looking at her favorite anime characters on her phone to notice.

A look of recognition flashed across Willem's face. He said in a ramble, "Oh yes, I remember her. At first, I thought she was a much older lady. When I brought the man the check, I was surprised to see she was much younger. She changed from baggy sweatpants into leggings." Willem paused and said, "I'm interested in people's fashion."

"Was she made-up to be older? A disguise perhaps?" Jack asked.

Jeremy put his finger to his lips and gave Jack a stern look.

Willem looked confused about their conversation but kept on talking. "I overheard the old man ask her, 'Why did you remove your make-up?' She'd gone to the *Damer*." Willem pointed to where the toilets were located. "She was in there quite a long time."

As Willem cleared napkins and plates from another table, Jack semi-apologized to Jeremy. "I get it. Keep my big mouth shut. And stop acting like the Keystone cops."

Jeremy scowled at Jack. He needn't say anymore.

When Willem returned to their table, he brought a crumpled pink napkin with him. "The man left this behind on the table." Willem handed it to Jeremy. "I think you call it doodles. Such a funny word. Like googles. I kept it in case they'd come back for it, if it was important for them."

Jeremy and Jack loved what they saw. Jeremy thanked Willem by leaving a big tip for the coffee. Little did Willem know that he'd just given them a huge clue.

On one side of the napkin were Lars' detailed sketches of a broad faced Asian woman. On the other, he'd drawn a line with Bergen on one end and "Russian border" on the other. A cross-hatched railroad connected Bergen to the town of Voss.

Jeremy glanced at Jack and said, "And our next destination is?"

"I got it, Jeremy. This tells us where Lars and Mai are headed and even their final destination."

To save time, they got a taxi from the funicular queue to the train station. En route, Jeremy let Max know they had a lead. Tiger Girl and Lars were headed out of Bergen by train to Voss. Their final destination was most likely Russia.

Lars planned to escape from Norway via an overland route to the Russian border. He arranged a car to pick them up in Voss. It would be a very long drive to the border, but there wasn't much choice. And there's only one border crossing point with stations on each side in Norway and Russia.

The Norwegian border guards were always on the lookout for illegal immigrants and refugees, mostly Nigerians and Afghans trying to slip into Europe. They would arrive on bicycles, travelling from Russia to Norway on the harsh "arctic migrant route".

On the Russian side, the border guards could easily be bribed not to scrutinize the hastily created visas. Lars' contact would supply the faked visas for Russia for him and his wife, Åsa. He banked on it all going according to plan.

Bergen's grand-old station, built over 100 years ago, is modern and efficient. The schedule on the digital display showed the train to Oslo, a seven-hour journey that passed through twenty stations. Voss was the third stop and just three-hours away.

Bergen station had only four platforms so it wouldn't be hard for Jeremy and Jack to find the two fugitives. Jeremy lead the way as he and Jack ascended a little used stairway. They found a vantage point that gave a better view of people boarding the Bergen line to Oslo.

"We haven't much time. But we need to be sure," Jeremy said, panting out of breath from the quick ascent. They could see the train on the platform, ready to depart.

"Do you see the woman, the bright yellow?" Jack asked as he pointed wildly towards the train's engine.

Jeremy panned the platform. "The only yellow I see is a small child in a bright canary raincoat."

"Not the kid. It's the ribbon, Mai had a yellow ribbon. It's tied to her black backpack!" Jack's voice crackled, he coughed as he tried to clear his throat. "I think…yes….its her. Look!" he pointed again to the first carriage behind the engine." Mai was at the door to the carriage.

Lars was alert and cautious, he had a heightened sense of vigilance. In his peripheral vision, he saw the swinging motion of Jack's arm, his finger aimed wildly in their direction. But Lars, who never forgets a face, focused on Jeremy. He tried to place where he'd seen him before and recalled the emergency room at the Stockholm hospital. But, he thought, why is that man in Bergen with this gesticulating idiot?

Lars remembered the busy hospital ER where the unusual couple stood out. Lars overheard the man's British accent as he watched them. The wife's exotic symptoms—her eyes a purple glow, her skin covered in massive red-black spots—he'd never seen those symptoms before. But he recognized the man hovering above the platform. And that man, the English tourist, was now watching him. A feeling inside him said it couldn't possibly be a coincidence. But where is the wife? He thought they were tourists. And why is this Brit in Bergen with this young man? They must be following us.

Just as Mai stepped up to the carriage, she looked at Lars. His eyes were fixed on the two men above, one of them pointing in their direction. To Mia's surprise, that young man looked surprisingly like Jack, her fling at the Riverside hotel. She quickly figured he was out to get her. And he was no lovesick Romeo. Mai nearly choked, she trembled in fear, she didn't want to be caught. She knew, no matter who got hold of her, she was doomed to a dark cell somewhere and likely sentenced to death. No matter what country, her lifespan was limited.

Mai boarded the passenger carriage with Lars right behind her. The platform guard closed the coach door behind Lars and signaled to the engine driver that all was clear.

Jeremy and Jack bolted down the stairs and ran towards the departing train, but a conductor stopped them from entering the platform.

"Late passengers must wait for the next train," the conductor reprimanded them. But with only four trains daily bound for Olso, they'd have to wait awhile.

"Shit!" Jeremy couldn't believe their bad luck.

"Fuck!" Jack complained even louder.

Jeremy wasted no time and got Max on his secure phone. "We saw them board the Bergen to Oslo train. But we were stopped getting on."

38

Spy vs. Spy

"In three hours, the train arrives in Voss. Get your teams there. Find her! Arrest her!" Max told his FBI colleague. "We'll get there anyway we can." The FBI director issued a directive to his agents. "I authorize helicopters, hell, mountain mules if you want. Whatever we get our hands on. We need to get her."

The FBI agents understood their dual role, law enforcement and intelligence. In a foreign country, they had to collaborate with national police and Intelligence.

"Get to Voss. Search the platforms. Board the train at Voss. Fugitives are on the first passenger coach behind the engine." Those were the instructions.

FBI called the Scandinavian Police. Swedish Intelligence were already on alert and notified Norwegian Intelligence. Norway sent for police reinforcements, their swat team in Voss could mobilize fastest.

The agencies agreed to keep the communication channels open. Stay in constant contact. No slip ups. No getting in each other's way. The Scandinavian Police would zero-in on Lars, FBI would target Mei Wong. Norwegian and Swedish Intelligence would protect their interests with a watching brief. But, all in all, mutual support was critical for the sting operation to be carried off without a hitch.

But China's MSS Central cyberspooks picked up the chatter and notified their undercover agents, including Chen and Hong's convoy. The convoy changed their route at Kinsarvik, shortening the distance to Voss. Other MSS agents—in the guise of Chinese "diplomats"—leased private jets that landed at Flesland airport in Bergen. From the airport, the drive to Voss would take about an hour and a half.

A complex spy game was unfolding in Norway with multiple cats chasing two mice.

Neither the FBI nor the MSS went unnoticed by Russia's Foreign Intelligence Service. The new Russian agency partly replaced the notorious KGB. They too wanted to arrest Mei Wong. After all, she murdered a Russian citizen in Stockholm. Their agents lie in wait. The US, China, and Russia all vied for the trophy, Mei Wong.

Spy vs Spy, it was always a competition. Which country is the potential winner? Which country's agency is most underhanded and sneaky? Which one can circumvent and out-think the others? Who can conduct the best cyber and communication surveillance? And with so many acronyms, who can really keep them straight? They're all pretty much same beast.

Lars' contacts were his Russian friends in Murmansk. On the promise of wired money, they primed in advance the Russian border guards with cash. The guards would agree to turn a blind eye for an easy crossing. Lars' friends had access to a network of fixers.

On the train, Lars told Mai, "I spotted two guys at Bergen train station. They were watching us."

Mai thought it odd and disconcerting. She told Lars, "I recognized the younger one. I met him at the Riverside hotel. A close friend of Hong."

"Hong? I don't see the connection? The man I saw in Stockholm was a random tourist. His wife in the Stockholm hospital was critically ill. It makes no sense."

Mai agreed, "Yes, confusing. I don't know how the couple in Stockholm are connected to Jack and Hong." She didn't have a clue.

Lars told Mai, "There may be others out to get us. Those two men know we are on this train." Lars' calm, usually stoic manner began to crack from agitation. People were in hot pursuit of them, Lars needed a back-up plan.

Mai felt the pressure. "Please tell me. What can I do?" Mai's anxiety grew. Never before did she feel so frayed and frazzled, her left eye twitched and her lips quivered. Lars stroked her forehead, then rubbed her temples to calm her down.

"Listen closely, Mai." Lars wrapped Mai under his shoulder. Protective and loving, he would save her like a valiant prince. "You are still my princess." But Mai squirmed under his caress. No old man could soothe her and ultimately love her. Only Mei Wong could save herself. And Mei Wong was the strongest woman she knew. She needed to rekindle those invincible feelings that she could overcome whatever adversities or adversaries were coming at her.

Lars told her, "Listen carefully to our alternative escape route, Plan B." Mai listened to Lars' Plan B knowing full well that she could always come up with a Plan C of her own.

"Let's check the schedule for the next train to Voss," Jeremy told Jack, "I'm afraid it might be hours from now." Both were still recovering from the failure at the station. Had their timing been just minutes earlier, they wouldn't have missed the opportunity, they would be following their quarry to Voss. They knew they were no longer vital players in how the game would end. They'd done their part. Now they were surplus.

As they walked towards the digital board, Jack asked Jeremy, "Will they be caught?"

Jeremy nodded and said, "They'd better be." He was still reeling from unspent adrenaline.

But as luck would have it, the next direct train to Voss was only an hour and a half away. Too late for Mei's anticipated capture, but they'd at least be there for the bloody or not so bloody aftermath. Neither wanted to miss out on the arrest of Mei Wong, even if for different reasons.

"We'll be able to sample Voss water right from the source," Jack quipped.

"You twit, they don't bottle the water in Voss. It comes from 250 miles away, the locals use the pretentious product, it's free tap water," Jeremy growled at Jack. He was exhausted from his travels in India and a wife who defied the gods of death. Any fondness Jeremy might have had for Jack was long gone. They're relationship was as flat as the misbranded water of Voss.

Jack persisted with his cornball optimism. "Look on the bright side, Jeremy."

His fatigue catching him, Jeremy quietly sang, "When you're chewing on life's gristle, Don't grumble, give a whistle." The Monty Python refrain played on in his head with images of Eric Idle hanging from the cross.

And together Jeremy and Jack whistled the happy tune, "Always look on the bright side of life."

39

Flam Bam

On the train platform at Voss station, sniffer dogs led by the police tugged hard. The dogs were primed for Mei Wong's scent from her sweatpants retrieved from the *Damer* trash bin at the Bar Barrista. The dogs sniffed out the tourists—some were alarmed at the not-so-friendly pups. Most of the travelers were just amused and curious about all the police activity.

As the train reached the platform, Lars didn't like what he saw. He peered over at the Voss station's parking lot where three marked Norwegian Police cars, one police van and an odd assortment of unmarked SUVs were parked. The police dogs on the platform were the final straw.

"Mai, the police are searching." Lars told her, "A group of young women, Chinese tourists, are three or four carriages behind us." Lars stopped to look over his shoulder. "Be quick. Join them. Hide among them. Pretend you are part of the group. Then go on to Myrdal. I'll find you there."

Mai grabbed her black bag and made her way between the passenger carriages so she could merge with this Chinese group. She never once looked back

※

At Voss station, the platform was crowded with police. When the two fugitives, Lars and Mai, didn't get off the train, agents from the FBI and the Scandinavian Police got on. A small group of Chinese men and a woman, undercover agents for the MSS, followed suit. Other Chinese agents kept a watch on the platform.

The police and FBI agents walked the corridors of the carriages, awkwardly passing each other as they looked for the elusive couple. Each agency recognized the others. More spooks and spies from all over walked along the platforms and peered into train carriage windows. Some inspected the train tracks. Others tried to blend in and commingle with passengers in transit. All were pointy-nosed Spy vs Spy caricatures in action.

Groups of Chinese tourists disembarked from the train, including the young women who headed towards their luggage. The local police attempted to corral them.

Three armed Scandinavian police officers boarded the train and searched the first carriage, but Lars and Mei Wong were nowhere to be found. They searched every nook and cranny of the east bound train until they found a locked toilet between the third and fourth carriages. They suspected someone barricaded themselves in.

"Open the door. We are police," they ordered. When no one responded after repeated demands, a conductor was summoned to unlock the toilet.

Lars spent his time in the locked toilet covering his face with a dark foundation, hoping to pass for southern European. He'd just finished brushing his sideburns and three-day beard with a tube of black mascara when the police knocked. He looked in the mirror and adjusted his wife's dark eyeglass frames, then pulled on his wooly cap to hide his gray-blond hair. Lars held the door handle tight as the conductor unlocked the plastic bolt.

"Do you mind? I am on the toilet," Lars said in protest.

After a brief tug of war, a policeman pulled open the door. A commotion began when another cop pulled off Lars' cap, knocked his glasses to the floor, and revealed his thin mat of hair. Lars struggled to regain possession of his cap and his composure. His shiny black side-burns smeared and swirled across his darkened bronze cheeks like a watercolor by Renoir.

While everyone's attention was drawn to the mayhem and madcap comedy surrounding the toilet, Mei got off the train and lingered near the group of trendy young Chinese women with their mountain of luggage, backpacks and handbags. They were enthusiastically chattering, taking selfies, posting photos and checking their social media. Mei strolled past them and quickly swapped out her black knapsack, the one with the yellow ribbon, with a similar black bag. The young women were so distracted, none of them noticed her stealthy exchange.

Mei calculated her every move, like a chess game she stayed steps ahead. With her new black bag slung across her shoulder, she nonchalantly walked back to the platform towards the first coach, it had already been thoroughly searched. Bound for Myrdal, the train was scheduled to depart soon.

A second commotion ensued and a motley bunch of agents descended upon the gaggle of young women. A sniffer dog clawed at their pile of baggage as though he were looking for his favorite toy. The dog's handler had a tough time restraining him. Chinese diplomats quickly surrounded the women while the Scandinavian Police tried to intervene.

Two Mandarin speaking Chinese officials wedged their way in and ordered the women, "Identify your luggage and handbags."

Jumping to their command, the young ladies gathered their belongings from the pile they'd constructed. The last woman recovered her roller suitcase, but then became frazzled and confused as she picked up the black knapsack with the hanging yellow ribbon.

"This is not mine," she said. But before she could say any more, two Chinese men grabbed her, one on each arm, and held her as she squealed and squirmed.

Her friends didn't protest and kept silent. Afraid that their "social credit" score would take a big hit; they knew their privilege of international travel might easily be lost. Only the most "trustworthy" in China can travel abroad on planes. Even trains are limited to those who pass muster. You can be blacklisted for offenses, whether it be smoking on a train, using drugs, or not promptly reacting to an official summons.

These young women knew they had too much to lose. And their friend, in their estimation, must have committed some minor infractions. She would have to fend for herself.

The Scandinavian police had encircled the Chinese officials. Like an army, they surrounded them to prevent the young woman from being abducted. The police demanded they show their identification.

The FBI then formed a secondary ring around the police.

Moving slowly, deliberately, the Chinese men peeled open and displayed their diplomatic passports.

"She is a Chinese citizen," one official countered in English. With diplomatic immunity, they couldn't be arrested.

The name "Mei Wong" went viral among the agents and police who were all on high alert. The Chinese officials, surrounded by Scandinavian Police and FBI, froze in place and dug in as they waited for backup. It was hard to tell just how many spies were mixed in among the hordes of the curious.

The Chinese "diplomats" directed the other young Chinese women to rejoin the large group of tourists.

The congregation of spectators grew, taking photos and videos to add to their travel collection. Every camera phone and tourist took telephoto images and video clips. Likely, a volume of snapshots and videos were posted to social media.

Mei, in all the confusion, had boarded the Myrdal bound train.

With Lars and Mei Wong, the two suspected fugitives, thought to be captive, the train to Myrdal was cleared for departure. It carried tourists who would then transfer at Myrdal to the famous Flam Railway, a highlight of their trip to Norway. They'd descend into the Flam valley with its harrowing switchbacks and spectacular waterfalls. But for this group of Myrdal bound tourists, on the scale of excitement, the dramatic events they witnessed in Voss might be hard to compete with.

Mei snuggled up to an elderly Chinese man, he could have been her grandfather. If anything, he was happy to have the attention of such a young beauty. He didn't resist as she whispered in his ear words he could barely hear. A smile of more than grandfatherly love emanated as he admired Mei's unadorned face, looking younger than her years. His grown son, wife, and grandson were in the next carriage where they found a cluster of seats. He told them he would stay where he was and meet up with them in Myrdal. The entire journey was about 45 minutes.

But Mei wasn't yet free and clear from capture and arrest, two agents stayed on the Myrdal-bound train.

For the first half of the journey, the law enforcers on board admired the valley's scenery. The steep river gorge and its sheer sides and the mountains on the other side were just so dramatic. Even the agents relaxed and took photos. Cell phone coverage was spotty, but with Mei Wong captured in Voss, they had little to worry about. Might as well sit back and take in the views.

Near the end of the train journey, they entered the 3.3 mile long stretch of the Gravhals tunnel. Communications with their units were lost entirely, but they didn't seem to care. It wasn't until they arrived at Myrdal station that their cell phones began to ping with text and voice messages. Their Voss colleagues alerted them with the news that the woman abducted by the Chinese did not match the profile. Mei Wong was possibly on their train.

The young, fresh-faced girl with her grandfather was not given more than a cursory glance. No one thought her in the least suspicious. Mai's only make-up was a thin eyeliner to enhance what was left of her Chinese features. Her bundled coat over her buried black bag disguised her figure.

Myrdal station had a miniscule police presence. After all, it was really nothing more than a train station in the mountains. There were seldom any problems other than the occasional stolen purse or wallet. They weren't prepared, nor did they have reason to be, for major crimes. With little traffic by car up the steep asphalt roads, not many people ventured out, especially in winter when the roads were icy.

At Myrdal, tourists change trains for the famous Flamsbana railway. It's busiest in summer, but many Chinese tourists booked the off-season cheap deals. Tourists scrambled to transfer to the Flam Railway while others travelled in the opposite direction. It was a hub of hubbub as tourists exchanged trains.

Before anyone could get organized to surveille the milling crowds of tourists, Mei got off the train. She kept her eyes down and glued to her phone—with its sim card destroyed in Gothenburg, it functioned only as a decoy. With only seven minutes to spare, she crossed the platform to the west bound train, returning to Bergen via Voss.

"When you are in doubt, reverse your direction," Mei mumbled to herself. It was an aphorism she adopted as her own. She would return to where she came from.

One lone Chinese agent also boarded behind her.

40

Extraordinary Voss

"We're on the next train to Voss." Jeremy left a message with Max but got no reply.

By the time Jeremy and Jack's Bergen train pulled into Voss, the crisis had subsided. There was still a profusion of police on the platform and a parking lot full of official cars. In addition to the police cars and wagons were vehicles with darkened windows and diplomatic plates of the US, Chinese, and Russian embassies.

Jack struck a pose like he was some American official and cornered a young news reporter. Before Jeremy could tamp Jack down, he was already acting like an official seeking information.

"Hey, what's up? Any new news?" Jack poked out his chest, trying to look authoritative.

The reporter spilled everything he knew. "Two fugitives arrived in Voss. The Scandinavian Police arrested Lars Lindon, a Swedish doctor."

"And Mei Wong, the terrorist?" Jack wouldn't stop. But Jeremy for once let him go with it. Those were the questions he wanted answered.

"A sniffer dog went after a black bag with a yellow ribbon. A woman was seized by Chinese diplomats from the Oslo Embassy."

"They captured Mei Wong." Jack assumed.

But the reporter said, "No. After a long standoff between the Chinese and Scandinavian Police, she was identified as Sugin Wei. Mistaken identity. The woman was finally released. People were appalled at how terrified she was. The Chinese officials apologized for their mistake—said they'd help her rejoin her group."

"So, where is Mei Wong?" Jeremy took over the questioning.

"I think she managed to escape. But who knows where?" The reporter shrugged and walked off.

Jeremy and Jack were flummoxed. Just where the hell *did* she go?

"Maybe we should focus on Hong's whereabouts," Jeremy said.

"I've called Hong's cell," Jack fessed up.

"Don't tell me. No luck. Call the Gothenburg Conference desk."

Jack had the conference registration number in his contacts. "Have you seen Hong?" he asked, then relayed to Jeremy, "Neither Amanda nor Olivia have any news on Hong."

"Ask them about the Swedish Police," Jeremy prompted.

"They swarmed the hotel and conference area. Asked questions about Mai Tran."

"Let's take a walk to the car park. See who's there." Jeremy thought it might be revealing. "I've always taken an interest in diplomatic plates. Since Moscow."

"Moscow? When were you there?" Jack asked, but Jeremy shook his head as if to say, not now.

Jeremy half-whispered, "Hmm, interesting." He had a good look around. "Standard plates in Norway for most vehicles is black text on a reflective white background. But there are blue plates here too."

"Yeah, different shades of blue, some have a shiny background. Oh, there's a green one on that truck." Jack waved his hand towards the truck.

"What interests me are the blue plates. Look at the cars with reflective blue plates and yellow text. They're foreign diplomats. In Norway, they've got the letters CD, *Corps Diplomatique*. The US is number 10, so the Americans are here. Russia is 72, interesting. And there's 52, that's code for China."

"China. Of course, they want Mei Wong." Jack didn't think it odd.

"Two others cars have blue plates with white text. Do you see them?" Jeremy asked as he scanned the other cars, SUVs, trucks and vans.

Jack squinted his eyes. "Yes. There's no CD on them. But they both start with AX."

"Sweden doesn't use the CD on its diplomatic plates. Instead, each country has its own code. In Sweden, AX is China." Jeremy gestured towards the two cars with his eyes. "So, the gangs all here."

"Jeremy, how the hell do you remember all that? The US, China, Russia, and the Scandinavians. Holy cow."

"Hey, everybody wants Mei Wong. More than we could ever know."

Hong was watching Jack and Jeremy's every move. He'd been secreted away, obscured by the darkened windows of the Swedish diplomatic car that he and Chen travelled in. Hong scrutinized the pair as they milled around, talked to the reporter, and checked out the fleet of Chinese diplomatic cars and SUVs.

A young woman had been watching Jeremy and Jack as they inspected the diplomatic plates in the station parking lot. They didn't take much notice of her, not until she approached them.

"FBI," she said. "Follow me. We need to talk." About the same age as Jack, she wore a hooded jacket. Her hazel eyes were her only distinguishing characteristic. She escorted them to a white van and slid open the side door.

Jeremy had noticed the van before. It had Norwegian plates, a reflective blue with yellow text, and the letters CD10-09— *Corps Diplomatique*, United States 10. He spotted the driver during his survey of the vehicles in the lot. Wearing a knitted cap and sunglasses, he was nondescript.

Once in the van, an FBI agent, an older blonde woman, asked the first questions, "Who are you and why are you in Voss?" She had a deep south accent.

Jeremy, a dual British-American citizen, said, "I'm here in Scandinavia under my American passport." He showed his two passports.

Jack said nothing for a change. He opened his American passport to the photo page.

Jeremy handed the FBI agent a card for his DHS contact, Max. "Ask Max about code name Tiger Girl. He'll vouch for me."

The agents chuckled and repeated the same silly name. "Tiger Girl?"

"Now that's a good one." The blonde woman rolled her eyes sarcastically at Jeremy. Her southern twang reminded Jeremy of country music. The agents poured over Jeremy's two passports and Jack Ashbell's American one. The younger woman made notes on her computer, while the other bulky-set blonde sequestered the seemingly two reprobates in the corner of the van, keeping a close eye on them.

A short time later, the hazel-eyed agent stepped out of the van, poked at her secure phone, and sent messages. The blonde said nothing as she watched suspiciously over the pair, Jeremy and Jack. When they tried to talk, she shut them up in no uncertain terms. She was in no mood to put up with any of their bullshit.

Once back in the van, the green-eyed lady pointed at Jack. "You're the one who had sex with Mei Wong."

Jack nodded 'yes' and hung his head. Jeremy had never seen him pull an embarrassed face before, but Jack's shy act didn't work with the hard-nosed hazelnut.

Shifting her gaze to Jeremy, she scrutinized the older man of the odd couple. "How do you two know each other?"

Jeremy started with the long version, but she cut him short.

After many awkward attempts at a believable explanation, Max confirmed their unlikely stories. FBI contacted Jo in Stockholm, but only to confirm what she knew, which wasn't much at this point. She was marginally coherent as it was.

"Other agents have some questions for you." When the blonde slid open the door, Jeremy hopped out of the van and looked around for other Norwegian diplomatic plates. He spotted a gray windowed SUV but couldn't see its occupants. The license plate read CD10-02—more Americans.

Jeremy then noticed two burly gentlemen as they stepped out of a Norwegian vehicle—plate number CD52-03, the Chinese embassy. He sensed a heightened awareness building around them. Jeremy elbowed Jack to pay attention.

The Norwegian police and FBI kept their eye on the Chinese dynamic duo as they approached an inbound train. It was the west bound train to Bergen that had just arrived from Myrdal. As the passengers, including Mei, disembarked at Voss, the platform jammed up with tourists.

Mei sandwiched herself in the crowd, moving slowly with a large Chinese group, then looped her arm on a surprised man. She wore the sweetest of smiles. Mei could elicit a glow of magnanimous virtue at a moment's notice. She had a brief reprieve when no one in the group of tourists challenged her.

But the Chinese agent who'd been on the train hung closely behind her. He nodded to the approaching Chinese heavyweights on the platform. As the two men drew near, Mei saw the look in their eyes, their gaze was directed at her. She unhooked her arm from her ruse and turned around to flee, only to be stopped by the agent who followed her off the train. The agent wrapped his arms around her shoulders, as if giving her an affectionate hug. The two burly brutes caught up and lingered close by.

Mei struggled to free herself, but the shorter, more bullish bruiser stealthily pricked her lower arm with a cluster of tiny needles. It transmitted a concoction of tranquilizers and sedatives. The agent from the train helped hold her upright as she began to falter and stumble. The taller, lanky guy tucked his arm around her waist. The bull led the way as they marched towards the parking lot. The agent from the train fell back to bring up the rear.

The reckless bull cleared the path for Mei and his colleagues. His attitude and solid build threatened whoever got in his way. With the Scandinavian Police in pursuit, the Chinese diplomatic abductors thrust her into a Norwegian SUV with Chinese embassy plates, CD52-03. The numbers were partially obscured under a dark gray plastic shield as a light snow began to fall.

Moments later, Hong appeared like a spooky apparition. Events unfolded like surreal scenes in a bizarre Swedish film. Jack stared in disbelief as Hong was escorted from the SUV with blue plates and white text, AX-14, a Chinese diplomatic vehicle from Sweden. Hong didn't resist the man holding his arm. Chen, just minutes before, had injected him with a sedative.

Jack yelled "Hong!", but Hong never looked back in Jack's direction, he appeared to see nothing.

Chen pushed Hong into the same Norwegian SUV that now confined Mei Wong— the SUV with CD52-03, the Chinese embassy.

Jack yelled again, "It's Hong. He's American!" Jeremy was focused on Tiger Girl but recognized Hong from photos Jack showed him. Things were even more complicated than they seemed.

Chen crammed himself in next to Hong. With their two captives in the vehicle, the Chinese didn't want to risk losing either one of them. Especially Mei Wong. They had so many questions to ask and expected her to have plenty of answers.

Jeremy and Jack's jaws gaped wide-open. Left in the cold, they were incredulous. They'd just witnessed China capture its own national, Mei Wong, on foreign soil. They had also seized an American, Hong, on foreign soil. The Chinese took one straight from the CIA playbook—extraordinary rendition. And this was as extraordinary as it came.

The Chinese embassy SUV, CD52-03, peeled out of the parking lot exit. The Norwegian Police followed in the chase. The two FBI women quickly shuffled Jack and Jeremy into the FBI's white van. The driver, a local hire who knew the surrounding area well, followed the Norwegian Police.

A second van from the Norwegian Chinese embassy, CD52-07, suddenly sped to the gate and blocked the entrance. But barreling up behind them, with no time to stop, was another diplomatic SUV, CD72-04. The Russian embassy.

Jeremy and Jack and the FBI agents flinched when they heard a sharp thump. They turned to look out the back of the van, almost in unison.

"It's the Chinese," Jeremy said, "they blocked the gate and it looks like a Russian SUV crashed into them."

The FBI's SUV came to an abrupt stop behind the crumpled Russian SUV. They called their counterparts in the white van. "The Chinese blocked the gate. The Russians hit them hard. No one else can get out of Voss station." The American caller sounded out of breath. "We're trapped in the parking lot. It's up to you to follow."

Jeremy called Max and asked, "What shall we do?" But the blonde agent grabbed his phone and put it on speaker.

"Shadow the Chinese vehicle with Tiger Girl," Max ordered.

"The Norwegian Police are in the lead," the southern blonde said in her husky drawl.

"Defer to them, do not interfere," Max ordered. "But do not lose Tiger Girl."

"You heard that Jack," Jeremy warned.

"Where could they be going?" the blonde agent asked.

"Who knows? Just follow," Max directed them, he was too far from the action to have a good read on the situation.

"They have an American citizen, Hong Min Chan," Jack said.

Jeremy agreed, "That's true."

❊

The FBI's white van drove through snow and ice and rough terrain as they followed the police on the road back to Bergen. In less than an hour, the Chinese SUV took a side road to a field where a double rotor helicopter awaited them.

The Norwegian police were already on foot when the white van pulled up behind them. The police surrounded the group of six Chinese diplomats—the two bruisers, one seasoned diplomat, two younger men, and the young woman.

Jack was the first to step out of the van, but no one complained. The FBI agents and Jeremy followed after him. They abutted three Norwegian police officers who stood opposed to the six Chinese diplomats. The entire assemblage had grown to a baker's dozen. They stood so close they could look each other in the eye. Jack glared at Hong, who avoided his gaze. Tiger Girl stared only at her feet.

Hong looked disheveled and appeared to be woozy. He no longer wore his jovial mask.

Jack and Jeremy shifted their gaze from Hong to Mai, or Mei, or whoever she was. She hugged her sore arms that ached from the needles and rough hands of the two bruisers. Weak from exhaustion, her skin pale and blotched, she was unmasked and no longer attractive. She was no longer Tiger Girl, the seductively evil, most wanted bioterrorist. No longer Mei Wong, the young woman from Shenzhen. No longer Mai Tran, the con artist and designer of babies. She no longer wore a disguise. Like a frightened chameleon, she showed her true colors. The ugly shades of a killer, a murderer and manipulator of men.

The police demanded, "Show us your passports."

The diplomats displayed a collection of purple passports. With his new identity as a Chinese diplomat, Hong could not be touched. But he could no longer hide from who he really was— a traitor, defector, a turncoat and spy. An undercover mole for Chinese intelligence.

Under the whir of the duel spinning blades, Jeremy wondered aloud to Jack, "How many secrets has your spy friend pilfered?" Jack shrugged and said nothing in return.

Hong and Mei never once looked at each other. Never once looked at Jack. Never once looked beyond their blank stares. They nodded 'yes' when asked to verify their identity and offered nothing more.

The Chinese arrested Mei Wong. Under Chinese law and their system of justice, she would be tried for her criminal acts as a murderer and terrorist. Deemed a threat to national security, she would be dealt with accordingly.

The FBI could do little, it was outside their jurisdiction. They stood there powerless, so close to their prey, the elusive Tiger Girl. But there was no way they could capture her now.

Jeremy reminded the Norwegian police, "What about our American citizen?" He pointed to Hong.

"What US citizen? He's a Chinese national with a diplomatic passport." The police knew only what they gleaned from the passports they were shown.

The six Chinese nationals then boarded the helicopter and disappeared into the dark evening sky.

The Norwegian police did what they could. They told Jeremy, Jack, and the FBI agents, "We had to let him go. He's a diplomat."

41

Who's What?

The next day, Jeremy and Jack flew to Stockholm. Jack checked in to the airport hotel.

That evening, we three dine together in the hotel restaurant, then Jeremy suggests a private de-brief in our room. I'm thrilled that I'll finally get some information even if it's their filtered version, there's plenty to learn.

"So, help me unpack all this. The international news is as far I got." I want the detail, but my brain is still clogged with dead little sausages and their poisonous waste. It would take time for my own filtering system to clear out the gunky mess.

"So, you want it first-hand," Jeremy asks, "where shall we begin?"

"Jack, how did you get involved with all this?" I ask, half knowing what to expect.

Jeremy laughed and gave a huge grin as Jack turned ten shades of scarlet. Jack became mute, not even an audible stutter or groan. He only winced a painful expression, like he'd just stepped on hot coals. He might as well have. At least he'd have the scars to show.

Jeremy got tired of waiting and dead-panned, "He wants to be a gentleman and censor his dalliance in Gothenburg with an international terrorist."

"Did you just say what I thought you said?" I know what Jack did but I play along with Jeremy.

They both nod yes. Jeremy enthusiastically. Jack meekly. I'd begun to put my finger on it, that Jack was a womanizing little shit. Was I ever glad I never succumbed to his advances.

"And now on to the bigger news." Jeremy smirks and nearly spits as he says to Jack, "pun intended."

Jack looked even more peevish that before. Jeremy's derisive attacks go beyond his usual sarcasm. I had a good idea how much animosity he'd amassed during their time together in Norway. So, I try to change the tone as well as the subject.

"What I've heard on the news might not be accurate. The story gets lost in translation. It's that language problem." I look at Jeremy who knows what I mean.

"Language, its use and what it means, depends on the listener as well as the speaker. It's subject to interpretation," Jeremy says in his erudite way.

"Right now, it's hard for me to interpret anything. Please give it to me in black and white." I'm doing my best to understand, despite the fog I'm in.

The boys buzz with an elaborate and highly entertaining rendition of spooks and spies and tales of extraordinary rendition. It's really hard for me to wrap my head around what seems like something out of a spy thriller novel.

"Jo, don't worry, I'll give you a recap later." Jeremy says and breaks out the Swedish beer. He seems to take on a more amicable tone with Jack. I defer on the booze. Mixing beer with my heavy-duty meds is probably not a good idea.

"So, you've got intelligence agencies from at least three countries involved." I say.

"*Truth* is all according to the big 'eyes in the sky'." Jeremy goes on about how each nation's intelligence will interpret what they see, "so that *truth* becomes clouded and obfuscated."

I imagine a randomly dripped painting by Jackson Pollock. And Pollock's abstract impressionism really always muddled my mind. Right now, it would take a lot of careful dissecting to unscramble the eggs in my brain.

"But where is Mei Wong now?" I ask, thinking they must know. They both shrug their shoulders.

"She's nowhere to be found. Last seen boarding that helicopter. There's speculation that she was flown somewhere on a private aircraft, a jet perhaps." Jeremy said but didn't know for sure.

"But where would the Chinese fly her to?" I ask.

"Your guess is as good as any," Jeremy says. "Just like the Americans did with suspected terrorists after 911, extraordinary rendition is no longer just the prerogative of the CIA. China and Russia have their own black ops too."

"Black Operations?" Jack asks.

"What can you see in the dark? Nothing." Jeremy reverts to mocking Jack again. I begin to think that Jeremy's carrying it all a bit too far.

"But how did China abduct her in the first place?" I still can't believe they got away with it. "She was on Norwegian soil."

Jeremy explains, "She's a Chinese national. Interpol had issued a Red Notice for Mei Wong, but that means she's suspected of committing a crime, they can't arrest her." Jeremy pauses to think. "Each country must decide for itself what it will do."

I think I understand. Sort of. "But why didn't Norway nab her?"

"During the confusion in Voss, the Chinese grabbed her. Norway has no extradition treaty with China. Norway and United States do. And Mei Wong is wanted by the US. But 'Finders, Keepers' seems to have been used." Jeremy's thinking out loud.

"So, if the FBI got her, would they've been able to extradite her? How did the FBI and Scandinavian Police miss the ball?" I ask.

Jack broke his silence. "China got the home run in this baseball game."

"When China's MSS diplomats swooped in, they claimed Mei Wong was not only a terrorist but a great threat to Chinese military security." Jeremy went on. "Here's another twist. Everyone had Chinese diplomatic passports. And Hong was in that Chinese convoy."

"Hong? You mean Jack's friend?" Now I'm really flummoxed. I look at Jack and he nods sort of sheepish.

Jeremy laughs before he says, "Yet another of Mei Wong's lovers." He rubs it in. "Speaking of Tiger Girl's other lovers. Besides Hong, there's Lars Lindon, the plastic surgeon."

"So, who the hell is Lars Lindon?" I'm wondering how long the list of Mei's lovers is.

"Long story short, an older Swedish doctor and business partner. More about that later." Jeremy keeps tossing out tantalizing morsels.

"Business? What kind of business?" I'm curious as hell.

"A designer baby scam," Jack interjects with a grin "human genome editing."

I think Jack is cheering up, now that were talking his language. "This story is starting to confuse me," I say.

"And there is so much more to tell." Jeremy shakes his head at the whole crazy mess.

"So, what'll happen to Mei Wong?" I could never understand her motives. A notorious bioterrorist who changes her identity and demeanor while managing to keep one step ahead of everyone. Her accomplices, her lovers, and mainly the law. She'd been on the run for so long, just how did she do it?

"She's a Chinese citizen, they'll take her home. Who knows what they'll do with her next." Jeremy gives me an ominous roll of his big brown eyes.

"I'd hate to be on the other side of Chinese justice." I'm thinking it won't be pleasant. Visions of torment and torture make me squirm. "What about the death of the Russian in Stockholm? The Swedish news said she's wanted in connection with it."

"Apparently, he's a mobster of some sort. Vladimir Petrov. But it looks like he was keeping her captive. Restraints, cuffs, and evil looking sex toys in his hotel room." Jeremy's never been shy when it comes to mentioning fetishes.

"So, maybe she killed him in self-defense?" I suggest, shrugging my shoulders.

"It looks like Vladimir was another victim of Tiger Flu. She still has a stash of her 'Honey Sweeties'. Slipped one to her abusive Russian lover, poor old Vlad." Jeremy looks over at Jack and says, "I wonder if she had one for you…"

"Fuck off, will you Jeremy?" Jack is still reeling from the mess he got himself in.

They're going at each other again so I reprimand them, "OK, settle down boys. Let's stick to the point here. It's not about you two. So, put on your big boy pants."

"It's about fucking Mei Wong," Jeremy says with a nod, smug with his entendre. I'm thinking, this bioterrorist nymphomaniac really gets around.

Jeremy's on a roll and he won't let up. He thinks he's clever when he says, "Jack, if I were you, I'd get tested for every possible venereal disease. She's literally been around-the-world—Russia, China, Europe, *and* the US."

Jack glares at Jeremy again, resorting to his now familiar selective mutism. He keeps chewing on his lip.

"Jeremy, please stop." I'm adamant and he knows it.

"OK, madam, I'll shut up." Jeremy finally relinquishes.

"I still don't get the whole picture. So, what did Hong have to do with all of this?" I ask, peering back and forth between Jack and Jeremy.

"That's a whole other chapter." Jack says and glances at Jeremy who nods in agreement. That story would have to wait to be told.

I hoped the temporary truce would hold.

42

Two Ticks

Jack flew to Gothenburg the next morning from Stockholm. We didn't see him at breakfast, he departed early morning.

My "Hong" questions wouldn't be answered until we returned to Rhode Island. After three more days in Stockholm, the doctors thought I could comfortably fly home via Boston.

A few weeks pass before my symptoms improve enough to rejoin the land of the living. My brain miasma, the fog and mist, has begun to settle. The muddled confusion dissipated enough to carry on a semi-coherent conversation. Just don't tax me with the details of the last couple months.

Another meal at our place, Jeremy lets me help with the cooking. Traditional Italian dishes. The ploy is to ply Jack with plenty of red wine. To be followed by extracting whatever salubrious morsels we can pry out of him on his sexual trysts with Tiger Girl and his violent assault by Hong.

We pluck at the meats, cheeses and olives on the charcuterie plate as Jack turns the table to pick on my brain. A distraction from questions about his sexual encounter.

"So, Jo, tell me about your tick encounter." Jack wants to know.

"I think it's my cue to go cook the spaghetti. *Aglio e olio.* My favorite." Jeremy says and gets up to leave the living room.

"Love the garlic. An extra helping please." Jack orders Jeremy, as if he's his waiter. I see Jeremy glare with resentment on his way out.

Jack always wants more of everything, so I pour him another class of Sangiovese.

He sips then asks, "How do you feel?" I think he's concerned or maybe it's just an academic interest.

"Still recovering. Nasty symptoms seem to linger. Deadly strain of *Rickettsia.* Tests in Boston confirmed it's one of the Spotted Fever group. Not Rocky Mountain. A more exotic beast."

I show him the gigantic spotty leg photos on my phone, then stand up and pull down my leggings.

"Look." I say as I expose myself. Jack grins, entertained by my gesture. The spots have faded some but are still visible.

Then I begin to rant. The wine has kicked in, I haven't drunk alcohol since the tick attack.

"It started with Delhi belly, then blurry eyes at the funeral pyres, a cascade of swollen joints, inflated knees, extreme fatigue, my guts on fire... a muddled malaise, disturbing delirium and a lack of equilibrium. There were frightening nightmares, bizarre hallucinations, a wild boar with mohawk hair and flashing electrified eyes. A thickening rash from pink to blood red to purple-black. And my eyes, a glowing shade of purple-red. I was blinded by the light. Close the shades. I'm a vampire, I'm a zombie...."

Jack listens in horror and amazement at my lightning-speed truncated synopsis.

"So, Jack, what's the probability that two ticks—one in Rhode Island, the other in Central India—would find me so irresistible? I was assaulted by two ticks nearly 8,000 miles apart. How could I be so lucky?"

Jack flinches and asks, "Jo, did you have Lyme too?"

"Yep, undiagnosed for a year. I never tested positive. By the summer of 2010, it was bad. Really bad. Started with a flu-like cold, then a goopy eye infection and extreme fatigue. I never noticed a bulls-eye rash. Over time, it went after me with a vengeance. Joints ballooning, legs pinging, jolting, stinging. Sending shivers down my spine, body's aching all the time … down to my very soul, I mean soles of my feet. Like they were pounded with a meat tenderizer."

Jack groaned as I recited my sing-song synopsis. "You got those nasty spirochetes. *Borrelia*."

"Those corkscrews spiraled their way into my brain. And I couldn't find my way home."

Jeremy walks in and sings a few bars, "And I'm wasted and I can't find my way home." He scratches his head, "I remember Blind Faith, Steve Winwood, Clapton. Ginger Baker was eccentric, to put it mildly."

"Who?" asks Jack.

"No, not The Who." Jeremy fires back and laughs at Jack's youthful ignorance.

I ignore their banter and continue with my story. "Electric bolts jolted my brain. What excruciating pain. Thunderbolts of lightening, very very frightening."

"Queen." Jack quips.

"Damn, I love Freddie." I reflect, mourning his loss.

"But you're still here, Jo," Jack says in amazement.

Jeremy looks at his watch, "We'll eat in about fifteen minutes. Gotta fry up the extra garlic and oil for the youngster."

"Lots of Parmesan, Molto Mario." Jack and Jeremy again take jabs at each other.

Jeremy flashes him the two-finger salute. "No, that's not a backwards peace sign or a Churchillian V for victory. Same as that middle digit. Sit and rotate." Jack ignores Jeremy's British attack. And Jeremy is off to the kitchen.

Jack returns to the subject. "Jo, which one is worse. Spotted Fever or Lyme? Not many people have had both."

"Hmm. Good question. I'm not sure which one's worse." I pause a bit to think about it. "With Spotted Fever, my symptoms were intense. Really god-awful. Without Doxy and the docs, I might have died. It robbed me for a while of my brain, did damage to my eyes, bright light can still be unbearable and there's black cobwebs that lurk in the darkness. Both Spotted Fever and Lyme reached my soul, as in S-O-U-L. Painful agony on the soles of my feet made it impossible to walk as well."

"So spotted fever is worse." Jack thinks it must be.

"On the short-term, yeah. But on the long-term, Lyme seemed like a never-ending bout of disabling things. The list of symptoms is infinite. I went untreated for way too long. The antibiotics finally killed the corkscrews, they died off, but then all hell broke loose. The treatment was almost worse than the disease."

"Herxheimer," Jack says, "those *Borrelia* spirochetes burst and release toxins. You're attacked again, a double whammy."

"For sure. Absolutely debilitating. A year of my life disappeared. I just wanted to die. Really. I wished I was dead."

Then Jack tosses in a surprise. "That's how Lyme is. It debilitates but seldom kills. Some say it's a biowarfare agent."

"What? A designed bio-weapon?" I ask. I'm confused. "Is it a designer bug?"

"Maybe or maybe not. Depends on who you listen to. Some say it came from research during the Cold War when bacteria and viruses were paired up with arthropods, like ticks, fleas, mosquitos. The aim, to incapacitate. If you dump infected ticks from planes, you can disable the enemy's workers, destroy their sugar plantations or other staple crops. Or you can weaken or disable their soldiers on the battlefield, you nix their ability to fight."

"Do you think? Is that what happened?" My mouth agape, my eyeballs on stalks, I must look like some odd designer bug.

"Plenty of military scientists say 'no'. The disease specie of *Borrelia* bacteria has been around for a long time. But they didn't show up until the outbreak in Lyme, Connecticut, around 1975. Then, not much later, ticks with the same *Borrelia* bug popped up in California and New Jersey. So, go figure."

"Hmm." I'm thinking, I'm absolutely confounded.

"People can be co-infected with other microbes. After all, a whole cocktail of microbes got injected into ticks by scientists in labs. And they might have escaped into the wild. Or so the story goes."

"So, I'm crawling with biowarfare weapons?" I'm getting scared.

Jack laughs, "Ha! I got ya." Why is Jack torturing me like this?

"But why did I never test positive?" I ask.

"Some think those coinfected bacteria might mute the Lyme antibodies, so they can't be detected. That might be why you tested negative for Lyme," Jack suggests. "Who knows?"

"Coinfections. I'm sure I got plenty of the little beasts." I say, but what Jack doesn't say scares me even more. And I'm not sure if he isn't just pulling my leg, he does like to tease.

"Who knows what else you've got?" Jack cracks a sinister smile.

"Jack, stop pulling my chain." I know he's trying to goad me. "Stop egging me on. Just stop it." I snarl at him ever so slightly.

"Some people wonder what designer weapons the Pentagon created." Jack gives me something else to fuel my conspiracy theories, if they are just that, I'm not too sure.

Jeremy appears from the kitchen. "Designer bugs, I should've known." I thought Jeremy might have been listening in.

"Plenty of speculation where Lyme *Borrelia* came from. Escaped from Plum Island? Experiments in Fort Detrick?" Jack says and shrugs.

"In my kitchen lab. I have finished my experiment." Jeremy quips and we laugh at the absurd.

"Your guess is as good as mine, as to the truth of all this." Jack shrugs again.

Then, as droll as an English butler, Jeremy announces, "Dinner is served."

43

Unintelligent Design

We sit on the patio and talk until sunset. The hummingbirds are at it again, dive-bombing and doing their aggressive dance. But this time, it's not the boys.

I point and say, "Look, those two don't have red chests. They're girls. Fighting over the honeysuckle nectar."

"Just as territorial as those boys." Jeremy reminds me.

"Maybe even more so." I look his way with squinty eyes.

Jeremy opens another bottle of Tuscan red. He doesn't wait to be prompted and begins where we left off in Stockholm. "Let's start with Lars Lindon."

"OK, we know he was part of Mei Wong's 'designer baby' business. She hatched her scam with the Swede, Lars Lindon," Jack says.

"So, what's going on with him?" I ask, we'd been following the Swedish news.

"After his arrested in Norway, the Swedes took him back to Stockholm. He's up on fraud charges and embezzlement. And possibly aiding and abetting a terrorist. That is, if he knew beforehand." Jeremy speculates, stroking his gray and black beard he mumbles, "Maybe I'll keep this."

"So, it's likely Lars didn't know Tiger Girl's true identity." I say, then ask, "But what about Hong?"

"Hong was their lab guy, to make the designer baby business look legit." Jack repeats what we already knew.

"So, what's the buzz in the world of gene hacking?" Jeremy asks.

Jack went on a tear, "Lots of baby designing going on. Well beyond China. Everybody knows it's easy to hack an embryo. Hong was working on the micro-injection technique."

"And I can add he's been a sleeper for years with China's military intel. How is it that you never picked up any cues?" Jeremy asked. "After all, he was your best friend."

"Jeremy, I would never have suspected him of MSS. Damn. I still can't believe what he was up to." Jack says, shaking his head incredulously. "He was good, I really got suckered."

"What's going to happen to Hong now?" I ask, wondering why China orchestrated his escape from Norway.

"Well, that depends, if they think he's important enough, they might keep him alive. It depends on what he knows. MMS has secret training camps for different types of spies. Rigid, grueling, heavy-duty indoctrination. They run most of their intelligence against US targets." Jeremy always know so much. Too much, I think.

"Maybe we need to target him too, that SOB," says Jack. I think he's frustrated and angry that he never caught on to Hong's duplicity.

Jeremy expounds on the inner dealings of MSS. "If Hong's done anything bad, like pass false information, then he's expendable—the Chinese will kill him. But scientists seldom have experience in clandestine work and Hong's been trained. If he shows himself to be valuable, his technical skills perhaps, then maybe they'll keep him hidden away in some secret lab. He won't be allowed out in public again, he's too recognizable."

"I know a lot about China's genomic science," Jack tells us. "Despite what they say, the Chinese have secret labs for human performance enhancement. The Chinese are doing it, human genome design—editing human DNA to re-invent their future population. Whether soldiers or athletes. Or brilliant scientists." Jack pulls us in and we banter back and forth, all on the same wavelength.

"How about their *intelligencia*? Their intellectual elite?" I ask, "Would they dare?"

"Or just plain functionals, designed to perform certain tasks, repeatedly? Happy to work in factories or out on the farms." Jeremy suggests with a hint of sarcasm.

"Yep, they'll want plenty of people with limited aspirations and imagination."

"Obedient citizens, fully compliant to the government."

"No questioning of authority or wanting a voice, no say in what they want since they'll want nothing special. Content to just live a mundane, uneventful life with no expectations or desires or dreams."

"No shooting for the stars."

We ran out of steam on that scenario, but I wonder aloud, "Would the Chinese really do such things? Could Hong play a role in some Chinese lab? There are calls for a global moratorium against human genome editing and design."

"Remember Jo, the Chinese are already working on increasing brain power. That CCR5 gene removed to make babies HIV resistant, it likely made those same children more intelligent. That was the real intention for those first designer babies. And the government…well, they've already got plans for the future." Jack had our attention on that piece of reality.

"Just think about all the possibilities…." I trail off. "Hmmm."

Jeremy asks, "But what about the ethical implications?" Moral philosopher that he is, he muses. "There's an ethical dilemma—changing the human genome by design and editing the genes of babies will alter the future of humanity. It will change what it means to be human."

"Yes," I agree "but at what point are we no longer human?"

"And who's to say it won't happen here in the US?" Jack gives me a faint smile, like he knows something that we don't.

"Orwellian." I wink at Jack and give him a wry smile in return. Jeremy and I want to learn more of Jack's thinking.

Jeremy carries the thought further. "In Orwellian societies— and with those who have the means—it could be a very different world indeed. Depending on who has the access, the money, or the power to make the decisions for 'their' people." Jeremy looks over at me and says, "Remember the golden rule." He already knows my reply.

"He who has the gold, makes the rules." I'm thinking how nothing ever changes. It's all about rulers, those with the resources and mega-wealth. And I think about an essay I'd read by the late great physicist, Stephen Hawking.

"Listen to what Hawking wrote." I pull out a quote. "… the wealthiest individuals in our society could fuel the creation of superhumans… and this could have deadly implications for un-improved humans. Presumably, they will die out, or become un-important."

"So, us naturals will die out." Jeremy concludes, he raises his eyebrows. "Extinction for the rest of us?"

"We've been breeding plants and animals for years, only now we design them by editing their DNA. Darwinian evolution is a thing of the past." Jack scoffs. "Unnatural selection will re-place it."

"And the future of human evolution is?" I ask.

"Powerful people will hack their genes to become smarter, stronger, and live longer." Jack doesn't seem to see a problem— he has no qualms. He nods and says, "Powerful people will de-sign other humans for special purposes. Humanity will be cus-tom-made by and for our future leaders."

"Did you mean dictators?" I ask.

"What's the difference?" Jack asks with a shrug. He laughs as if he's said something funny.

Jeremy's face was deadpan, but I could tell what he was bot-tling up inside. I didn't push things any further.

Jack hadn't yet finished. "Look, every species on earth could have its genes edited. The country that invests the most in gene editing will gain control over life as we know it…" Jack hesitates before adding, "on this planet."

We sit in silence as an ominous orange sun lights up our faces, the same odd sodium glow I remember from halogen street lamps. The sun sank lower and lower until darkness brought a natural end to our conversation.

Jack thanked us and departed.

🧬

"Are we Luddites?" I ask Jeremy. "Or have they crossed the red line?"

"Welcome to the age of the superhuman overlords." Jeremy's droll sarcasm is laced with sadness.

"Damn. We're doomed," I say.

"But it's even more sinister than that, Jo." Jeremy stands up and bends down as if to kiss me, but he has something else to say. "A few will have enhanced free will. And the many will not."

"Hmm. To paraphrase Hawkings, we'll have a race of self-designing people, constantly improving themselves. At an exponential rate."

"Perhaps, someday they'll escape the earth," Jeremy says with his head in the stars.

"Let's hope they do leave before they decide to destroy the rest of us. Good riddance," I say.

"Some people won't be able to resist the temptation. Have you heard of space force?" Jeremy asks, he's always somewhere extraterrestrial.

I shake my head "no".

"It's the selfish domination of the new frontier. A new type of exploitation by the super-rich." Jeremy pauses. "And superhuman edits are only for the super-rich."

"Will someone please stop them." I always get emotional about global idiots with more money than sense.

"But the editing technology could just as easily backfire on those who seek to exploit it." Jeremy pauses and smiles. "It could come back and bite them in the ass."

"Let's hope it does."

44

Designer Weapon

At last, I'm alone. Jeremy's out batting tennis balls at an all-day tournament.

My brain's working overtime, trying to put square pegs into round wholes. But most of all, I'm thinking about Jack. Where does he fit into all of this? And then I remember that night alone, just him and I, and me a bit loopy on Pinot. How he excited me, but also scared me with what he knew—and what he had done.

During his early experiments with Hong, they tried to create deadly flus. The fact was, that labs around the world already succeeded in doing just that. As did other rogues like Mei Wong and her Tiger Flu. There was no stopping those bioterrorists now. The gene genie was out of the bottle.

Everything Jack told me that evening was so fanciful it sounded like science fiction. Genetic weapons, gene-edited viruses that target only select ethnic groups, killing one group of people while leaving others unscathed.

"Racist bombs?" I asked. I thought he was messing with me. But he explained how different ethnic groups have different RNA. These RNA messengers control your brain, your heart, your kidneys, your liver, your lungs.

"If you shoot these RNA messengers with a genetic weapon, well, you know what happens. Those organs shut down. Like you heart. These weapons can make your heart stop beating." His grin was just so evil. I think about what he said.

It was Saturday morning. My heart pounded as I called Jack. He'd swing by for coffee before heading off to meet with colleagues. I didn't ask who.

I had questions. "Jack, those genetic weapons, the ones that shoot the messengers. That make hearts stop beating. Tell me again."

"If you shoot the RNA messengers, then all major organs shut down… the lungs, kidneys, the heart." course."

"Yes, the brain too. My memory is coming back." I point to my head. "At least my brain didn't shut down completely."

Jack reaches across the kitchen table, puts his hands on my shoulders. "I'm so relieved you're getting better. Jeremy thought he might lose you. You had him really worried."

"I thought I was a goner too." I chuckle. "Hey, they don't call me Rasputin for nothing."

"Rasputin?" Jack knew the general story. "Nothing could kill him."

"No, well, almost nothing. Not the old peasant woman who stabbed him in the stomach. Not the tea and cakes and wine laced with cyanide. Not until they found the right weapon. Three gunshots wounds. The fatal one to his forehead, finally brought him down. They threw his body into the river. But later, they discover he struggled to get out." I knew the gory details. "Now, that is super creepy."

"Funny how assassination weapons have changed. Instead of cyanide, tea is spiked with radioactive polonium. Or umbrella tips are spiked with Ricin pellets." Jack says.

"The newest, those neurotoxins. Like Novichuk. Those two Russian FSB thugs were so obvious." I know the story.

"They're just isolated incidents. Small scale assassinations." Jack tells me. "Genetic weapons are on a whole other level—they could wipe out millions."

"But who would want to kill so many people?" I ask.

"That's what weapons do. They kill people. They can be used as weapons of war. Think about it. If I were to edit a virus, I'd make sure it didn't affect everyone. Not you. Not me." Jack trailed off, "Just our enemies. Maybe a specific set of people."

"I got it. But what if terrorists could use those same weapons too? Could they set off a genetic plague? Or start a race war?" My voice nearly chokes on the terms, "genetic plague" and "race wars". I've never used those exact words before.

"Precisely, a genetic plague would kill targeted groups of people. It's a precision instrument. And terrorists could be plotting the demise of an entire population. Ethnic purity makes for the easiest targets. Even people like Hong with ethnic Han genes." Jack was as precise as his targeted instrument. I had no idea how much he'd come to hate Hong.

"Woah! You'd wipe out whole segments of humanity?" My eureka moment finally arrived. I wonder just how deadly this new tech has evolved. "How would you deliver it?" I ask Jack.

"By infecting people like you and me. Or infecting a non-vulnerable group with the altered virus. Maybe Turkic people, for example the Uighurs. They'd carry it around and infect their vulnerable oppressors. There's over a billion Han in China. Hong is part Han, so who knows how susceptible he might be?"

"Would you wish that on Hong? Would you wish that on an entire race of people?" I can't believe Jack could even suggest such an egregious attack. Using humans as weapons. I'd never really thought about the full implications, all its genocidal possibilities.

Jack shrugged.

"Jack, stop kidding around."

I see Jack flinch. As if tasered to the heart, he bolts upright, places his hand over his mouth. I think he is trying to silence himself.

"Hey, it ain't rocket science. It's just child's play," he says before he goes.

I hug him as though he were an errant child and wonder where Jack will someday end up.

⟨⊂⊐⊏⟩

Jack never told me where he was headed. He flew out of T.F. Green airport to Washington, DC.

He'd been thinking hard about editing the genes of humans. And even harder about the potential for transforming humans into lethal weapons. Populations of assassins who would, wittingly or not, turn their victims' livers into pate. And their brains into pottage.

Jack crossed the Potomac River in a taxi, headed to the head-quarters of the Genetic Strategic Command. He'd brainstorm with others on a new program: The future of biological warfare and weaponry. What are the goals?

But this was a program that was not. It would never be acknowledged that it existed. Since acknowledging its existence was antithetical to its implicit goals.

Forget the conventional arms, the cyber wars, even the nu-clear missiles, bombs, chemical, and biological weapons. It's all about who can outsmart the others. Becoming the superior race to outthink the others. And finding the newest infallible weapons to annihilate the others. *En masse*. The buzz in the room ranged from superhumans to human weapons to genetic weapons that target crops and people.

A senior agricultural scientist from the Pentagon said, "We can target crops with insects. Aphids or leaf hoppers or white flies. They are our 'little buddies'. Our insect allies can carry destructive viruses to kill crops, like wheat or rice." And Jack listened.

Another scientist countered. "But what about US corn? The Chinese, the Russians, maybe others, are capable of doing the same to us." He warned, "In the new arms race, do not ignore the possibilities of genetic weapons turned against us." And Jack listened.

A panel of military scientists talked of designing soldiers for future warfare. "Military personal could be edited and designed to enhance their performance. Super-soldiers." And Jack listened.

"Not only can soldiers be engineered to be superhuman in every way possible, but our own genetic make-up can be at-tacked. Think about that. There are those who wish to do us harm. What works for us can work for them. It's the yin and the yang of it. Dual use technology both creates and destroys." And Jack listened.

"Human Weapons are not far off. Just think about the Chi-nese Army, if even 5% of the Chinese population could be ge-netically engineered....just think, just think….." someone said and Jack listened.

"Every scientific weapon that has ever been invented has been put to use. So, what weapon should we adopt for use in our future wars?" The final question was asked. The room went silent.

And Jack said, "The weapon is yet to be designed. We'll design the next generation, the new weapons of war. And we'll carry the genetic weapons with us wherever we go. We'll create human neutron bombs. We can wipe out a race while leaving the perpetrators intact. We'll select human targets based on their DNA. We'll target the enemy we wish to eliminate by going to the core of their very existence. Only us chosen few will survive."

"We have met the enemy and he is us," someone said and people laughed.

"It's Pogo," a voice said.

And Jack shrugged.